ISHA SCHWALLER DE LUBICZ spent her youth studying first Christian, then Hindu, Buddhist and Hebrew theology and mysticism. As pupil of R. A. Schwaller de Lubicz and later as his wife she went on to study other religious and philosophic systems, including Taoism and Islam. Her studies came to completion in Egypt, where she spent fifteen years among temples and tombs, probing the symbolism of the hieroglyphs. Her discoveries aroused the enthusiasm of the Egyptologist Alexander Varille, who gave the last ten years of his life to the work of verification. Her description uncovers a system of thought, a pattern of knowledge by insight, that is altogether stimulating.

Sir Ronald Fraser's translation is to some extent 'free'. The English text has been read line by line with the original by Mademoiselle Lucie Lamy, daughter of the author, and Professor Gertie Englund of the University of Stockholm: their suggestions have been incorporated. The French edition included some massive commentaries which would have had little interest for the general reader and these have been omitted.

Also by Isha Schwaller de Lubicz:

HER-BAK 'CHICK-PEA':
The Living Face of Ancient Egypt
English translation by Charles Edgar Sprague

HER-BAK

Egyptian Initiate

by

Isha Schwaller de Lubicz

Translated by
Ronald Fraser

HODDER AND STOUGHTON

CONTENTS

INTRODUCTION

This is the successor to a book that was published in French by Flammarion in 1955 and in English by Hodder and Stoughton in 1954 under the title *Her-Bak, 'Chick-Pea'*. The authoress, Isha Schwaller de Lubicz, spent her youth studying first Christian, then Hindu, Buddhist and Hebrew theology and mysticism. As pupil of R. A. Schwaller de Lubicz and later as his wife she went on to study other religious and philosophic systems, including Taoism and Islam. Her studies came to completion in Egypt, where she spent fifteen years without social amenities, among temples and tombs, probing the symbolism of the hieroglyphs, the key to which was put in her hands. Her discoveries roused the enthusiasm of the Egyptologist Alexander Varille, who gave the last ten years of his life to the work of verification. Her description uncovers a system of thought, a pattern of knowledge by insight, that is altogether stimulating. It reads like a complete, intelligible account of what seems to have been abridged for children in the first four chapters of Genesis.

The preceding volume concerns the earlier stages of Her-Bak's experience. In boyhood he was called Chick-Pea. The name Her-Bak means at the same time Falcon-Face and Face-of-Horus; it also serves for the chick-pea, which has the pattern of the bird's face with the characteristic eye. Chick-Pea then is the name of a boy who seeks his way until the time when Face-of-Horus will be his name and his light. Horus is what the authoress calls 'the principle of purposeful super-evolution'.

The story, she tells us, shews in one individual's life a path of progress through temple-training. By temple we are to understand the whole structure of Egyptian science, knowledge or wisdom. The living temple is man, who is an embodiment of cosmic principles and functions, the 'Neters'; material sanctuaries are 'houses' in which he can learn through the symbology to recognise the constituents of macrocosm in himself. This is a progress of consciousness and the whole secret of what we call salvation or redemption lies in it. Her-Bak embodies it, as schoolboy, student and disciple of that Master who is Egypt, the ancient wisdom, itself.

As a small boy, son of a head farmer in the domain of the Lord Menkh, grand-master of craftsmen, Chick-Pea comes under the notice of a Sage who, perceiving the lad's exceptional gifts, advises him to begin the training and development of his innate powers and to do this by cultivating the earth and watching the life of plants and animals. As soon as his experience of nature is found adequate, Menkh puts him first, to a school for scribes, then, by apprenticeship in various crafts such as pot-making and carpentry, to studying the laws of matter. At a given stage he becomes sandal-bearer to the great Lord.

During four preparatory years this precocious and predestined lad meets with problems of conscience and understanding that develop a sense of responsibility and form his mind. In the end, shocked by social inequalities and the weakness of certain leaders, he is seized with desire to know the secrets of the temple. The Sage then comes into the picture and presents Chick-Pea with a choice between two paths: the normal training of an official and the training of an Adept. Having pondered some urgent considerations suggested by his instinctive nature against the call of his destiny, he chooses the way of knowledge, the mystical or gnostic way. The Sage gives him his name, Her-Bak, Face-of-Horus, and leads him to the temple.

At first, of course, he is a pupil in the outer temple or Peristyle. His teachers, who are not initiates, put Her-Bak off with the formality and utilitarianism of their thinking, but he accepts the discipline, along with certain tests in discrimination and other qualities. Finally, a vision of his own Neter, his real self, opens the inner temple, the Hypostyle, to him and at this point the present volume begins.

The events related take place between the twentieth and twenty-first dynasties in the temple of Karnak in face of the Theban mountain whose peak dominates the Valley of the Kings.

The translation of this most intricate cosmogony is to some extent 'free'. The English text has been read line by line with the original by Mademoiselle Lucie Lamy, daughter of the authoress, and Miss Gertie Englund, fil. mag., an expert in languages, including French and English, at the University of Stockholm: their suggestions have been incorporated. I also consulted M. Henry Bourgeot, L.ès L., on a number of points and am greatly indebted to him. But it has by no means always been easy to find the word or phrase that corresponds with the somewhat elaborate French and expresses its meaning, or even to divine the intention. Meaning for the Egyptian initiate lay not in a word but very closely in its history, composition and relation with others. This will be clear enough in the chapter on BA and KA, which may seem like an attempt to bottle and catalogue the invisible.

The first volume, 'Chick-Pea', includes a number of plates and illustrations that are helpful in studies of a technical character. Some massive commentaries which would have little interest for the general reader have been omitted from this volume.

Egypt is referred to in our text by more than one name: Kemit, the black one or black Earth; Ta-meri, the beloved or magnetic Earth, which attracts the powers and gifts of its Neters; the Two-Lands, North and South, allied under the Pharaonic authority, each with its crown and symbol.

The word from which we derive 'Pharaoh' means 'Great House'; the expression 'Twofold Great House' is sometimes found. This gives Pharaoh the impersonal character of a royal House, seat and embodiment of the royal Presence, which is considered to be in a state of becoming or unfoldment through successive dynasties. His names disclose the nature of the Principle which he incarnates (as in Râ-meses, product of Râ) and his symbolic role in the becoming of the Two-Lands. His active part is to pass on the royal blood and decisions that affect the destiny of his people, as well as his own. Passively, he becomes for his people the 'leaven' of the principle he embodies; accepts the character ordained by the astrological moment he represents; bears the names assigned him; obeys by doing what devolves on him in the way of religious and warlike acts, the issue of symbolic decrees and writings, the building or renovation of monuments in accordance with the times and with rules laid down by the Sages behind the throne. Temples are seen as seats of the Neters, each a dwelling-place of the principle, cause or agent in continuous creation to which it is dedicated; its plan, dedication and emblem make it the projection on Earth of some aspect of the cosmic organism. The projection of macrocosm into man or microcosm was the teaching given at Luxor; its projection into Egypt gave rise, we are told, to the organisation of Egypt in nomes, whose sanctuaries reveal their function and character. The history of the Pharaohs is seen as a genesis or becoming, a succession of stages in the becoming or development of man, who, in the first, abstract or ideal creation was the perfection and totality of all functions, made in the image of Light, androgynous; man who will, as Eckhart put it, 'again enter and eternally possess Paradise'. Pharaoh is the expression in history of a corresponding moment in the archetypal myth; and this demands changes in the measurements and proportions of temples and monuments, for Numbers as well as Neters are factors in the cosmic process. Thus, from time to time changes are made in grammatical forms, the use of signs and so forth. A particular Neter becomes dominant or reappears in some principle that is exalted for the moment. Emphasis is laid on one or other sanctuary at certain times of year or of the precessional cycle. Temples are renovated or rebuilt; ancient sculptured stones are embedded in the foundations if their symbols bear relation to the principle expounded in the new building. A Neter's name is modified; the names of kings and officials are chosen in accordance with the note of the epoch. The measurements of Pharaoh's image are changed periodically, leaving traces of earlier measurements to accentuate the idea behind the change. Theses are taken up again or personages from the past brought back to public memory. All this happens abruptly, as if an act of will ordained it; indeed, the astronomical data with other circumstances reveal a pattern that must have been worked out beforehand and put into execution with a continuity that is not deflected even by internal crisis or foreign domination.

      •   •   •

The Egyptian Sages seem to have seen reality as consciousness, the phenomenal world as an incarnation of ideas, principles, functions, stages of consciousness in process of becoming. We are to think of the beginning, Genesis, as an abstract, principial creation, timeless and spaceless, antecedent to those conditions; a creation in principle of possibilities, patterns, functions. Next follows a continuous creation in time and space, a process of generation, actualisation, becoming, of what was potential in absolute Cause. Manifestation in the realm of forms and appearances that are real inasmuch as they embody Cause itself is called the 'fall into matter'. The agents of this procedure are the Neters, causal powers, themselves the principles and modes of such manifestation, immanent and virtually contained in nature, subject to the law of the principle they embody, its prisoner until the phase of return is complete. For it is a cyclic process. The history of mankind is a progress of consciousness through selfness to original selflessness; through consciousness and control of the principles and functions of which Man is the sum to reintegration with the ideal Man that was born of the abstract Imagination, fusion of consciousness with the prime reality from which all derives. We see it happen before our eyes, or in ourselves, when we experience nature and ourselves as phases of generation, regeneration and return. This is the principle of 'purposeful evolution'.

The aim of temple-instruction and the arduous, dedicated life required of teacher and pupil was to awaken and develop the intuitive gift of those who were called to it and capable of achieving consciousness of the facts by fusion with Fact. The method is initiatory, progressive, but the word 'initiation' is not used in reference to occult practices or mysterious rites. To initiate, as the authoress points out, is to introduce or set going. An initiate is one who gains not a mass of mere information by observation and comparison of phenomena but knowledge and power by entry into experience. The disciple is repeatedly warned against taking symbol or word for the reality. What he acquires, if he endures, is a dynamic, like the Gnostics; by which and his effort of study, faithfulness, silence and impersonality he comes to a mode of intercourse with the Real, fusion with it. This is done through 'the intelligence of the heart'. It is insisted that the mind, the cerebral function, can never know the Real: in this especially, Egyptian wisdom agrees with the Vedic, Buddhist, Taoist and esoteric Christian.

.   .   .

We risk mis-statement, of course, when we translate a mode of experience, the theology and cosmology that flow from it, from one language into another, especially when the original is hieroglyphic. But it is difficult not to see correspondences in what this book sets out with other perhaps more familiar systems and it is convenient to use their terms. We are used to the Unnameable Source and Cause. The Abstract in which the principial creation takes place and from which it is projected is an idea we can easily grasp. Such themes as a second creation that proceeds by division, a kind of cell-fission . . . 'I am One that becomes Two, Two that becomes Four', division in the indivisible, the co-existence of opposites in unity, simultaneity in sequence: these are not altogether foreign to our mode of thought. And is not Maât, 'cosmic consciousness, universal ideation, essential wisdom' akin to what Eckhart called the first substance of godhead? Mention is made of the cosmic Virgin who is ceaselessly united with the fiery Word that fecundates her and whom she bears eternally, mother of the uncreated light that is called divine Râ; and we may see in Horus Redeemer a reference to the light we call Christ, Apollo or some other name. But it would be hazardous to press these analogies. The aim of Her-Bak's training was, in part, to free him from obsession with analogy and appearance.

The words BA and KA, however, require provisional treatment. Roughly, but only roughly, they can be translated by 'spirit' and 'psyche'.

Any translation of the word KA, says our authoress, is helpless to give the meaning that arises from its composition. No explanation can do any more than indicate various aspects the word originally contained, differentiated by the subtleties of hieroglyphical writing, without evoking the idea of multiplicity in the thing-in-itself. The meaning of BA is more easily given, she suggests, by using the French word 'âme'; but this word is no more satisfactory than our own 'soul': both are often used when it is 'spirit' that is in mind, or an amalgam of spirit and psyche. The word *'âme'* is used nevertheless in the French text and 'soul' in the English. This will do if it is borne in mind that 'soul' is however remotely phenomenal, while its reality is pure spirit, pure being.

.   .   .

We must, in fact, take into account three prime factors of a principial and causative order.

First, *akh*, pure spirit, yet not spirit as it is in itself but a birth of spiritual light, spirit revealing itself, immanent in nature, creative.

Second, BA, or a man's BA, pure spirit, formless, neutral, impassible, indifferent to personal matters because concerned with the immortal, an individualisation of pure spirit as it were.

Third, KA, or a man's KA, the principle of concretion, individualising factor, medium of attraction that draws BA and fixes it in the personality.

In the beginning KA is form that gives form to principial substance in the making of matter. It is KA that in the process of becoming will undergo manifold changes from the lowest of forms to perfection of the 'indestructible body'. KA is the carrier of all powers of manifestation and activator of cosmic functions. It is the actualising factor, agent of realisation; the force without which, for example, a father would be impotent.

Original KA, creator of all KAS, proceeds from universal consciousness, Maât, and takes character in the man who embodies it from his natural, organic and instinctive constituents. It becomes a bundle of incarnate principles and functions, spiritual, psychic, animal, vegetable, mineral, elemental; it includes an ego-principle. Spirit, if it is to manifest, needs a means, what our text calls a support, a *point d'appui*, and with a man this means is the selective affinity or magnetic power that inheres in his higher KA which draws spirit into incarnation. Actually, a man has several KAS, for every part and organ has one; and it is the KAS of his animal constituents that hold him to the instinctive life of Earth: when Cleopatra says, 'I am fire and air; my other elements I give to baser life', she might have been reading *Her-Bak* (and other passages suggest it). Thus, one man's KA differs from another's in the particularity of its selective action. Universal BA is in continuous relation with the man to whom it gives life, and with his KA; but it is KA that assimilates, lends form, individuality, to an immortal spirit that is conditioned, so to say, by affinity with the KA's specificness. Only the higher KA can link with the potential of immortality in which a man must gain consciousness or perish.

BA, then, is like a migrant bird, a stork, that wanders between *akh* and a mortal body, drawn to Earth by the KA and the *kas*. But we are warned that, whereas imagination tries to separate the different aspects of the being, in reality all is in all. Each part contains the principle of all the others, with accentuation of the properties that are specifically its own. It is wrong to think of the various states of the being as discontinuous; there is continuity from the most material to the most spiritual. Each part, corporal or spiritual, participates in the whole: thus, the heart, which is the man's sun in his bodily aspect as it is in his divine reality, is involved with the rest of his make-up. His higher KA, a ray of universal Maât, is in the same relations with his BA as those which unite Maât with the divine Râ whose daughter and nourishment she is.

.   .   .

Neters are causal Ideas immanent or virtually contained in nature, themselves the principles and agents of manifestation, from Nile mud to the galaxies. They are therefore immanent or virtually contained in Man and can be awakened in him, brought into consciousness. Indeed, the central theme of this book, the aim of Her-Bak's course of instruction, is the awakening and enhancement of consciousness, the consciousness of these principles and functions in himself and of his own Neter. More generally, it is the development of this process in men who are capable of it and of the discipline, such men as Her-Bak, until there arises the possibility of liberation through self-conquest and fusion of personal consciousness with universal Maât, identification of their own Neter with the Neter of Neters.

The worlds or states of being in which the Neters function are called Heaven, the Dwat and Earth, celestial, intermediate and terrestrial. Heaven is the realm of principles, not the absolute, sole Principle itself that is immobile and unintelligible, but of the imagined and projected causal powers, properties-in-themselves, which act because there they are, so to say, and in their inherent mode. It is an abstract, impersonal state that contains all possibilities such as may be evoked in successive becomings, manifestations or states of nature which is the realm of Earth.

The intermediate state, the Dwat, is a sphere of transition between abstract and concrete, the state of that which moves towards becoming or disbecoming, not so much the Hades we read about in the Aeneid, for instance, as a stage in the recurrent processes of 'purposeful evolution'. There are, in fact, two Dwats . . . the state of that which moves towards generation on Earth and the state of that which has emerged from terrestrial existence and waits, whether for a return into Earth-life or for the reascent through necessary metamorphoses into Heaven, a post mortem condition in which all that has taken shape in the terrestrial world retains such consciousness as it may have acquired and suffers transformation according to what new possibilities this opens up.

Man, the Sages taught, is a complex of organs and functions each of which is a replica or miniature of its cosmic original. He is a bundle of animal instincts and selfnesses, associated, loosely in the undeveloped, closely when the individual is further advanced, with the subtle element called 'higher KA' and an uncreated factor called BA which the KA attracts, captures, individualises, characterises according to its own proclivities and holds in embodiment until, through self-discipline and self-conquest, liberation is gained. Liberation consists in fusion of the individualised consciousness, now grown impersonal, selfless, with Maât, vehicle of Râ's essence. A man only lives in spirit and in truth when his lower KA or complex of selves is assimilated to the higher, which is a ray of Maât become his own wisdom. All that belongs to the lower self, mortal, cerebral, fictitious, perishes; whereas the higher KA links with BA, imperishable spirit, as Maât links with supreme Râ. This change is effected by the patient weaving over a long time of the Horus spirit-soul into the Osirian body.

There is rebirth when an individual begins to be aware of the reality that dwells in himself and in cosmos; when he 'takes possession of his BA and his KA'. He is then ready for spiritual evolution. Until that stage there is no reincarnation, no evolution; nothing to reincarnate and evolve; nothing but a repetitive continuity of instinctive life. Evolution involves preparation, for the KA cannot link with the BA which it draws to itself until it has itself become incorruptible, freed itself by the weaving process from the ego-principle. Short of this a man is merely the sum of his lower elements and the nightly sleep may lead to eternal sleep if he fails to cultivate affinity with his real self: in that case spirit returns to its own country and evolution of its individualised existence ceases. Whereas the search for reality, the development of consciousness, changes the lower self's quality and diminishes its reign. Evolution begins on Earth and in the Dwat until perfection is attained, integration with cosmic man, sum of all functions and principles, true Adam, and return into the Cause.

All words? Notions and images that don't conform with reality? Readers will soon understand that the real meaning of words and symbols in this formidable structure can only be obtained by a process of meditation. But parallels with other systems are easily discernible, suggesting that the truths which they disclose and at the same time veil derive from a common source, an original Gnosis. The essence is the same. It is for man to become what he was when he was first thought of, a fully conscious being. What is a fully conscious being? One whose will and consciousness are reality, being itself. To attain this the ostensible self, the sum of ostensible selves, must die.

I am grateful to Miss Ingrid Lind, Vice-Principal, the Faculty of Astrological Studies, for help with the passages relating to astrology, and to Miss Diana Higgins, B.A., as well as to Miss Gertie Englund, for help with the proofs.

It remains to add that the initiative in introducing this book to the British public comes from Mr Paul Beard, President, the College of Psychic Science, and author of *Survival of Death*.

RONALD FRASER

PART I

I

THE QUESTION

There is silence at the uncertain moment when dawn ends night. The teaching Her-Bak had received in the Peristyle was in the past: what promised light was to shine?

The Master had said, 'An answer is profitable in proportion to the intensity of the quest. A problem clearly envisaged, a point succinctly made, hold the elements of the solution in themselves. We must impose a test before introducing you among the disciples: if we authorise one question, to what question do you attach first importance? Consider the grounds of your choice attentively and write them in your memory. You will set them out in exact terms when you are called.'

Her-Bak bowed. He re-examined the themes of his impassioned research, looked deeply into their bases, strove to throw out the superfluous and uncover the essential. Now he waited.

.   .   .

Dawn whitened the ground. The first golden rays drew a silhouette on the stone, a messenger's. Her-Bak followed him without fear, conscious of having given the fullness of what was possible to him.

The candidate was led into the Hypostyle, where bright light fought with shadow. Guards had been posted at the approaches. He walked towards a voice that called him from the eastern side, where, at the far end of a colonnade, three men were seated on the Master's right, the Master of Mysticism, the Master of Measures, the Master of Symbology. Her-Bak was struck with the majesty of this group: nothing in their costume proclaimed it, but clearly they were the true pillars of the temple.

To what new world had he been transported? Only a few steps separated him from the Peristyle, but its gossip and quarrelling were already far away. If I am not received here may I at least live here as humble servant of its majesty! With this aspiration Her-Bak prostrated himself and in his ardour forgot all else, even the test to which he must now submit. At the Master's voice he rose. 'Approach, Her-Bak. Now is the time to prove that endeavour equals your ambition. Have you framed your question?'

'Master, may I put it in the order in which it evolved? I've got hold of one end of a clue but I don't know where it will take me.'

'My son, this isn't the place for unnecessary words. Announce your problem as you conceive it.'

The novice replied, 'This is the first question that comes from my heart. "Why am I on this earth?" But discussing it with myself I haven't found it very astute. Do I know what I am? Do I know what Earth is? It is that which is neither Heaven nor the Dwat. It is written, "All that is in Heaven, on Earth and in the Dwat": Earth is under Heaven and under my feet . . . therefore I am on Earth and under Heaven. What is man doing on Earth? He is born, lives and dies. Where was he before he was born? In his father and his mother. Whence came the first father? When man dies he goes back into Earth; when he ends Earth goes on. Will it exist always? Earth changes with the seasons: I have been told it is the Sun, Moon and Sirius that make the seasons, so earthly existence depends on them. Do I too depend on them, since I live on Earth? On what do Sun, Moon and Sirius depend? Are they stronger than all Heaven? I have been told of stars even greater than these: which is the most powerful? But still my question eludes me. If I know the answer I shall know who rules the world. Is it true, what I say?

'If Earth changes, why not Sun, Moon and Sirius? Mustn't what changes die? If so, death is stronger than all else: is death fundamental? Death ends something. What thing? A life? This brings me back to the same point . . . what is the object of existence? It can't be death. There must be other purposes, or the world is horror and madness. Of course, this isn't my definitive question. I must first answer another: did I choose my goal or was it imposed on me? Is there a will that compels mine? Is there a law that governs me as Sun, Moon and Sirius are governed? I've heard about the laws of nature . . . if they rule me I have no liberty, no goal. What then do we look for? What purpose does the temple serve?

'One thing is certain . . . I can deserve or forfeit admittance, so I have a measure of liberty. The getting of wisdom could be my aim. Is it absurd? It would be if there were no real knowledge in the temple. I haven't the right, because I know nothing, to conclude that the Sages have lied; yet, since they say I can accept or refuse the way of truth this is liberty. How do I get it? Is it above the laws of nature, stronger than they? What in nature is less free than I? I don't know if the animal has liberty . . . certainly less than mine. I don't believe an animal can conquer the laws of nature. The plant can't, nor the stone: here's a difference between me and them. Therefore, if I'm to know whence my liberty comes I must ask, what is man? If man is the most complete being on Earth, I ought, knowing this, to be able to know all else; but I'm a man and I don't know myself. I don't know who or what is in me. The doctor who teaches in the Peristyle doesn't explain where the first man comes from, nor the purpose of life, nor the meaning of death.

.   .   .

'Masters, doubts of this sort brought me up short before ever I watched a funeral. Now I've seen death and I ask myself, if death is the final end what use is knowledge? The singer was right . . . better enjoy life without care. In which case temple and wisdom are absurdities, funeral rites are absurdities. Yes, that's what I've thought. But I also told myself it would be another absurdity to reach this conclusion without proofs.'

'Do you yourself believe, Her-Bak, that death is a final end?' asked the Master of Mysticism.

'My heart refuses it. But I must find the "question" I'm to put without asking what I believe.'

The Masters received this with satisfaction and Her-Bak resumed. 'The funeral rites affected me through my love for Nadjar. I understood what separation means. Before death he was like ourselves . . . he breathed the same air, saw the same things. Now his eyes see nothing, his nostrils breathe nothing. Is there some part of him that still sees? If not, it's total annihilation. If so, does he see what we don't? In which case, are our eyes dead to that world we don't see? If it were so would our life and his only be separated by a difference? Where is his life, his personal life? Is what he learnt dead with him? A master-carpenter said to me, "Death is change." If the body is mummified it can change no longer: in what does the change lie? People talk of the BA and KA that can, as they say, return. What are they? Where? Their body is dead. How can they live if they have no body to eat with? And here's another question . . . what is it to be alive? But there's too much I don't know. I don't know if this is the fundamental question.'

.   .   .

The Masters looked at each other, smiling. 'He is a true seeker,' the Sage said. 'He has dared to speak. Let us help him with his question.'

They assented. 'To frame a question,' said the Mystic, 'first go to the heart of the problem. Everyone is moved by an urge that governs his life. What urge is yours?'

'To learn what I must know if my life is to reach its goal.'

'Then begin by seeking the goal.'

'How am I to do this?'

The Geometer said, 'Every axiom, every truth, must be susceptible of geometrical expression. For every phenomenon is the resultant of movements and rhythms that give it form and character by the law of Number. Make your own life, your phenomenal self, the centre of enquiry if you wish to know its goal. Where does it come from? Where is it going?'

'It comes from my birth.'

'Lines of force and numbers determined your birth. Your life demonstrates the harmonious characteristics that lead you to a goal. That gives the field in which you have to search.'

Smiling at Her-Bak's perplexity, the Sage said, 'Start from some point you know. In what does life end?'

'In death. And perhaps something I don't know about.'

'You can't know your goal unless you know your ending. But your real aim will guide you to knowledge. For lines of force in a man, let us say his disposition, determine his real aim, so that he is fatally directed by the true facts of his aim and ending.'

'Actually my aim is to know how I really end.'

The Symbolist replied, 'Then establish the relationship between this your own disposition and that of other existences. The mineral's is limited by its inertia: it waits and suffers changes imposed on its passivity. The vegetable's, expressed in various movements, limited by its being rooted in the ground, consists in finding conditions favourable to breathing, nourishment and fertilisation. The animal's is to seek food, shelter and the opportunity of copulation. These tendencies reveal each individual's aim. In the mineral inertia and the slow rate of change make its aim all but imperceptible. The vegetable's is the production of seed. The animal's is to continue the species and satisfy its instincts. Do the disposition and aim of animal nature fulfil your aspirations?'

'They will never satisfy me.'

'Seek then in this difference the difference between your own real ending and theirs. The measure in which your disposition and aim surpass theirs will indicate the quality of your own real aim and ending.'

The Mystic questioned the candidate. 'Do you believe that life can go on after the body's death?'

'My heart desires it. After what has been said my heart believes it, but nothing proves it to me.'

'What matter? Listen first to your convictions, even if they seem absurd to your reason.'

'A sound precept,' agreed the Sage, 'in spite of its dangers. In effect, if there exists a body of law that binds all forms of life together, this establishes between them sensorially imperceptible relations which, since they are outside the range of reasonable logic, may well be called absurd until experience shews that concrete fact can emerge from the abstract. To reject what seems absurd, without discrimination, is to reject the possibility of knowing the laws in question. Learn then to distinguish between the certainties of the heart, or faith, and belief, or blind adherence to words. Such belief must be rejected; but faith is indispensable if you will enter into the divine knowing. Accept then, provisionally, your heart's certainty; then seek proof of its truth or falsehood.'

'Where shall I look?' asked Her-Bak. 'I don't know what death is.'

'Proceed by elimination,' said the Geometer. 'Death is an undeniable fact, whereas life isn't a fact but a sum of effects that derive from an abstract and incomprehensible cause. Begin then with the fact of death. If you consider death according to the look of it how would you define it?'

'As an ending. What seems to result is nothing.'

'Your conclusion is inexact, Her-Bak. There is a tangible residue, the corpse. As to the process that changed a body into a corpse you can envisage two possibilities. Either there remains a body whose vital activity has been simply annihilated, in which case there has been subtraction, or, over and above the cadaver, there remains something that came out of it, in which case you have division. Well then, death is subtraction if life has definitely ceased, if it has simply been annihilated; or it is division if something has been separated from the body.'

Having reflected, Her-Bak submitted his conclusion. 'Look for what left the body . . . is this what I am to do?'

'To find it,' answered the Symbolist, 'observe what brings about death in nature and how it shews itself. What brings it about is the cessation, or the accomplishment, of the reason for living; in which case death shews what the reason for living was.'

'If the cause of death is accident?'

'Cessation of the reason for living may permit or provoke it. Nature exhibits the connexion between death and aim. The flower dies at the birth of the seed, corn when the grain ripens. Certain male insects die in copulation. In all animals decrepitude begins with the exhaustion of the procreative function. Among men you see the same law with a difference: there are men and women who thanks to their intellectual gifts are no longer enslaved by this function, with the result that their reason for living outlasts the merely animal aim and for them death may have another meaning. How does death shew itself?'

Her-Bak replied with some hesitation, 'By the disappearance of movement and warmth.'

'Correct. The first obvious effect is the ending of that incomprehensible drive that gave heart and body movement; after which the body is abandoned to destructive changes, shewing that what left the body is what kept it going.'

The Mystic added, 'We call it the quickening soul.'

'But whence comes the first activity?' asked Her-Bak.

The Symbolist replied, basing himself on nature. 'From the incomprehensible moment when the seed awakes in the womb . . . how could the seed do without one? Nature scatters seed in profusion and much is lost, finding no womb. The female, who receives the seed, conceives the germ and feeds it with her own substance. The mother withers when this function is exhausted; but there is one mother who brings forth and nourishes germs incessantly, Earth, nurse of all vegetables and other beings whose food they are. She is the mother of minerals. All bodies return into her bosom.'

An ironic light in his eye, the Sage murmured, 'True, but meanwhile the bodies have lived and Earth is not dead.'

'Earth is the perpetual nursing-mother,' the Symbolist agreed. 'Giving, she may be depleted, but she draws afresh on the resources of nature in order to transmit life. Only an overwhelming Sethian fire can stem her regenerative power: it is in this way that the "red earth", the desert, arises. Tell me, Her-Bak, do you know a mother who cannot die?'

'How could it be possible? Mustn't all that is born suffer death?'

'Then such a mother can neither be born nor have bodily form, for it is on the body that death exercises its power. And such a mother, nurse of life itself, must have the same nature as that which gives life and which we call soul.'

The Sage offered a provisional conclusion. 'The problem of life is not yet fathomed, but the possibility of a Mother-who-dies-not brings you nearer a solution, for she reveals the meaning of death, which is no more than a passing of the creature into the belly of the great mother Nut who brings about all changes.'

'If death is a moment of change,' said Her-Bak, 'there must remain over and above the body something that goes on living . . .'

The Sage corrected him. 'Something that is life itself.'

Her-Bak strove to remember every word. At last he put his question.

'Then the fundamental problem is, what is life? What is life if it is other than a fleeting appearance, a ripening of seed, a transit between birth and death?'

None of the Masters spoke. 'Before we answer,' the Sage said at length, 'each of us will question you. For my part I ask why you didn't choose for your question the theme that has always troubled you, "What is a Neter?"'

Her-Bak replied without hesitation. 'I've passed my whole time asking it. I'm beginning to think it's the last thing to look for.'

The Masters smiled. The Sage approved. 'You can add that it's the thing it's useless to look for. If the Neter isn't in you you'll find it nowhere. If it is, it will disclose itself and you'll find it everywhere. Now let each Master put his question.'

'What is your inmost desire, Her-Bak?' asked the Mystic.

'To feel the life in me and in everything.'

'Learn then to know the world in yourself. Never look for yourself in the world, for this would be to project your illusions.'

'What do you wish to know, Her-Bak?' asked the Geometer.

'The truest truth.'

'Even if it were to prove disagreeable?'

'I wish only to know what is most true.'

'Then seek it in Number and geometrical function. They will give you facts that are inescapable and no person or sentimental consideration can set them aside.'

'What do you wish to do, Her-Bak?' asked the Symbolist.

'To give others what I get.'

'To give one must have. To teach one must know the nature of those whom one is teaching, their symbol, that is to say. Study men and things through their symbolism.'

'My son,' said the Sage, 'the three Masters have let you taste the very essence of their subject. May it please them to add a definition of man.'

The Mystic said, 'Man is the tabernacle of the divine Word.'

The Geometer said, 'Man is the measure of Cosmos.'

The Symbolist said, 'Man is a living statue of the Great World and sum of its symbols.'

'As for me,' declared the Sage, 'I owe you the reply to your question, what is life? I will give it tomorrow, on your entry to the inner temple. What will you give, Her-Bak?'

Her-Bak prostrated himself. 'My obedience and my faith.' Rising he added, 'That is only natural. But Master, if you teach me what life is I will give you my life.'

II

THE ANSWER

Now it is full day. In the hall of the Hypostyle Her-Bak has awaited the Sage since dawn, his impatience diminishing as the hours pass.

Astonishing magic of the place! He came in as a conqueror, exalted, swelling ambition to the size of the edifice. Now the great bulk has disappeared, the columns too; he goes to and fro among them like a somnambulist unconscious of height or depth. But it exhausts his elation; he becomes aware that he is waiting; the Sage's absence begins to disquiet him. Can he have forgotten Her-Bak?

Another hour goes by. He grows impatient once more, sees himself alone in the colonnade where priest and student, silent, busy with their work, ignore him. Little by little he becomes aware of physical disproportion; the enormous shafts crush him, he goes among them like a pigmy amid the work of giants.

Yet another hour. His thoughts go round and round. Were not the giants men like himself? They weren't afraid of size. His work reveals the craftsman and the craftsman exhibits luxuriant thought, thought that evades measurement. What matters the pigmy? Her-Bak lifts his face . . . am I not heir to all that? With a thrill of pride he sets himself to search for the secret meaning of the texts. An hour goes by and head in hands he gauges the darkness that lurks in ignorance.

.   .   .

The Sage appeared. 'Admittance to the inner temple,' he said, 'demands absolute silence about instruction received there. It isn't enough never to repeat the spoken word. To interpret, to comment, is treason, until you are judged to be "established in the heart's intelligence". Are you ready?'

'I hear and will obey.'

'So may it be. Her-Bak, you are to cross the threshold. Go.'

The novice approached the main entrance, great folding doors of wood worked with gold. The Sage stopped him. 'My son, where are you going? Into a place unknown to you. Between what you will be and what you were there is a path. In every vital activity it is the path that matters, for it involves all possible relationships of time, space and means between a beginning and its end, an unfolding of law through the means. The relationships may vary according to the means, according to the direction of the path, whose point of departure, material or ideal, is the door that determines the nature and direction of the way. This above all is what the Sages have taught by symbol, inscription and the orientation of doors. Always attend to words that relate to them, for they are in every case revelatory. Our language is not vulgar but initiative.

'A door is power and it is ineluctable destiny. Power because it reveals the meaning of that to which it opens the way. Destiny because the threshold once crossed, direction and meaning are imposed on you. The main door gives passage to the Master of the House when he shews himself: it is an outward door that opens to two knocks. Other is the door that admits.'

The Sage led Her-Bak leftwards to a low doorway hardly visible in the shadows. 'Here is the beginning of your path, a beginning proportionate to it. The way of knowledge is narrow. It allows neither detour nor wilful complexity: the law is strict, the canon not indulgent. He who seeks the real no longer puts any trust in appearance.' The Sage studied Her-Bak's clouded face. 'Are you afraid of strictness?'

'I am afraid of cold.'

'Coldness is in the exactitude of the law, but life moves and fire is hot. You will choose the instruction that suits you, on condition that you allow yourself to be guided in its use, for with every departure from rule you will slip into error. Listen.

'The teaching of the three Masters is integral, each in itself. The Mystic will teach you the joy of giving. The Symbolist will awaken your intuition to the vital connexion between things and beings. The Geometer will initiate you into the properties of Number and the becoming of forms. But it would be wrong to confuse and transpose their methods.

'The science of measurement gives knowledge of "imperturbable laws", provided it starts out from reality and not from a supposition, a thing that only the Sages our Masters have known how to do. All philosophical axioms, which are the very basis of theology, should be susceptible of translation into mathematics, necessarily geometrical, for a mathematic that isn't expressed in geometrical terms opens the door to rationalistic hypotheses which lead to error. Mysticism consists in direct consciousness by con-fusion, fusion; a state of transparency that gives direct, total vision of a harmony, not at all a matter of understanding. To seek this result by a play of thought and weaving of notions is to fall into the fanciful and erroneous.'

'How can one achieve it?'

'By abolishing screens that intervene. Until you reach it be precise in your studies, avoid fantasy, be careful not to transpose the procedures of the three modes of instruction: such indiscipline turns the disciple from that path that leads to the subtlest revelations.'

The Sage fell silent. The silence lengthened. Having weighed the implications of what he was told Her-Bak spoke up. 'Master, I hear what you say. Dare I acknowledge a regret? If your science is strictly defined, measured and written down I don't see what fields of research remain open to the student.'

'Overweening Chick-Pea still imposes his presence on Her-Bak? Let Her-Bak open his heart and his ears. Written down or not, truth stands for ever, whereas your spirit is incarnate in you but for a time . . . it came to acquire consciousness of all this. What matters is the growth of your consciousness, which is the relation between the personal you and the causal Power. Don't be anxious. Each truth you learn will be, for you, as new as if it had never been written. It will always have the importance of a discovery, through its resonance through your own number and particular function in cosmos. For this is particular to each student, as well as his use of acquired consciousness in his private life.'

The disciple bowed low. 'I understand.'

·   ·   ·

At a given signal the door opened from within. The Sage embraced Her-Bak. 'Go in then, my son, and may your destiny be fulfilled.'

Shaking all over Her-Bak crossed the threshold under the eyes of a keeper who closed the heavy door. 'We enter an inner world,' said the Sage, 'where all the mysteries of the Word are at work, the Word whose face, *hr*, is a mirror. Your own face, Her-Bak, opens to the outer world by seven doors: three are double, opening eastward and westward; the seventh is one and central, yet it has a double interior canal with double function. The air of Shu bathes them all equally; but each takes from this same air, by adaptation, a different quality. The eyes, *ar-ti*, receive Shu's light. The nostrils, *sher-ti*, breathe his air. The central door, the mouth, *ra*, has a dual function, to admit offerings of food and to let the Master of the House, the active Word, emerge and shew himself. Each door is specialised as to name and function; but the central door is known by the generic name of *ra*, opening, entry. Note that the eye, *ar-t*, the nostril, *sher-t*, and the ear, *mesdjer*, have the same letter, *r*. You must learn the meaning of each door and, if you want to know where it leads you, study its form, name, place, and symbolism and it will tell you its function.'

'Master, did you forget to speak of the ear, that hears all Shu's voices?'

'The Master knows when he leaves something out. You can speak of Shu's air, his light, his shadow, his dryness, because Shu is a primordial, elemental Neter. That is to say, with his twin Tefnut, without whom he couldn't have existed, he contains the four constitutive qualities of the world; but he causes the manifestation of the Word which becomes word, voice, *kherw*, all the voices of nature. That is why the ears are said to be living, for they are the doors that receive him.'

Shyly Her-Bak expressed surprise. 'But . . . haven't I heard this about Amon?'

'Shu is immanent in perpetual creation, as primordial principle. His name evokes air and space. His symbol, a feather, is light and undivided, while Amon's is rigid, dual, divided into compartments, coloured and pervades the sky. For the universal Neter Amon, whose nature and power are likewise aerial, containing the four qualities of Shu and Tefnut, is essentially the generative environment of being in cosmos. The name Amon is that of an aerial water that carries in itself the principle of stability. While Shu gives our atmosphere its qualities of fire, light and air, the generation of a being in the world is surrounded by the amniotic water of Amon like a foetus in the womb.'

The disciple didn't hide his feelings. 'Master, I'm hardly through the first door and already so many symbols are shewn me. But I still don't know where I am.'

'This is the entrance to the inner temple,' said the Sage. 'In this hall offerings received in the hall leading to it are consecrated.'

Her-Bak considered the strong columns, the altar-table, the dressers for offerings and various articles used in the rite. 'I don't understand the principle of the offering,' he said. 'If the Neters are the powers that rule nature they don't need what is brought to them.'

'They don't need it,' said the Sage, 'but man needs them. Don't let yourself be deceived by a too facile confusion of the abstract, causal Neters with the concrete form in which they have had to be depicted so as to avoid the mistaken transpositions an abstract theological teaching might lead to. As man is always tempted to invent gods in his own image it is better to give him pictures whose hieratic style and peculiarities of composition exclude the possibility of sentimental error and interpretation of the divine in terms of the human. The Neters are an expression of the principles and functions of divine Power manifesting in nature. Their names and images as pictured in the myths define such principles and functions and they are offered that the student may learn to know them and seek them in himself.

'For the Neters are within you and this can't be explained to the masses, though an effective rite may awaken consciousness of it. That is one reason for the offering. An offering, made at the offerer's expense, arouses in him the consciousness and effective desire of the Neter's action. Such desire is the force of attraction, the magnetic power, we call *mer*. It means a want, a need, a void that longs to be filled. This is the active principle of the sacrifice, which is based on the law of compensation.

'But there is a risk that you will be deceived as to the meaning of "compensation" unless you understand the action of "crossing" and the reactive force in all nature. You must habituate yourself to this mode of thinking if you wish to read our symbols, for we "cross" every idea. Bear in mind then that every phenomenon is a reactive effect, that an active cause never produces a direct effect, since it remains abstract, imperceptible, unless there is resistance. When a resistance of the same kind as the cause absorbs and annuls it, regard this as a first "crossing" that is also a death; but when the resistance becomes active in its turn, as an anvil throws back the hammer that strikes it, the effect will be a life-phenomenon, which is what we mean by the "second crossing".'

'Does the law of crossing as applied to an offering mean that the sacrifice to the Neter should produce by reaction its effect in myself?'

'Correct, as far as the moral magic of sacrifice is concerned. The practice of sacrifice is a defence of human consciousness against the deadly effect of the search for satisfaction. Animal man obeys the desire of satisfaction as nature obeys the law of inertia. Now satisfaction of a desire neutralises it and this is a kind of death . . . such is possession of a thing ardently sought. The only active force that arises out of possession is fear of losing the object possessed: this is an egoism, constrictive, which consequently diminishes more or less the power of its appeal.'

'I see,' said Her-Bak eagerly. 'Then the object in sacrificing the firstlings of the herds and firstfruits of the harvest is to counter the possessive instinct that interrupts an exchange between man and Neter?'

'Her-Bak, you still seem to forget that the Neters are also in yourself. It isn't at all a question of exchange as the profane understand it. An offering of firstlings, like all true sacrifice, arouses in the giver faith in the thing he desires or the power to bring it about, whereas there is risk that the effect of simple prayer will be compromised by the unconscious doubt it evokes, by way of reaction, in the man who makes it.'

'Still, a sacrifice or gift offered against something desired is an exchange,' said Her-Bak.

'Not as understood in the market, a deal in quantities, but a "compensation" according to the law of Maât or the law of equilibrium immanent in dualised nature, as night for instance balances day, outbreathing inbreathing. What troubles you is the confusion of various intentions in the act of sacrifice, the object of which may be magically to awaken creative faith in the thing desired, to evoke the thing by desire or the magic of analogues, or to provoke its realisation by reaction.'

'What is the difference between evocation and provocation?'

'To provoke is to excite reaction in the thing, being or power to which provocation is addressed by resisting it. If you defy an enemy by doubting his courage you double it. Wind strengthens the trunks of trees and the ears of corn by provoking their reactive, their vital, power. A bone, eaten by dog or vulture, stimulates the action of juices that facilitate its digestion.'

'Then these animals run the risk of perishing if they are deprived of this kind of food?' asked Her-Bak, attentive.

'Want of lime atrophies their characteristic digestive function, which is specialised for it. As to evocation, it invites actualisation of the desired object by offering the thing, principle or idea that will act towards it magnetically, direct or by the magic of analogues. In the first case it works by creating a want or void that becomes the *mer*, or attractive force, for a thing of its own kind. If you wish to drain a piece of land you have only to dig a canal deeper than the level of the adjacent waters so that they gather there: the depth of the canal is your magnet for them. If your stomach feels no desire of food you can stimulate hunger by evoking a favourite dish. If you plant shrubs in the desert, giving them the water strictly necessary if they are to live, their roots will go deeper seeking water underground and their leaves will draw humidity from the air. In this way your plantation may transform sterile soil into fertile. What will you have done to gain victory over the Sethian fire of the desert? You evoked the Amon-Osiris functions of nature by offering Osiris vegetation.

'In the second case, evocation uses the magic of analogues, which is the intelligent choice of an analogue with the characteristics of the desired thing: funeral offerings are often made in the form of flowers in elongated bouquets, as if by some freak of growth they sprang from one another. You evoke by analogy what you wish for the dead. The flower bears seed; the symbol or analogy of such bouquets is the rearising of life that no longer depends on Earth. It even happens that the mummy's image is given excessive height to accentuate and intensify the symbol's power.'

'Doesn't this say the same thing as the prayer so often repeated in our texts, "May your name flower again"?'

The Master approved. 'This is true. Funeral ceremonies give further evidence of it in the dress of the mourners, whose robes and hair evoke the water of rejuvenation.'

'Don't the myths confirm it,' Her-Bak asked, 'by depicting the resurrection of Osiris through the tears of Isis and Nephtys?'

'Correct. Enrich your understanding with this other thought: evocation by the magic of analogues has an aspect of which the profane are ignorant. The offering in this case is not a gift but a symbol of what the Neter invoked can give.'

Her-Bak made a point. 'It doesn't seem that what is offered need be identical with the thing asked for. If I sacrifice a bull's thigh . . .'

'. . . it is because you need what it represents. To judge well of the matter you must acquire what you still lack, knowledge of analogues in nature, which we always use in our symbolic images. Begin by noting the characteristics of the thing offered. The nourishing flesh of a quadruped's thigh hasn't the same functional meaning as the forefoot, which gives measure and direction to the power that resides in the thigh. Learn also to distinguish the gestures of the arms and hands of the one who makes the offering or performs the rite. An arm held up offers an emblem of what is desired. Hands lifted in opposition to the Neter provoke him. The supplicant gesture of hands cupped to receive is an evocation. Consider without neglecting any one of them the details of an offering: each is a word, each picture a book.'

Musing, the disciple contemplated the sculptured walls. 'Then each of these commonplace scenes teaches something?'

'Can you doubt it from now on? In default of other proofs wouldn't the meticulous care over details, their coincidence with the relevant texts, the opportune rearrangements of proportion in successive epochs, the strict correspondence of gesture with the intention of an offering be enough? But experience is the real proof, if you use our method of thinking in the consideration of the themes. Their true value lies in an integral correspondence with the laws of nature that gives them the character of universality. If you discern the principle that a picture interprets you will be able to explain what corresponds with it in the becoming of chick or foetus, or of a man, or a being in the Dwat, on condition that you are not mistaken as to what phase is symbolised.'

'Master of Wisdom! I have seen the whole meaning of the sacrifice.'

'No.' The Sage pointed to the offertory table. 'In spite of all I have said you haven't grasped the most inward meaning. You passed the night before a statue of Ptah in swaddling-bands and you didn't understand that *pth* is creative force bound through the fall into matter. It is the cause of life but it only lives when peace, *hotep, htp* or *pth* in reverse, releases it: that is to say when peace or union has been made between the creative energy and what is to be given life. For there is a destroying fire in Ptah that becomes creative when this union is achieved. That is why *hotep* is the word for peace as well as for an offering; peace, conciliation, between opposites is the most perfect of offerings, peace in which the giver gives himself in communion and becomes mediator, a leaven.'

Marvelling, Her-Bak studied the symbols the Sage shewed him. 'How can this teaching be secret when it is written in the words *pth* and *htp*?' he asked.

'Alas, man looks to the semblance and fears the reality.'

'Master, the gift you have made me demands a recompense. The only thing I'm attached to is the jewel you gave me.' Her-Bak restored it to the Sage. 'I tear out a piece of my heart . . . is it enough?'

'No gift compares with the gift of Heaven. But sacrifice pride and an offering acquires efficacy.' The Sage placed the jewel on an altar. He crossed his disciple's arms, took his hands in his own crossed hands and said, 'What Ptah made is returned to him, that he may make peace, *hotep*, in you and live in what he created.'

. . .

The Sage was the first to break silence. He touched the novice's brow. 'What are you waiting for, Her-Bak? You have forgotten something?'

'Master, I have been fed and fortified during this hour more than in a year of the Peristyle.'

'What is astonishing in that? They aren't the same doors. But were you not awaiting an answer? Or do you think you have had it?'

'Master, I know you were talking about life when you were telling me about peace. But I have still everything to learn, everything to receive . . . would you make me the gift of the promised answer?'

The Sage led his disciple into a shadowy room. A lamp with feeble flame lit walls covered with texts and carved scenes. A great image of Min presided. He made Her-Bak sit facing the Neter, limbs crossed, hands open on the knees; he burned incense in a dish and waited until silence calmed the disciple. Then in the serenity of this atmosphere he

c

spoke, grave with unusual gravity, asking, 'What is life? It is a form of the divine presence. It is the power, immanent in created things, to change themselves by successive destructions of form until the spirit or activating force of the original life-stream is freed. This power resides in the very nature of things. Successive destruction of forms, metamorphoses, by the divine fire with rebirth of forms new and living is an expression of consciousness. It is the spiritual aim of all human life to attain a state of consciousness that is independent of bodily circumstance.

'What I have just said concerns the living spirit bestowed on the man already quickened, like every living thing, by a rudimentary soul, which makes of such a man a creature superior to the animal-human kingdom. He who recognises the divine meaning of life knows that knowledge has but one aim, which is to achieve the successive stages that liberate him from the perishable. For things only die in their body: the spirit, the divine Word, returns to its source and dies not. Unhappy is the KA that fails to recover its soul.'

.   .   .

Eyes closed, Her-Bak took in every word of an answer whose importance he realised. When after long silence he expressed his gratitude he no longer spoke out of unquiet curiosity but in the certainty of a heart that has found its anchorage. The Sage allowed him to savour the joy of it, then gave the impetus for a new effort. 'Don't be satisfied with the terms of my answer: the nut doesn't reveal the tree it contains. Bury my word in your heart that it may put out root and seed; then return untiring to seek your nourishment in it until you have exhausted its substance.'

III

THE THREE CIRCLES

Her-Bak thought he knew the chief features of the great city that surrounds the temples, but a few days in his new environment shewed him he was wrong. He found that whereas he had used certain roads, always the same, frequented the same temple-courts, the same gardens, visited a craftsmen's quarter, some granaries and outhouses, the city, fortified by sentry-walks and bastions on the circumference, comprised certain quarters sequestered between the walls of the sanctuaries, their gardens enclosed, their paths bordered with workshops for secret processes. This labyrinth hid from profane visitors the life of a closed world.

One such sheltered the retreat of some who were never seen in the Peristyle, among whom Her-Bak recognised the three Masters and Nefer-Sekheru. A group of low houses made a home for students and disciples; a thin-sown palm-grove shaded some private dwellings, temporary residence of distinguished visitors. Roads linked them all with the principal services of the temple without touching the common ways. This was the cause of turnings and windings that had puzzled the novice, for in the course of his walks Her-Bak had touched without knowing it this inner world whose activity in no way resembled the to-ing and fro-ing of the outer world that was so close to it. No one in it took any notice of others apart from the common life and work; each went his way, within his own boundaries, without envying his neighbour. From highest to lowest teaching and experience were for each his only preoccupation. Working so hard one acquired a habit of forgetting egoistic interests on pain of being expelled as a hindrance. The common welfare safeguarded peace and in face of these invisible defences storms from the outer world, intrigues, jealousies, died away like waves on the river.

This astonished Her-Bak. So did much else. After his first surprise at finding an old friend, Aqer, next to him in his lodging, he plagued him with questions. But today Aqer didn't respond with his usual patience. 'It amazes me,' he said, 'you, so greedy for knowledge . . . you should know that peace is an indispensable condition of getting it.'

'Of course I know it,' said Her-Bak. 'But I didn't expect to find it among men who must have their faults, angers, ambitions, like others.'

Aqer exploded with laughter, 'As to faults, don't doubt it: isn't the best of us a marsh in course of evolution? But it's no obstacle, if one doesn't annoy one's neighbours. As for ambition, you'll soon be reassured ... or disappointed if it is in your heart. You'll see that it does to intuition what the weevil does in a granary. Besides, anyone who works out of ambition is soon recognised and the door shut in his face.'

'Isn't ambition a powerful and often legitimate motive?'

'Powerful, with a man who seeks to dominate others. For one whose interest is not in effects but in causes ambition loses its reason for existing: he will occupy himself with the play of natural forces, destiny, the laws that govern things, rather than with acquiring power.'

'But it can happen that the desire to make a show predominates?'

'If it does the man is driven from the inner circle.'

'Out of the inner temple?'

Aqer hesitated. Seeing it Her-Bak apologised. 'Don't say anything if your heart isn't free to speak. But questions are swarming in my own ... must I suppress them? I notice that venerable men treat you as a familiar. My old professor Pasab, now Upuat, speaks to me with deference and I am more ignorant than he ...'

Aqer took Her-Bak's hands and regarded him with pleasure. 'We are fortunate, you and I. We shall always find friendly ears for our questions and mouths to answer them. How many can say as much? Get up and come along, for you are bidden by a great man and we mustn't keep him waiting. Put on your robe of fine linen and follow me.'

Much excited Her-Bak hurried to obey and followed his friend in silence.

.   .   .

They soon left the city walls for a countryside empurpled by the setting sun. At the roadsides pavilions stood among sycamores and date-palms before one of which Aqer stopped that his friend might take a look at the charming little house, rectangular, miniature, perfect. The walls were of plastered brick, smooth as plates of sawn lime-stone. Small windows, placed high, patterned the lateral walls with blinds in Nubian basket-work; the cornice was heightened with lively colours, the door fastened with a wrought lock. The one-time carpenter admired the joints of the door-frame in wood of red *meri* and ebony, 'What marvellous work, Aqer!' he cried. 'How everything fits! Truly this is perfectly put together, *menkh*.'

Aqer agreed. 'You couldn't put it better, my friend.'

A porter admitted them to a room with four small columns in the middle of which three personages, well known to Her-Bak, were talking. One of them, the master of the house, watched the young men come in, smiling. Her-Bak, dumb with astonishment, was pinned to the spot. 'My Lord Menkh!' He threw himself at Menkh's feet, but the great lord raised him and held him in his arms, saying, 'Don't tremble, my son. Are you not my guest?'

Recovering self-possession Her-Bak saluted the Sage and Nefer-Sekheru in turn. They welcomed him and Aqer cordially and he took his place on a stool Menkh assigned him. Aqer seemed perfectly at ease: his deference to his hosts was matched by the friendly tone of the three seniors. And so great was the one-time sandal-bearer's pleasure that he forgot to feel embarrassment in his new role as guest.

Two little Nubian servants busied themselves about a sideboard loaded with bowls of fruit kept fresh under leaves, honey-cakes, boiled milk, wine made from dates and from grapes. They put a low table with the necessary vessels before the two friends and Her-Bak, occupied with Menkh's questions, watched without seeing them. A young negro brought a bronze jug in a basin. 'The water-jug, Excellency.'

Following Aqer's example Her-Bak wetted fingers and lips.

'The towel, Excellency.' The second young negro respectfully dried his fingers. Somewhat troubled, yet quickly adapting himself to the surroundings, he let them wait on him and answered Menkh eagerly, recovering all Chick-Pea's verve with his old Master.

The Sage and Nefer-Sekheru were well aware of the reactions of Her-Bak, schoolboy, neophyte, disciple. Menkh waited for the enthusiasm of reunion to cool down and they watched the novice, noting the salient traits of his disposition. The novice talked, while his plate was filled with cakes and sweetmeats which he ate abstractedly. The young negroes took pleasure in this game. Their sly glances put him on guard . . . he pushed his stool away. 'What am I doing? I'm not a performing crocodile.'

The Sage smiled, 'One learns from everything. For the disciple every gesture is a theme to be mastered.'

Her-Bak accepted the lesson, apologised for his loquacity. Menkh stopped him. 'Today you are a friend among friends. Let your heart speak.'

'In that case,' Her-Bak replied, 'you will know that my eyes are not yet used to my surroundings . . . could you throw some light? I have asked questions of Aqer and no doubt I have been indiscreet . . . he couldn't answer.'

The Sage interrogated Aqer who repeated Her-Bak's questions, leaving out nothing. They listened, but no one opened his mouth to satisfy the novice's curiosity. The young negroes brought lamps, offered wine made from dates: they were chased away like sparrows and evening calm filled the air. A circle was formed; then said the Sage to Nefer-Sekheru, 'You are the expert on social relations. Will you give my disciple some light on the subject? If he doesn't forfeit the privilege he will live in intimacy with us: it is good that he should know how things are planned and ordained.'

Nefer-Sekheru said to Her-Bak, 'You have known communal and social life in various aspects. You have lived among peasants. You have watched managers, scribes, officials. You have had opportunity to assess the worth of good or bad craftsmen. What impression have you concerning those so employed?'

Her-Bak reflected and didn't dare speak his mind. 'Your presence among us,' said Menkh, 'demands absolute frankness. Tell us all your thought, Her-Bak.'

The novice saw he must reply. 'I give my love and admiration to my Masters here present, to my teacher Pasab, to Nadjar, to the master-potter, the harpist Mesdjer and several exceptional craftsmen. Apart from these I have only known peasants, workmen, officials, scribes, even priests, greedy for gain and the favour of the great rather than in love with their work and the truth. It astonishes me that with such a difference between such men and the Masters great things are possible in this country.'

Menkh looked at the Sage, who said, 'The problem is clearly put.'

'In effect,' Menkh said, 'though there is no possibility whatever of systematically infusing the masses with wisdom, we must look at the facts. You can travel the Two-Lands in every direction and throughout the cultivated regions, marking the desert tracks, all along the banks of the Nile, you will find temples, funerary monuments, steles, covered with carved texts, often ornamented with precious substances perfectly wrought. Everywhere you will come across sanctuaries under construction or in course of alteration, stone-yards, quarrymen, master-masons erecting columns, statues or steles. You will find teams of sculptors and painters who incessantly modify monumental inscriptions. Picture an innumerable crowd of workers spread through the nomes of the Two-Lands, since the temples are altered or renewed according to the necessities of the epoch. Later on you will learn what complex forms the language of architecture requires in the shaping of each stone, differences in proportion according to purpose, a complexity of irregular details

that inscribe secrets of date and number. Such inconceivable precision
and the difficulties of calculation and execution demand the co-operation
of experts, as much as the making of overall plans as in the technical
work of construction and carving. Try to imagine what the renovation
of one single sanctuary requires in the way of initiate overseers and
expert teams. Multiply them by the number of stone-yards and ask
yourself how such a multitude is recruited.'

'After what I've seen I can't understand it,' murmured Her-Bak.
'Where do they come from?'

'Learn to reason from evidence,' said Menkh. 'Draw a parallel between
the small craftsmen who supply the necessities of the people and the
technicians employed in more lasting work, not to mention the Masters
who watch over the perpetuity of tradition. Could you put them in the
same category? The smelters of rare alloys used in tools for shaping the
hardest materials . . . are they to be compared with the makers of common
implements? Are the owners of estates whose sole care is their personal
advantage to be put on the same footing as those who have traditional
knowledge such as can make the vines of Khonsu flourish extra-
ordinarily as well as the magnificent cattle of Amon? Among our Sages
you will find men who claim to possess these gifts and at the same time to
have created such a *chef d'œuvre* as a colossal statue or the building of a
temple. You must either recognise, in face of the evidence, the universal
character of their knowledge or allow for symbolic functions . . . which
takes nothing from the fact that these men have left indisputable testimony
to their science in their architectural work.'

'Did they really perform several functions at once?'

'It isn't the daily performance of a function that matters,' the Sage
said, 'but the fundamental knowledge that gives mastery and allows of
its being communicated. The first thing necessary in teaching is a master;
the second is a pupil capable of carrying on the tradition. But let the
Chief Technician complete what he wished to say.'

'There is a paradox in our situation,' said Menkh, 'that is inexplicable
to one unacquainted with our inner organisation. You have felt it, Her-
Bak. You will find in the priesthood the same difference as in other
professions: call to mind priests, even among the top grades, who make
sure of their material and social life by a title, often hereditary, and you
will never confuse them with the initiates of our high sciences, who
gained their knowledge by strict detachment and impersonality,
guarantees of discretion. The proofs are, continuity of traditional teaching
on temple walls in every age, an inviolate secrecy that protects it and

the anonymity of the work. You know the world of officials and scribes well enough to see that one can't normally endow them with such impersonality by governing their passions. There has to be some means of picking out, among the various classes, those capable of a teaching that will give their activities an unusual quality and ensure their silence and incorruptibility. But if there is such a means it explains why we have no castes or classes, since the constituents of an *élite* are taken from all of them. They pass from one occupation or profession to another and in the end accumulate the know-how of several.'

This delighted Her-Bak. 'I have seen examples, as the Lord Menkh knows.'

'Without doubt, Her-Bak. But don't lose sight of the ditch that separates the two elements of the problem. The men of our country are ranked by occupation and this can be changed on request with good reason shewn, if those who rule agree. This state of affairs, which applies to officials, scribes and even priests, craftsmen, clerks and peasants who take part in Egypt's functional life, is open to injustices and the weaknesses inherent in human nature. If our sciences and techniques depended on it they would as in other countries have deviated from the straight line following private caprice and interpretation. Whereas our monuments and texts display continuous fidelity to the wholeness of our tradition. Thus, two realities co-exist: on the one hand the imperfection of men, great or small, who have no other horizon than the coercive duties of material and social life; on the other the splendour and perfection of work done for the temple. Such co-existence seems unlikely to those who are unaware of the secret classification we are going to disclose to you, which is based on the fact that individual worth is assessed by competent Masters, according to qualities of heart and professional capacity.'

The Sage confirmed this and added, 'The difficulty is to discern, in each grade of society, those who are likely to develop, those with unappreciated gifts, those capable of rapid progress. And when they are discovered it remains to give them the means of shewing what is in them. One can't impose virtues that passion thwarts on every occasion. It is necessary that the pleasure the awakening of their gifts excites shall bring them the consciousness of real nobility; the nobility of altruism, work done for an impersonal motive, incorruptibility. To get this result a social constitution isn't enough, for it judges individual effort by material success, whatever means are used. There must be a subtler method of weighing things: the incorruptible judgment of Maât. But no man is competent in that sphere who hasn't been trained in the proper school:

that's why there must be a higher organisation, an organisation with what we may call psychological consciousness that permeates the social order without violating it and prevents suffocation of the lotus that is trying to reach light at the surface.'

At the Sage's request Nefer-Sekheru undertook to explain the structure of this organisation. 'Our society is conceived of as a tree with roots, trunk, leaves and fruit. Each of the tree's organs has its laws of generation and production: we must shew you how the cells of the trunk are selected in such a way that the cells of the pith may be powerful, capable of giving the whole tree life and of maintaining its strength throughout, no matter what difficulties. The root or fixed point of the tree is wisdom. Now imagine a centre or nucleus round which are three circles or discs of increasing circumference, concentric, like the rings of a trunk round the pith. This nucleus is the vital heart of our society; it comprises the source of wisdom of which the King, life, health and power, is the active arm. I won't deal with the nucleus today. The first of the circles that surround it is the inner circle of initiates in the temple. The second is composite. The third, the outer, has no relation with the specific life of the first. Many officials form part of it, craftsmen, minor priests, scribes, cultivators and managers. The three circles are so to say incorporate, without open distinction, in the various classes; and just as the generative layer of cells in a treetrunk is next the bark, and as some cells push outward, some towards the inner rings, so men are found among the people who can make their way circle by circle to the centre. Are you not an example, Her-Bak, seeing your father remains among the cells of the mass?

'Consider now the intermediate, composite circle in which people of various classes move . . . priests, scribes, officials of all grades, technicians, craftsmen, who shew comprehensive possibilities without as yet sufficient guarantee that further instruction will be fruitful. It is a circle under observation, in which means of education are offered through groups and organisations, by means of rites, feasts, and various techniques. It is there that those admissible to the inner circle are picked out.'

Her-Bak was more and more amazed. 'How is it I didn't know this? Have I been part of a circle without knowing it?'

'No one knows until he is on the inside: there are no visible barriers. Those on the outside have no secrets. The composites receive suitable advantages: there's nothing for them to desire, unless it's wisdom. Those of the inner ring alone must know who the others are, that they may know what to hide or disclose. For our techniques and sciences hold certain secrets that are not to be given to the ambitious who would profane them, to the undisciplined who would distort them, to the wicked who would abuse them.'

Her-Bak pondered over this surprising organisation. 'To accept part in it carries the obligation of obedience and demands qualities that are not demanded of others?' he asked.

'Isn't it obvious? Doesn't participation in such blessings require a higher consciousness?'

'To win it I'll be my animal self's worst enemy!'

'We accept your undertaking,' said the Sage. 'If you weren't capable of it you wouldn't have been invited to join us. For this group's life is lived in retreat from worldly stupidities, that there may be no intrigue, no hindrance, such as personal preoccupations inevitably arouse. In this way we secure the peace and harmony that surprise you. But peace is the fruit of activity, not of sleep. Our friends are alive, but as their aim is ours the quest comes before self-interest and our struggles are in ourselves, never against the neighbour.'

'I would like to make an essential point,' said Nefer-Sekheru. 'In a figure of three concentric circles draw two triangles whose bases touch the outermost and whose apexes meet at the centre. Place the temple in one, Pharoah's court in the other, and you will get an idea, schematic but exact, of how thoroughly these two powers permeate the circles. In the inner, the composite and the outer you will find members of the court, the priesthood and the schools, for there is no question of honorific distinctions but of qualities and tried states of consciousness. A dignitary may be an "outsider" while his colleague is picked for the inner teaching: that is why one sees some among them who perform more than one function, apparently irreconcilable, of which one may be practical, another symbolic and comprehensible only to those who know.'

'Am I then,' Her-Bak asked, 'to mistrust titles that give their possessors the right to steles and monuments?'

'All such, if they have been authorised to perpetuate their memory in this way, must have adapted themselves to the symbol of the name that was imposed on them. Their function may be practical because it fits their nature; but if it is good that they should add one that is purely symbolic they don't hesitate since it is a teaching they inscribe on the monument, not their personal life.'

'I shall never again be astonished,' said Her-Bak, 'over work done with such self-sacrifice. Here are men who accepted the annihilation of their personality to be representatives of a symbol.'

The Masters were touched: they were of one mind. Her-Bak prostrated himself, saying, 'You have done me the honour to summon me. I wish to serve as you serve, were I the least of your servants.'

Rising, Menkh filled a cup with wine and offered it to the Sage who when he had raised it to his lips handed it to his disciple. 'We haven't yet drunk wine together,' he said. 'Drink, Her-Bak, and may silence be in your mouth from henceforth.'

.　　　.　　　.

When they had all drunk wine Menkh resumed his place at the Sage's side. Her-Bak seated himself at their feet as one of a family and said, 'When I was Chick-Pea my behind got the answer to indiscreet questions. Now I see why. Dare I ask questions now without being thought insolent?'

'You may,' said Menkh, laughing, 'since the Master of Wisdom has done you the honour of taking you as his disciple without your having gone through the student stage.'

'Do you make such difference between student and disciple? How can such honour be accorded to your servant?'

'All this time I have answered for you to speed your training,' the Sage said. 'Have I been unwise?'

'Master, I will be deaf, blind and dumb sooner than betray you.'

'To be dumb will do. Open on the contrary your eyes and ears, for an exceptional effort will be required of you. There is a great difference between students instructed in our sciences and techniques and disciples initiated into their causes.'

'Are students of the temple members of the inner circle?'

'Not until they have completed what includes certain secrets. Some expert technicians, some high officials, are in with us though without a disciple's training. This requires a change in them that opens intuition to the knowledge of causes. But a disciple is always part of our circle, and obliged to make total submission.'

'Who wouldn't, for such a prize!'

'Willingness is by no means enough. Predestination is necessary.'

'Who can discern the predestined?'

'Those who are trained to it. You'll learn the way of it, if you get that far.'

'I am discovering a new world,' Her-Bak murmured. 'How does such a world keep in harmony with the world of other men?'

Nefer-Sekheru replied, 'It is this world that makes harmony possible. If the masses follow instinct the strong among them will bully the weak in spite of all their resistance. Passion will hold the sceptre whatever class governs, for envious greed must govern to possess and ambition must possess to govern: their sceptre is the whip.'

'Hasn't there been rebellion in such case?'

'Anarchy changes masters. The oppressed becomes the oppressor. It is always so when privilege is given to goods and revenues, or birth.'

'Isn't this too often the case?'

'As regards certain offices, but not at all as regards our secret techniques or for functions that demand knowledge of universal law. One can't wholly prevent injustice in the outer world, for human passions are unmanageable; but an inner circle, if it is alive, gives the country an impetus just as fire in the marrow quickens all organs. The channels are our Brothers, trained in the traditions of a hierarchy that is qualitative. They uphold the principle that gives supremacy to true professional and moral worth.'

'Are they high dignitaries of the kingdom?'

'Dignitaries or not, it isn't their titles that matter. They are a leaven that vitalises the dough according to the specific requirement of the time.'

'Are they then Sages?'

'They follow the instructions of the Sages of their time.'

'Have they sometimes governed the country?'

'In the great days yes, and effectively. But in every age they drew their strength from the Brotherhood and this allowed them to affirm their wisdom without vanity: for wisdom isn't the work of a man but of a traditional training. In times of decadence those who survived played a hidden part, averting destruction of the roots, safeguarding the treasures and legacies of truth, so as to hand them on to their successors.'

Aqer, who had listened attentively, made a point. 'It isn't any the less astonishing that the traditional foundations should have held, in spite of disorders and invasions. Our letters, our symbols, the secrets of the canon and of measurement, have never been lost or profaned since very ancient times.'

'That is so,' the Sage agreed. 'The science of Number and certain keys that derive from it enabled us to foresee days of ill omen and take precautions. The immunity you refer to is evidence of this.'

Nefer-Sekheru added, 'That invaders have never succeeded in imposing their doctrines on us but have adapted themselves to ours is yet one more proof of the value of our knowledge.'

'History confirms this,' Menkh said. 'As to interior disturbances, the simplicity of our customs helped us to avoid a definite collapse. Our mineral wealth would have made a considerable trade with our neighbours possible, but we reduced such exchanges to what was essential; we avoided what might have led to personal luxury and obliged us to substitute a rate of exchange between individuals for barter. For when luxury becomes a necessity preponderance is given to wealth. Society is no longer governed by the principle of quality but by favouritism and greed.'

'Luxury would have increased the craftsmen's skill,' said Aqer.

'We use luxury in impersonal matters,' Nefer-Sekheru replied. 'In matters of religion, monuments, symbolic art. We use it in private life, when some rare object gives the idea of quality for instance, without falling into the error of complexity and the lust after quantity. Menkh was right. When the governing class isn't chosen for quality it is chosen for material wealth: this always means decadence, the lowest stage a society can reach.'

'I don't clearly see the importance of the idea of quality,' Her-Bak said to his Master.

'Two tendencies govern human choice and effort,' the Sage replied, 'the search after quantity and the search after quality. They classify mankind. Some follow the way of Maât, others seek the satisfaction of animal instinct. Quantity relates to material goods and their possession. It belongs to the terrestrial goddess of fecundity, Apet-Taurt, Apet, symbol of numbers and material treasures, Taurt, the belly ever full of seeds that grow and multiply. Quantity is given by *âsh* or *âsha*, numerous, multiplicity: notice that the opposite of *âsh* is *shâ*, sand, a characteristic of which is multiplicity of grains. Quantitative mentality, an expression of cerebral consciousness, consists in the analytical consideration of parts without vital connexion.

'Quality in itself is creative power. Creation manifests a hierarchy of specific qualities or multiple aspects of the Great Neter and attributes of the Neters; they belong to the world of causes, the values that form and rule matter; but they become perceptible, assessable, by way of comparison, in the world of phenomena. We assign to various forms of perfection names determined by a material aspect, *menkh*, *âqer*, *ân*. *Menkh*, a putting together with tenon and mortice, designates the idea of excellence in the sense of unified diversity, perfect joining together, exactitude, conformity, precision.

'As to *âqer*, the material picture is a polished surface, precisely defined, flawless; a woman shining with *âqeret*, smooth complexion, creamed; the final dressing of a wall, polished, stuccoed, before texts are carved on it. This designates the idea of excellence in the sense of the completion of a phase, the accomplishment of a function, a state achieved or the end of a road reached; *àqer* gives the idea of a quality acquired, a result achieved.

'As to *ân*, the eye was chosen for this word, which gives the individual-isation of a quality, the manifestation, exteriorisation, of the quality proper to a being or thing. The symbol is happy, for by its colour and shape an eye discloses a man's energy qualities as well as his organic and moral reactions. But two essentials precede all particular qualities. One is a relation of harmony between a thing and its properties, *her*; the other is the vital intensity that belongs to the thing, an intensity that gives it power of accomplishment and continuity, *nefer*.

'This word, in regard to the thing thus qualified, means what air means for the blood, nervous force for the body, seminal power for the individual. The *nefer* principle is the qualitative principle. It can't be calculated or measured. Our cerebral and sensorial faculties only allow us to assess qualities through quantitative comparison, a substance more or less hard, a man more or less strong, more or less able: such assessment is relative to an individual's means of perception. Qualities of a moral order are measured by deeds. A plant has several qualities that are per-ceptible sensorially, its colour, taste, scent; but it has also a certain healing quality that is subtler than these, a power that is one of the characteristics of its vital quality or qualitative principle *nefer*, perceptible to us through the intelligence of the heart.'

'Is my Master saying that the intelligence of the heart is never deceived?'

'We are saying, Her-Bak, that the intelligence of the heart is vision of the real or communion with it, with what in reality *is*, or again with the essential nature and quality of the thing. Integral vision or knowledge of this order excludes all possibility of personal interpretation whether intellectual or emotional . . . otherwise it is no longer intelligence of the heart. It is personal interpretation that is fallible, being susceptible to subjective judgment. In the animal, above all the savage animal, such intelligence lies in what we call instinct, which runs no danger of being affected by mental activity. In man, when cerebral consciousness can read it without mistake, it becomes intuition.'

'Then we must cultivate intuition if we are to perceive the vital qualities, the *nefer*, of things and beings, and their relation of harmony, *her*?'

'We cultivate it,' the Sage replied, 'when we encourage the craftsman to put quality first in the smallest piece of work, when we awaken in our students a consciousness of the relations that link the things of this Earth with Heaven, in general when we formulate the laws of analogy, and finally when by representations of the Neters and by the symbolism of letters we describe the functions and qualities of nature. A man who will learn by this symbolism quickly becomes open-hearted.'

Nefer-Sekheru finished by answering what was behind one of Her-Bak's questions. 'As to the social problem that interests you, the qualitative selection of individuals is a choice of perception and judgment . . . are their faculties and gifts such as guarantee perfect accomplishment in a trade or profession? Have they the qualities of energy, constancy, loyalty, that will foster and enhance them?'

'That is true,' said the Sage, 'but it would never be feasible without the three circles. One can't stifle the masses by obliging them to practise what is as yet beyond their capacity. They must have scope for their turpitude and opportunity to gain consciousness of it through suffering. Selective activity can only proceed by experiment and indirect test, which is really the aim of the system. In this way we can guide those chosen in the use of their real aptitudes and give them effective means of developing their gifts.'

'The perfection of your work proves the success of your methods,' said Her-Bak. 'But isn't the being chosen a blow to individual consciousness and an attack on the joy of life?'

'All that makes for the joy of life among men of Earth is accorded to each class within the limit of its real needs. It is an individual's training and aspiration that determines the choice that is made of him, which besides leads him step by step to pleasures of higher quality. No one is forced to prefer the austere and impersonal quest in which those of the inner circle and centre are engaged. Those who take this path are a minority and the majority would never relish their pleasures; but the minority understands the majority's aspirations and tries to give them due satisfaction, as the cells of the pith dispense vitality to the cells of the bark. It is this that justifies and necessitates the three circles.'

Aqer accepted this, but he looked for some other way of maintaining the progress gained through selection in this mode. 'Do you not believe in the law of heredity? Can't heredity give a basis of continuity for a governing class?'

'Heredity,' answered the Sage himself, 'concerns blood and body; it has nothing to do with the reincarnation of an individualised soul. There is a line of incarnation in the same blood for the ancestral soul, but it follows certain laws of Number. A son merely receives from his parents some physical, emotional and mental traits; that is tendencies and characteristics that make up the mortal body, the animating soul and the lower KA . . . I speak now of hereditary germs that incarnate in liver and spleen. Such personal characteristics create envelopes of a specific rhythm; transmitted from father to son they constitute a channel by which the ancestral soul may find, after several generations, an environment apt to its rhythm. We may say then that there is heredity in principle; but it would be wrong to ascribe powers and qualities to immediate heredity without verification. Besides, considerations of time and coincidence come into play. But we must take into account such atavistic legacies, held so to speak in reserve, so that when the hour of rebirth comes the soul may find its proper environment.'

Aqer shewed gratitude. 'You teach us what should be the key to several problems, Master of Wisdom.'

'We won't attack them today. Now you understand that the continuity of our traditions necessitates constant selection; but in spite of an impersonal centre that exercises hidden control it would be impracticable without the progressive testings of the three circles. But participation in secret knowledge is the object of a severe choice; for while our symbolic writing and theological art speaks to the profane in religious imagery it speaks to the "open-hearted" as a revelation of principles.'

The Sage rose. The two disciples followed his example. Her-Bak marvelled over what he had heard. He thanked Menkh for having summoned him and Menkh replied, 'You will come back, if you make what you've received bear fruit.'

Her-Bak couldn't repress curiosity. 'Does Monseigneur always live in this pavilion? What has become of the fine house where I was sandal-bearer?'

'All remains in the state in which you knew it. You are here in my place of retreat during the days I shall pass with my Brothers. If we are life-giving channels mustn't we sometimes renew the life in us?'

This increased Her-Bak's joy. He had found his aim and his path.

IV

THE DIVINE WORD

Seated among the students Her-Bak, for the first time, received instruction from the Linguist, assisted by the Symbolist. 'Her-Bak,' said the Linguist, having watched him in silence, 'have you, newly come among us, been taught concerning the *mdw-Neters?*'

'Indeed, Master. I was a pupil in the school for scribes.'

'Then instruct us. What is the number of our fundamental letters?'

'Am I to answer regarding the signs that represent an idea, the groups of letters, or the letters apart?'

'My question was clear. The fundamental letters are the elementary principles of word-making. No perspicacious man can fail to see that each comes in numerical order, itself necessarily a number. You can't be ignorant of this since you know . . .'

Her-Bak stammered an apology. The Linguist pressed him. 'No doubt you can explain to us the properties of the letter *u* . . .'No answer came from Her-Bak. '. . . and of the letter *m* . . .'

'Forgive me . . . our teachers never mentioned these details . . .'

'Don't apologise for your ignorance, Her-Bak, but for having pretended to know. These are not details. They are the essential bases of our teaching. Nevertheless, they are not disclosed to scribes and students. No hand was ever entitled to write them. They are a sacred treasure of the House of Life.'

The Linguist fell silent and no one dared question him. Presently he spoke again, weighing each word. 'These are secrets of Thoth and Seshat. Sefekht writes them into nature: none can undo the sevenfold seal without her aid.'

'This is obscure to a beginner. Can one learn about this without understanding it?'

'The Master's mouth speaks fundamental principles in the disciple's ear. The disciple hears them according to the openness of his heart.'

'If this is so, the unworthy can never see their real meaning: why wrap them in such secrecy?'

'The tongue may falsify teaching not well understood. False doctrine arises in this way.'

'May I put one more question? Many scribes seem learned in the letters

D

and signs of various epochs: can this be possible without their knowing the bases?'

'A judicious question, Her-Bak. As regards essential truths, the sacred teaching begins with the complexity of becoming and ends with the simplicity of beginning, for there lie the secrets that are not to be spoken.'

The students listened greedily, astonished that they had never elicited this answer. Her-Bak watched their reaction and voiced his own astonishment. 'How is it that this doesn't make students rebel?'

'Man is so made that he takes pleasure in complex doctrines and details of appearance. The subtle connexion between one thing and another only interests those rare predestined ones who don't let themselves be put off by a dry simplicity. Concise teaching asks for personal effort and development of the intuitive gift on the student's part. Selection comes about naturally in this way.'

The disciple's face cleared and the Linguist questioned him again. 'When, ignorant, you joined the school for young scribes how did you learn to read hieroglyphs?'

'By writing words.'

'Just so. How do you discern the meaning of words spelt with the same letters?'

'By the sign-image that specifies each, such as the sign of three flowers that designates a vegetable.'

'How do you recognise a word that expresses an idea?'

'By the image that signifies what is without form and body.'

'What is this image?'

'A papyrus, rolled, sealed.'

'The papyrus has form and body. Why was it chosen to express an idea that has neither?'

Her-Bak stammered a vague reply. 'It must be expressed by something . . .'

'Couldn't the something be a point, a dash, a sign that isn't an object?'

'My answer was stupid. What the Master says is right . . . why not have chosen one of these signs?'

'First because they would be conventional. Then to shew that nothing in nature is pure quality. Quality in itself is imperceptible to the senses, unknowable, we can't name it. But the initiate knows that inasmuch as they are numbers our letters shew aspects of pure quality.'

The Symbolist supplemented this. 'Everything in nature, Her-Bak, rests on something material or it is in some sort of relation with a material fact.'

'Is thought material?' asked the novice, shocked.

'You can't think without attaching your idea to some tangible fact or thing. If you think of cold, the idea of cold is referred to what your body knows of it. If you think of good or evil, you refer the good or the evil to the man who does it. If you think of the formation of an idea the idea proceeds from a brain. If you think of space, the extent of the sky, you measure it with reference to Earth and the stars. Everything your brain can reflect on is compared with some thing that is sensorially perceptible, and is therefore relative. That is why ideas, which you call non-material, are represented by concrete objects. But the sign you spoke of shews a papyrus rolled and sealed; the eye doesn't see its contents. One is to look for the hidden meaning, which often calls for the intelligence of the heart.'

.   .   .

Aqer spoke up. 'Master, is it right to say that in the old days this sign hadn't the meaning of immateriality but signified objects used by a writer?'

'The thinking of the ancients didn't separate matter and spirit as we are beginning to do,' the Linguist replied. 'Human mentality changes and with it its mode of expression.'

'May we infer that our own is growing subtler?'

'More complex, a symptom of decadence. What does it matter? Every age accomplishes its destiny. But throughout the ages the meaning of essential symbols is the same: the rolled papyrus will always indicate a hidden meaning behind the obvious. This shews you where you were wrong, Her-Bak . . . you know how to write the *mdw-Neters* but you don't know them. What you must learn today is their educative importance: how is it that having a cursive script which represents our hieroglyphs by signs easier to write we should have chosen sign-images that need skill on the draughtsman's part for our initiatory texts?'

'This question often puzzled the teachers in the Peristyle,' said a newly-promoted student.

'That isn't surprising,' replied the Linguist. 'They are often led astray by love of the complex, where the play of thought has free scope. This tendency is bound to become more marked with development of the mental faculties. It takes a strong disciple to breast the current and go constantly to the source.'

'Master, where are we to look for the source?' asked Her-Bak.

'In the legacy of our earliest Sages. Humanity dates from far back.

Cataclysms have smitten Earth. Certain men great in true science came to organise our country in Heaven's image that wisdom might be preserved and cultivated here in a "sealed jar". They set going the system best suited for its transmission, which could only have come about through the pre-existence of a philosophical tradition and because at the outset exact thinking co-ordinated all its elements, existing and to come'.

'It was thus,' the Symbolist put in, 'that the *mdw-Neters* were chosen in such a way as really to signify all the qualities and functions implicit in the image. Each hieroglyph is therefore in itself the living symbol of the meaning sought. All that exists, all that is known to us, is a fact or hangs on a fact: that is why our symbols illustrate something tangible that leads thought to the exact idea, of a vital order, the thing suggests.'

Her-Bak shewed surprise. 'If this is so I don't see why they are called *mdw-Neters*. Neters aren't tangible powers surely?'

'You are wrong. If Geb is Neter of Earth it is because he gives his own character, himself, to the substance that makes it. Without him Earth wouldn't exist. He is the dry, cold, principle incarnate in terrestrial matter. All that exists on Earth is an incarnation of the principial Neters.'

'This Neter's name is sometimes written *Gebb*,' Her-Bak remarked.

'The doubling of the *b* materialises the principle.'

The Symbolist asked his colleague to carry on. The Linguist said to Her-Bak, 'I shall give you neither the properties nor the number of our letters until you are well aware of the importance of these secrets. But you need an example if you are to understand our manner of thinking. I will give you two hieroglyphs on which to exercise your powers of research, the letter *r* and the letter *n*.

'The letter *r* is written in the lenticular shape of a half open mouth. Now look for the ideas, qualities and functions this sign represents. First, its nature. The mouth, *ra*, is the upper opening of the body, an entrance that communicates by two channels with the lungs and stomach: that is why this hieroglyph is also the generic word for an entrance, *ra*. The mouth opens and shuts to eat, breathe and speak as the eye, *ar.t*, opens and shuts to receive or refuse light. The mouth's function is dual, passive and active; it receives air and food, emits breath and voice. The eye's function is dual likewise: the reception of light and the expression of organic and emotional reaction. The mouth's shape changes by separation of the lips for the performance of its functions. Opening, it widens or narrows, like the shadow thrown on a disc by another disc which gradually eclipses it. In the partially occulted disc, the lentil or dark mouth is the complement of the crescent still visible. This gradual change of shape produces portions of different size that represent parts of the occulted disc. This characteristic has given the name *ra* to parts of a whole such as numerical fractions, chapters and so forth. In the same way enlargement of the lentil by diminution of the crescent justifies the choice of *r* to mean augmentation, more than *r*. You, scribe learned in the theme of the *mdw-Neters*, will note the determinative of the word *abed*, month, a small lentil in a crescent.'

'No one has been able to explain to me the meaning of this device.'

'But you will understand now the meaning we attach to the month, the continual increase and waning of the lentil or dark mouth in the luminous crescent.'

'Bear in mind,' said the Symbolist, 'that all our concepts are based on natural functions. Eye and mouth are related to the two luminaries: the eyes are their symbols. The word for an eye, *ar.t*, means also to make, to create. And isn't the name Râ written with a mouth, *r*? Heaven is our model and Râ is its sovereign master. His Word is manifested by a shadow or thing. That is to say, everything is a shadow of Râ, which grows or diminishes, ascends or descends, becomes or disbecomes. The hieroglyph *r* symbolises this.'

'The letter *r*,' said the Linguist, 'is of solar nature. The ideas of activity, circular movement, revolution whether of stars or beings in a cyclical orbit, attach to it.'

.   .   .

Her-Bak tried to arrange these new thoughts. 'Isn't there some relation here with the sign *shen* that surrounds the name, *ren*, of our kings?' he asked.

'In effect, yes. A name betokens a cycle, a loop on the thread of a soul's existence. The loop betokens a life, or an incarnation, under the name *ren* that is its actual destiny. If you know the letter *n* you have the full meaning of *ren*. *n* isn't the image of an object or being, but, by the wave-sign, it denotes a function. Open your ears, Her-Bak. The sun rises and sets. Day follows night. Man and woman attract or repel one another. A pendulum swings to and fro. Duality is in being and not-being, a yes and a no, a high and a low: hence manifestation through the possibility of comparison. All nature is an affirmation of duality, an alternation more or less rapid. Alternation is the wave-movement of nature, energic, aerial or liquid; for original Energy is like still water which, under impulsion, manifests itself in waves and these, growing as they go, carry the energy from centre to circumference. The letter *n* and its figuration give this wave-character and this justifies the use of *n* in *nwn*, primordial and chaotic water; *nw*, primordial and aerial water; Nut, whose waves encompass Earth. One can also say that *n* is that which environs.'

'It gives the measure of a wave or a totality of waves,' the Symbolist explained, 'that encloses the atmosphere of a sky, Nut, a place, *nwt*, a time, *wnwt*. Every city, every hour, has its own character, which differs with the emanations, passions, activities, of the organisms, whether stars or beings, that the wave or totality of waves encloses. And you must learn that *n*, by its wave-nature that exhibits alternation, analyses and reveals constituent qualities that complement one another. Everything is disclosed by the *n*-function.'

'In this,' added the Linguist, 'you find the rationale of the locution *ànedj her k*, shew your face; for *nedj*, in its exact meaning, expresses the making evident of the constitutive elements of a thing, organism or word. If you wish to speak precisely, you will use this term for an enquiry by dissociation of constituents, never by synthesis.'

'What is *dj*'s role in the word *nedj*?' asked Her-Bak.

'Didn't I say I would explain two letters, no more?'

'Can I by myself try to understand the others?'

'You can study their living character in their symbols: this will be fruitful. But see that you don't draw fanciful conclusions beyond the concrete meaning. What I have explained with regard to *r* and *n* is summary and very incomplete, for I don't wish to reveal either their number or their secret role. Later on you will understand the reason for this: when you do your mouth will be shut, like our own. But this is by no means the time to speak of such things . . .'

'We may still impart the meaning of the three essential words that are formed from *r* and *n*,' the Symbolist proposed. '*n* is that by which appearances manifest; that is to say, that which reveals the content of the container. It is also the letter that expresses the relation "of", "to", "which". And *n* is the vibration that carries and transmits energy, like all that proceeds from Nut. If to *n* you add the active and outgiving significance of *r* you have *ner*, quantified energy. *Ner* is the energy which, as shewn in the loop that encloses a name, *ren*, is absorbed and imprisoned in a name. It is the proper activity of a thing, the power of its name and nature. That's why it is said, "To know a thing's real name is to know its power. To pronounce it exactly is to free its energy".'

'Is that then the magic power of the name?' asked Her-Bak.

'Indeed yes. And it is formidable. It is most fortunate for men that true names are hidden from them, given the state of unconsciousness that is normally theirs.'

Her-Bak sighed. 'It is more prudent, but what a pity!'

The students burst out laughing. The Masters nodded indulgently. 'Are you sure, Her-Bak,' asked the Symbolist, 'that you take the point of this lesson?'

Crestfallen, the disciple defended himself. 'May the Master please not doubt it. My heart isn't as light as my tongue; it has understood at once that attention must be paid to inversions of letters such as *rn* and *nr*, that hieroglyphical pictures must be studied in minutest detail, and that knowledge of nature is necessary to understanding of the letters in words.'

.   .   .

'Correct. You have heard and understood. Then I will discuss the second word. Between *n* and *r* the letter *f* is inserted, the letter for breath and for the air that quickens primitive life. *Ner* is energy, limited in nature by the matter in which it works. *f* brings animation and gives it a vital quality, *nefer*. Its symbol is a heart hanging by a tube from a horizontal bolt like the propelling stern-oar that by pressure on the liquid element turns a boat right or left. The image is absurd, but the symbol is true: the heart's movement is rhythmic like the alternations of the world. Contraction and dilatation are an essential alternation, cause of all formation. The air-channel conveys breath, *nef*. The heart gives alternate movement. Breath and movement, mover and engine of mobility, generate heat, life's essential quality, hence the vital quality of energy, *nefer*.'

'We have other words,' Her-Bak suggested, 'for this idea. *Qd* for example.'

The Linguist reproved the novice sharply. '*Qd* has a more quantitative and concrete meaning than *nefer*. It expresses a manner of being, modalities, material characteristics. If you would profit by this lesson, compare the third of these essential words, *neter*, with *nefer*. In *neter f* is replaced by *th*, a terrestrial letter, or by *t*, which is terrestrial and passive.'

Impatient, Her-Bak interrupted once more. 'This seems unlikely. The Neters can be neither terrestrial nor passive, or I know nothing about divinity.'

This got the answer it deserved. 'It is well for men that the Neters don't depend on their intelligence. All that is terrestrial is natural, Her-Bak. But what is nature if not a manifestation of the Neters? And what is passivity? The passive is that which is submitted. What is submitted to the laws of nature with never a possibility of derogation if not those who are its principles?'

When Her-Bak had acknowledged his mistake and his impudence the Linguist addressed himself to the disciples who were listening in silence. 'We have instructed our young brother,' he said, 'in subjects of which you know the elements already. If any of you is uncertain on any point let him speak without hesitation.'

. . .

'I thought a Neter was an entity,' said Abushed to the Symbolist, 'and that *nefer* meant fulfilment.'

'The meaning you give these words is exact as regards some particular aspect, not their intrinsic meaning. An entity is made up of the essential characteristics and properties of a type-principle. Every number is an entity, but Apet is the Neter of Number. Each of our letters is an entity, but Sefekht is the Neter of all written symbols. The Neters are Ideas immanent or virtually contained in nature which give substance form throughout the phases of continuous creation and all genesis. *Nefer* is a vital quality in its state of maturity. It is the moment of fulfilment that gives generative potency to a thing or being, whether of its own seed, its particular quality, or its proper energy. *Neter-nefer* then is a principle in a state of generative potency in the quality or function it stands for. As to the ordinary meanings the vulgar tongue ascribes to *nefer*, they offer, with less precision, some confirmation of the absolute meaning, since they express perfection, beauty, goodness, puberty, virility and other states of fulfilment, bad qualities as well as good.'

Abushed thanked the Symbolist. 'It is a great theme for reflection, what you have told us. It would help me if it could be fixed by an example. Isn't it the vital quality of the Neter Osiris in seed that accounts for the seed's awakening, its death and resurrection in the living germ?'

'It is so in truth. But you bring together in this definition various phases or aspects of the Neter's function and quality. According to the phase or aspect under consideration Osiris is qualified by a different epithet, *Neter-nefer*, *Neter-âa*, or *wn-nefer*. The epithet *Neter-nefer* refers Osiris to the moment when he exercises his generative power to revitalise the thing to which it relates. The epithet *Neter-âa* specifies the Osirian function in its aspect as cyclic principle of the eternal return in which the subject runs his course, going to the maximum of what is possible, then returning on itself in perpetual reiteration. The epithet *wn-nefer* likewise gives the idea of an endless cycle, as applied to earthly life. In the word *wn*, existence, the choice of the symbol of the hare shews that terrestrial existence is meant. The hare, an extremely prolific animal, lives alone nevertheless. It makes its form among mounds of earth. Our hieroglyphic emphasises its ears. Note the word for an ear, *mesdjer*; *mes*, to give birth, produce; *djer*, limit, to reach limits. In fact *djer* denotes the delimitation of a place or thing, defines its horizon, its orientation. *Mesdjer*, then, signifies that which gives orientation, the very sense of the orientation not only of a terrestrial horizon but the horizon of all existence. And there is another relation between the hare and Osiris. Osiris has a dual aspect. He is the Neter of periodic renewal in vegetable life, the transformation of essential life into vegetable life, the passage of potency into act, the power latent in substance to manifest in matter within the limit of its kind. But by the very fact of such transformation or manifestation the Neter becomes the vegetative power of the plant and is subjected to the laws that govern it. The rhythm of Osiris is the rhythm of becoming, in which the necessity of disbecoming or return is latent. His activity is in the ascent of the sap, his passivity in the inevitability of exhaustion, life and death in perpetual rebeginning. If his activity is drawn from the source of universal life it is nevertheless subject to the laws that govern a particular form of it, the rhythms of number and nature. Osiris then is Neter of the natural order. The necessity of perpetual rebeginning is Sethian, for Seth is the greed of possession and continuity which seizes and would appropriate the vital Osirian activity. The hare has a dual sign likewise; Sethian by its reddish colour, its form in desert ground and the duality shewn by its ears; Osirian because having a highly developed sense of hearing it symbolises the Osirian function that defines the spatial dimensions that condition all existence. It is this function that is given in the epithet *neb r djer*, ascribed to Osiris. Osirian again because its fertility-season coincides with the time of Osiris' rebirth. And finally because the hare's solitary life and sexual excitability make it a formidable intruder among rabbits which will attack a hare in quest of females and emasculate it with their teeth . . . it is said that the sexual organs of Osiris were devoured by a fish.

'The epithet *wn-nefer* situates the Osirian principle in a specific terrestrial existence, with a Sethian and concretive aspect.'

'This throws a strong light,' said Abushed. 'Now I can distinguish the cosmic and particular Osirian principles.'

The Symbolist approved. 'The cosmic aspect of this principle is the cycle that turns on heavenly conditions. The particular aspect relates to the life of a species. If you speak of the cosmic principle as at work in the generation of seed you call it *Neter-âa*. If you speak of the genesis of a specific seed Osiris becomes *wn-nefer*. It is the same with his other functions.'

'If one of these terms is used for another Neter, how is it to be understood?' Abushed asked.

'In the same way, by applying it to the Neter's principle or function. Thus, Râ, in the quality of *Neter-âa*, is the perpetual going and returning between the horizons of East and West.'

'Is it correct to say *Neter-wr* as one says *Neter-âa*?'

'Study each word. The idea of greatness in *wr* differs from the idea of it in *âa*. *Âa* means great to the limit of possibility in the thing thus qualified, its greatest size, greatest value, greatest yield . . . this with the understanding that having attained it it can only return on itself and repeat. The idea of "limit", particular to every being and thing, is in *âa*. *Wr* is amplitude with the possibility of growth, a meaning connected with the idea of origin and universality. Although the idea of a cycle is in it as well, it is less restrictive than in *âa* by the possibility of enlargement, amplification, in volume and growth. But a Neter is a cosmic principle; it defines a law and as such has its own limits. The epithet *wr* is only appropriate therefore to the Neters whose property of growth is part of their functional quality; as for instance Isis, Nephtys, Neith, Mut and Osiris. The universal Neter is himself the principle of *wr*, for which reason Horus is also called *Horus-wr*.'

.   .   .

Her-Bak drank the Master's words as thirsty earth drinks water. A world of possibilities opened; he was impatient to attack the difficulties. 'Dare I say that one of your answers troubles me?' he asked the Linguist. 'You told Abushed to study each word. To do this, isn't it indispensable to know the meaning of the essential letters, since each has its number and properties?'

The Symbolist exchanged a few words with the Linguist, who said to Her-Bak, 'Our reply will be the last part of this lesson. It is true that you can't understand the secret texts, or even get the real meaning of essential words or of names or gods, without this knowledge. But knowledge of this order will not be given in this first initiation . . . you'll see the reason later. This much may be said however. The word, *djed*, is an audible expression of a Word-Idea. Visibility, concretion, is effected by signs or characters which, in our sacred writings, give the Idea form. Each sign-character-letter then is a concrete word, *mdw*, with an appropriate image.

In this we follow the example of Sefekht who gives every natural form the lines, shapes and colours that display its character. Every sign-letter has three attributes, form, number, sound. Sound is its essential attribute, its Word, the principle of its magical action. That is why initiates are asked not to read certain texts aloud if they know the secret meaning. Number is a letter's intrinsic nature. Numbers, the determinative principles of form, are the real and fundamental letters. The sound and form of a letter are obvious attributes: its real number has always been more or less hidden by various devices. The form of a letter is characteristic of its author's philosophical thinking and educative method. A number expressed by signs constitutes our writing: the *mdw-Neters*.

'All written language is a construct whose principal elements, words and numbers, are given form by natural or conventional symbols: the truest language is that in which the conventional is reduced to a minimum. The architecture of such writing is an assemblage of signs. In our *mdw-Neter* combinations there is a play of relationships between the numbers and functions of the letters assembled, in such a mode that it is possible to write down the elements of a secret teaching, such as the phases of a genesis or the interpretation of an allegory, by choosing words and disposing the letters in them so as to compose phrases that seem commonplace. A knowledge of analogies and the discovery of certain easily-read clues might lead, after profound study, to decipherment of the secret; but there remains this difficulty, that the Sage who chose one of the "lines of becoming" for his linguistic method left and intended a certain obstacle on which we are silent, with the result that no one can reach the secret by study alone.'

'Why this cruel game, Master?'

'Because our word-architecture is conceived on the scale of the cosmic architecture. To reveal its construction would be to reveal the secrets of genesis and becoming; and this must never be accorded but to the tried and tested who will on no account make ill use of it. This is what justifies the Temple and its secrecies.'

.   .   .

Her-Bak bowed and put questions to his Master. 'Is our language the only possible form for the communication of knowledge?'

'It is the most perfect,' said the Sage. 'But it isn't the only possibility. Another system, based on the same knowledge, may lead to wisdom. But the ancients constructed our language in such a way that we can use it as a mirror in which to watch the development of our history with its epochs and phases of decadence or regeneration, as one might discern the superimposed phases of a monument that has been built and written on in stages if one knew the pre-established design. It is possible to name and describe events by means of letters and combinations of letters that form a word. In short, we can read what destiny writes. Sometimes, even, we name historical events after what we have read in this way.'

The disciple was divided between wonder and vague disappointment. 'If I can't find the secret by my own efforts what use is my search?'

'You may gain the right to knowledge through the training of a mind that will never betray it.'

'What must I do to acquire such a mind?'

'Begin by avoiding procedures that hinder it. Don't try to explain the formation of our language as a progressive experiment: its elements were given in their entirety by Sages who laid down its rules and line of evolution at the beginning. Don't look for the beginning in a hetero-geneous collection of idioms . . . all languages that have common roots with our own derive from one source farther back in time than any time you know of. Never doubt the philosophic unity of our language because of nuances arising from conditions of time and place, for such differences are but secondary, sometimes willed, sometimes accidental, and have never touched the essentials. Certain variations, brought about according to rules foreordained for certain epochs, are in themselves a teaching that confirms the existence of a pre-established order. Doubt this if you must, but if you watch sincerely for evidence it will come to you in the form of solved problems.'

'Master, I see what mustn't be done. May it be given me to learn how I am to go about my researches?'

'The cardinal rule is this,' said the Linguist. 'Think simply. Eschew criticism and specious argument. The thinking of our Masters was simpler the closer it was to the source. The further we depart from it the more we complicate things. Go straight to the natural fact that a symbol exhibits. Then, having closely examined it in all its aspects, you will discern the universal law which the natural fact itself symbolises. Never neglect the image or form of a hieroglyph. Whether it is a representation of thing or animal, or a mythical composition such as the animal Seth or Anubis, it is made up of natural constituents every detail of which has symbolic meaning. But don't make the mistake of substituting a word for an image, by saying for instance "the owl is *m*". Consider the nature, qualities and function of the thing represented. An example . . . the image of a foot, *b*, evokes the idea of that which places itself, the idea of support, the idea of duality because one foot isn't enough to walk with.

'Look for the simple and vitally true reasons for the choice. If several letters are grouped under one symbol, compare the other words that are spelt by the same group, under the same symbol or another. Meditate on the letters, whose number you don't know but whose image suggests certain functions. The search for the natural relationships of such analogous groups will itself awaken in you the vital logic that moved those who composed them. Refrain from accusing a scribe of negligence or an author of childishness in face of textual anomalies or some harmless detail: only a fool, who trusting in gross appearance, throws away the key to a treasury acts in this way. Learn to put natural evidence before sceptical argument. Learn to reject compromise. Learn to approach truth by daring what looks absurd. The man who has never suffered because of his quest will never know the value of an answer given him. Learn to sacrifice gladly a long stretch of misconceived effort for a moment of truth. Then you will be able to receive the knowledge of the Ancients without danger of ingratitude and profanation.'

V

THE VOYAGE

A north wind filled the sail and helped the oarsmen, attacking the resistant stream and covering it with foaming crests. The falling river left thick, limy beds that were cracking already in the sun and bristling with green stems. Slowly on either bank scene after scene opened to the voyagers, cultivated land chequered with thousands of trenches, framed in desert horizons; groups of palm trees protecting brown earth huts in their shade, restful dark stains in the pitiless light. Strange land of Egypt, never watered by rain! Black earth that drinks the waters of Nile which must be drawn ceaselessly when the river goes back to its source! Naked men toil night and day at *shadoofs* spaced along the banks, pulling the beam, dipping the cistern which a counterweight lifts to the trench-level. Their sad song and the grating of the shadoofs give rhythm to labour that fertilises the banks. Man doesn't complain. Râ's power and Nile's riches increase the fruits of his endeavour. Slowly the boat glides south, letting the stream pass by as the days pass, the centuries and millennia, before unmindful earth.

.   .   .

The Master recited the names of temple and village like one telling beads in a necklace. Fortunate disciples of the wisest country in the world, where the precisest of symbolisms leads even the least eager to perception of universal truth and offers them understanding of natural law in themselves!

'Open your eyes, Her-Bak, to the colours of the plover, the swoopings of the falcon, the habits of the vultures. Open your ears to the names of our nomes and cities. Breast Hapi's stream to the source of sources. Islets will get in your way: study the lesson of those chaotic rocks; go and read the signatures of pilgrims who added to the symbolism of the place the symbol of their names. Go and seek in the stone of Elephantine, grey as an elephant's skin, the secret of Khnum, divine potter who moulds earth and brings all things into existence. Contemplate the stony chaos of the Isle of Senmwt, Biggah, Senmwt of the meagre body, syren brutal as a lioness, aquatic and solar Sekhmet. The two-sexed rock of Kenset that marks the southern limit of the territory of Kemit, the holy mountains of Sethet, Sehel, and the red granite of Sunu, Aswan . . . these will tell you of the beginnings of the world, as they told the students and Sages who wrote the proof of their understanding on the rock. Follow the tracks of travellers who marked the road to Rohenu, Wadi Hammamât, with steles. Go upstream to the marsh-country where grow the rushes of the South: everywhere you will see temples, statues, steles, erected at the right moment, in a style suitable to the heavy and original black earth.

'But we must return. The decades roll by, the caves of the South recall Hapi; soon there will be danger that sandbanks will wreck the boat. We must return, Her-Bak. Within the temple walls you must meditate the enigmas you have glimpsed. The names and symbols of places will only yield their secrets when your heart reflects on them. The flagstones of the school are hard, the gods' faces severe: the discipline is pitiless. But your Master awaits you.'

.   .   .

It was a year of fruitful studies. Her-Bak had the joy of breaking the seal of a new door that gave access to a more inward teaching. Once more Nile poured forth his abundance, once more the flood retreated. The whirlpools vanished, the banks reappeared.

Sailors got the boat under way. They embarked for a voyage that would take them on the smooth, swift stream to the great temples of the North. The disciples, languid in the heat, somnolent, abandoned themselves to the boat's rhythm.

'What are you at, lazy ones? Are you not the conqueror's escort? Her-Bak, do you not see Sobek, Seth's crocodile, hidden in the mud?'

'There is no crocodile.'

'Your eyes are too realist, Her-Bak. Was it not here that Horus conquered Râ's enemies? Look at that grey back.'

'Isn't it simply an islet?'

'It's Seth's hippopotamus. He lies under water, but his head breaks surface . . . head? No, three points, two eyes and a nose that comes up for a breath of air. Horus will master him. Watch the "secret land", Shetu the tortoise whom the divine lance will pin to the river bottom.'

Her-Bak went with this fancy and the voyage became an evocation of myth known only to initiates. Horus manœuvred before his eyes, fighting, changing shape: one saw how the names of regions and cities arose. Through half-closed lids he watched the falcon's proud face . . . changed into a winged disc it hovered on the prow with the cobras Nekhbet and Uadjt. Amazed to see how Isis' son changes himself into Horus Behedty, he resolved to go into the meaning of such mysteries.

'Have patience, disciple. Learn to see and understand before trying to fathom the reality of the Neters.'

.   .   .

As they approached Abydos funeral barges became more and more numerous. The boat sailed on: they were to visit the sanctuary of Osiris on their way South.

The country had changed; the banks were flat, the palm-groves far apart; there were great stretches of cultivated land. And now a cry of joy burst from every mouth, for pyramids rose on the horizon. Many marvels awaited them, the temple of Hat-Ka-Ptah at Memphis, the schools of Iunu at Heliopolis, cities of the dead and funerary temples, those gigantic triangular masses that defy man's inconstancy and witness to the greatness of the old masters and the perpetuity of their declarations.

'Unfailing witness of the pyramids that cannot err! The word is a definition. A pyramid is the magnet that brings Heaven and Earth together. Its ramp is the way to revelation, ramp that joins the black earth of the valley with the red sand of the desert, that symbolises the ascent of life from earthworm to that royal Man who governs all the phases of nature and writes history in the most abstract of symbolisms. Power of Pharaoh, greatest of houses, power of conscious nobility and religious majesty, it pleases Him to contemplate the long succession of monuments that will establish the teaching for posterity. All-powerful and silent during his life, he watches over the legacy of knowledge that will speak for him after his death. Pyramid, cosmic monument, tomb, you will speak, not of the personal life of your builder, but of the immense experience of his patriarchate on Earth through a long line of tradition; you will tell of man's ascent, of which Pharaoh's reign marks a stage. It is thus that Pharaoh, who as he waxes becomes son of Râ, pays tribute in secret to Himself.

'Forms whether drawn, carved or constructed always mean something. They are characters of a universal script that everyone reads without knowing it. The pyramid images a descent. It may enshrine a corpse, but it is also in image and in truth the descent and cradle of Spirit.'

Grouped round the Master the disciples stored up each word as if it were the echo of ancient voices. 'At the beginning of our time,' he said, 'there was high simplicity, the teaching of Number through forms, to which the student must in the end return, when he has learnt how to find his way to the fundamental things through the complexity of our myths. The pyramid is a cosmic truth. Its base is square, its four sides

triangular: in principle these four trinities form the quadrangular foundation of a primitive five-pointed shape. This constitutes the pyramids'
mystical statement, since all the elements of Number are present in their
abstract aspect. The fact that this shape is constructed in certain proportions imposes geometrical relations which of themselves determined
the principles of measurement as regards length and volume. Here is the
connexion between the pyramid's mystical and geometrical character.
They are vitally, strictly, linked.'

.   .   .

Her-Bak scanned the desert levels where gigantic pyramids stood over
a city of tombs. The Sphinx, witness from very ancient times, watched
over the secret of dead and living, pointing the one and the other to the
Orient of resurrection. The disciple tried to count the temples they had
seen during their pilgrimage. He sighed. 'I shall never remember them
all . . . and we visted but few.'

The Master gave their voyage its true significance. 'All existence is a
voyage in the course of which the soul, carried in its corporal boat, is
impregnated with consciousness as your eyes with the colours, your
ears with the words, of nature. Thus do migrating birds. Each makes
its flight in response to the vital call of its own being. One seeks the
marshes, another Râ's beams; a third follows the ripening of the grain.
Each one's path is governed by Râ's course and by its own capacity for
adaptation to changing conditions of land and climate. And on the
journey its consciousness reawakens, enriched with fresh experience.
Thus, your soul is an immortal wanderer in the short courses of Earth,
the changes of the Dwat, the glorious reaches of Heaven. It isn't the
number of images perceived that counts but the ineffaceable impressions
that enrich your consciousness, above all the possibilities they awaken
and bring out in you. Remember the migratory birds. Each is called by
its desires and the aim of its existence. The aim determines the journey;
but otherwise is the passive pilgrimage of a mortal in his Osirian passion,
otherwise the conscious peregrination of Horus who wins his mastership
by subduing the animal forces one by one. Do not be held by the charm
and variety of this riverine landscape. Seek a wider horizon. Plan your
journey. It will have the scope of your desire.'

.   .   .

Her-Bak, on his return, had the pleasure of finding Auab among the
students of the inner temple. It surprised him, for naïvety gave Auab's

E

intelligence a childlike character that seemed ill-adapted to the arduous research that was imposed on the students. The Sage took occasion to recall the teaching of the three Masters on the day of the Question. 'If you would be an adept of the Wisdom, Her-Bak, don't forget that the ways of Maât are identical as to aim but threefold as to means. Understanding may be awakened by knowledge of symbols and analogies, by knowledge of Numbers, or by absolute surrender of Me in total fusion with Self. It is true that the three ways mingle, since awareness of one brings awareness of the others: still, every seeker drawn by Maât must choose the way that suits his capacities. Auab's gift of impersonality and his altruism offer a disposition that the Mystic finds acceptable. If he has the courage to acquire the consciousness of relative good and evil without losing his pure and simple love for the sole absolute Good he will attain wisdom by the simplest path, the way of Fusion.'

'What you say gives me great pleasure for Auab's sake,' Her-Bak replied. 'But can you explain what is meant by a Sage?'

'A Sage is a man who is conscious, able to conceive the three ways in himself, able to love impersonally, to know *what is* without prejudice, to obey the laws of nature and to write down what he knows. There is no room for self-pity, my disciple.'

VI

ILLUSION

It was full moon over a desert tract surrounded by palm trees. Students and disciples, seated in a semi-circle, looked like statues. Pale light illuminated perplexed faces; silence closed every mouth while the magician withdrew. When, a shadow among shadows, he disappeared, every eye went to a circle drawn on the ground, as if expecting some fresh enchantment.

Mystic and Symbolist watched, talking in low voices. The Mystic questioned Abushed. 'What do you think of the spectacle that was offered? Speak without hesitation.'

Abushed made a face of disgust. 'I don't like such phantasmagorias. If they're illusion I don't like being taken in. If they aren't it affronts my reason. I reject the world of absurdity.'

'A man who is seeking the real can't say "I don't like, I reject" without leaving the path.'

Auab, his eyes still dazed, cried, 'This magician is fantastic . . . everything he did was a miracle.'

'For me,' said Upuat, 'the phenomena haven't all the same importance. I think one should distinguish . . .'

The Master approved. 'Upuat speaks truth. We will sort the tricks into three categories. Auab, will you describe what your eyes saw.'

Auab didn't have to be asked twice. 'He took a stick and threw it on the ground. The stick became a snake and crept like a snake. He seized it by the tail and pulled . . . the snake became a stick. Then he did a terrible thing. He cut off a duck's head and the duck walked and its head came back on its body. And the third trick was so astonishing I no longer knew where I was. He took some wax, made a monkey with it, recited from a book and it became a live monkey which ran off among the palms to get dates for its master. When it came back he recited again and all that was left was the wax image.'

The Mystic questioned the others. 'Did each of you see with his own eyes what Auab tells us?'

They confirmed it with one voice. The Masters' laughter surprised the students. 'Did you see blood flow from the headless duck?' asked the Mystic.

'Certainly. The magician drew attention to it.'

'Perfect. Then look for some drops of blood.'

The students examined the entire surface of the circle but found no blood. The Mystic made them sit down. 'You won't find what doesn't exist,' he said; then, when they expressed their astonishment, he explained. 'A man who sets himself to study causes should be forearmed against illusion. The phenomena produced before you were typical of the chief illusions of which you may become the plaything. The cheapest trick of the three was the severed head: the magician existed, the duck existed, so did the spectators, but decapitation took place in your imaginations.'

Auab protested. The Mystic checked him. 'You saw the duck and the knife, but from then on the magician created the scene of decapitation and replacement in his thought. He imposed it on you as if you really saw it until the moment when, released from his suggestions, you saw the duck alive at his feet, which it never left.'

.   .   .

Deeply interested, Her-Bak asked, 'How could the magician work this miracle?'

'A magician can never go against nature. He can change its course, but he must always obey its laws. He can never replace a limb that has been cut off. He can't modify a star's orbit or alter the working of any essential law. But he can arrest or alter the cerebral consciousness of the spectators, for our senses serve to affirm, not to know.'

'There's a process,' said Upuat, 'between seeing and being conscious of what one has seen.'

'Just so. The brain is part of it, instrument of memory and comparison, seat of illusion and Seth's laboratory. Its work is good or bad according to the use we make of it, but the intelligence of the heart is truth and indeceptible. It is awake, or asleep, or stifled; but there is never evil in it.'

Abushed, humiliated at having let himself be deceived, complained. 'How can we have submitted to the imposture? It was an abuse of power.'

The Master rebuked his bitterness. 'It was a precious experience. You are wrong to regret it. Cerebral illusion is the most frequent of aberrations. The magician, by his control of thought, put your own out of action and made you see a mirage, making illusion, to which you are constantly subject in some small degree, perceptible to you. It is unconsciousness of the mistake that is dangerous.'

'How can one become aware of it?' asked Her-Bak.

'Train consciousness by incessant observation. Observe, for example, the data on which you base your thought. Look at the landscape now . . . what do you see between those two palm trees?'

'A hill.'

'Is it larger or smaller than the trees?'

'I know it's larger, but it looks smaller because it's farther off.'

'Note then what you see. Note too that with or without your will it is a process of thought that measures distance and makes you see what you don't see. Without thought you wouldn't be aware of distance.'

'Does the sparrow-hawk use thought to measure his distance from his prey?' asked Abushed, who dissected every process of reasoning.

'He doesn't think. He feels it, knows it by experience. Just as an ant knows from far off where the tempting morsel is and goes straight to it. The ant will seek for a long time some way of overcoming an obstacle that as it can't reason it can't understand. An automatic crossing of notions takes place through our senses and this is illusion. If you aren't aware of the relativity of your perceptions how can you detect a reflection thrown into your mind by a master of evocation?'

.   .   .

Her-Bak didn't hide his disquiet. 'Master, what can we think of as true?'

'Nothing we ascertain with our senses,' replied the Sage. 'For every sensorial conclusion arises through a play of relationships such that a thing is always defined by other things. Whereas each of the things can only be known to us by what sense can perceive. The qualities sense can't record escape us. It is this kind of failure that made the illusion of a miracle possible when the wax monkey climbed the tree.'

This shocked the naïve Auab. 'But . . . I ate one of the dates.'

'Illusion doesn't lie in the fact, which in this case is true. We are talking now, not about suggestion, but about a world, or state, of whose existence you know nothing because it isn't normally perceptible to your senses. Forces without form and discarnate beings move through our atmosphere without apparent contact with us because their substance isn't the same as ours. We have but one thing in common with them, an emotional life. That in us which yields to emotion delivers itself to the influences of this strange world. By rigid discipline a man can master these forces and make them serve him, for they are eager to borrow a substance in which they can materialise, so as to gain contact with our mode of existence. The magician furnished a substance, wax, and the image of a monkey. But to activate them he had to pronounce a magic formula, by which he put

them in his power. Then, by his breath and word, they took possession
of the image and brought off the desired result.'

'Marvellous!' cried Auab. 'The man can do anything he wants.'

'Doesn't he sum up the possibilities in nature? Magic of this kind isn't
a marvel but a danger it's hardly useful to challenge, for emotion is
attended by the risk that we shall become the blind victim of invisible
powers. It is too easy unconsciously to stir up undesirable phenomena,
and too common. We must learn not to accept projections of the
imagination that create fear, sensorial illusion and forms or phenomena
that can be tangible. But such things are no more real than cerebral
consciousness itself.'

'But what is our criterion to be?' asked Abushed eagerly. 'What are
we to call real? What subsists outside our subjective judgment? There
can be collective illusion. It can extend to the whole of mankind when
it comes to ideas that a line of reasoning, apparently correct, seems to
force on us.'

'Your argument is sound,' said the Mystic. 'We must have recourse then
to experimental and sensorially perceptible proof. Even this will only be
valid for things of the same kind: body affects body, not the emotions.
Emotion affects the emotional sense, spirit the spiritual. However,
bodily fact can be such as to affect the emotions through the attitude we
take. Your decapitated duck would have meant nothing to an animal
incapable of emotional imagination, since it could only have reacted to
the physical fact, so that as the head hadn't been severed the animal
wouldn't have been deceived. The case is otherwise with a dog, which
feels fear at a gesture that looks like picking up a stone. What makes
illusion then is an association of ideas, memory superimposed on a
physical fact. The threat of a sharp point can give the sensation of pricking,
fire that of being burnt: can we say that the pricking and burning are
illusion?'

'The absence of injury would serve as proof,' said Abushed.

'Unquestionably. But imagination can produce a wound . . . where
then is reality? If we are only willing to consider sensorially recorded
experience without subjective reaction as real, our knowledge will be
limited to what is material in the universe and can never go outside the
bounds of mineral and vegetable life, since the higher animal has reactions
that aren't wholly physical. There are a thousand proofs that animal
instinct can obey influences that are analogous and not identical with what
lies in its nature. In the complexity of the higher ranges of living creatures,
above all in men, are possibilities of events that we may call subjective

and disputable but which, for the individual, are not less real than the common facts of sensory experience, since the physical effect arises from vital activity.'

Abushed seemed uneasy. 'Doesn't this open the door to dangerous knowledge?'

'Dangerous indeed when it isn't wisely controlled, but infinitely wider than the scope of purely materialist thinking. Note too that we are talking now about knowledge, not practice. Try to understand the nature of the phenomenon and your reaction to it without prejudice. Your duck shed no blood: it was only decapitated by your emotions. Emotion acted so strongly on sense and imagination that you saw what the magician's words, his evocative gestures and his thought, created in your vision. It's exactly the same as the sensation produced by a threat of fire, or of fear in the dog which howls because it feels the stone no one throws. One can die of fright. Thus, however illusory the phenomenon the magician created, for you, spectators affected by what they thought they saw, it is a reality . . . to the extent that you yourselves are real as live human beings and to that extent only.'

'Then illusion and reality must be indissociable for the man who would pass beyond his mortal nature?' suggested Upuat.

'That way of looking at it is wise. If one adopts it one may discover an immaterial world, and this progressively, even to fusion with the Cause which, although immaterial to our sense, is the sole absolute Reality for ever and ever. What distinguishes man from animal is precisely this order of consciousness, fruit of a certain independence of the spirit that lives in a mortal body. There flows from this a complex play of feeling and imagination, with reaction on the sense, and if it becomes a source of illusion as regards physical fact it is also the manifestation of an incorporal mode of existence.'

. . .

The Sage confirmed what the Master said. 'All nature feeds on spirit and subsists by spirit, spirit that is non-corporal energy, sensible only by its effects. We are certain of the descent of the imponderable into the ponderable, invisible into visible. It is this that gives force to our teaching; and if the illusions you have just experienced had led only to this consideration they would have fulfilled their chief purpose. Now if we put you on guard, not against illusion but ignorance of its possibilities, I must also advise you not to blunt in yourselves, through excessive mistrust, the perception of what is truthful in nature. Mineral, vegetable and lower animal are not subject to imaginative illusion: you must conclude, you that are human, and subject to it, that something in you distinguishes you from the lower kingdoms. To know that illusion is possible is to have a means of gaining the mastery, through the demonstration of sensorial error and discernment of the consciousness-complex by which illusion arises.'

Abushed and Her-Bak listened eagerly, but Auab's curiosity wasn't satisfied, for nothing had been said about the snake-trick. He remarked on this to the Master, who replied, 'I have shewn you two unhealthy aspects of magic . . . may it please the Symbolist to speak about the real thing. Then you'll understand the changing of a stick into a snake.'

'True magic is always positive,' the Symbolist said. 'That is to say, it never creates either mental or emotional phantasmagorias. It knows that actual forms are worth nothing, but it recognises the reality of the causal spirit incarnate in them. It is therefore a use of symbolism in its true meaning, a revelation of abstract Cause in the concrete form. This is a cardinal teaching, for causal Spirit, discarnate, is incomprehensible. But forms constitute a reality which however relative it may be becomes a reality through such revelation.'

'There are then,' remarked Her-Bak, bringing all his attention to bear, 'as many possibilities of knowing the universal Neter as there are forms?'

'Your heart said that,' answered the Master. 'For it is by way of those possibilities that the causal Spirit must have passed to become "things".

'When you have learnt the science of "forms in space" you will see how wonderful such possibility is, truth declaring itself *a priori*. It is through this, and intuition, that symbolism can explore a world that is closed to rational thought. Knowing the possibilities of a living form we can retrace the road that its causal nature, its Neter, took, and one can evoke it. But these terms are too dry for the child Auab . . . he is asleep. Wake up, Auab. I'm going to speak your language. When dog-headed Hetet salutes the young morning sun, when in the name of Benti he sings the glory of Râ at his setting, when at the equinoxes he urinates every hour, when he shews his respiratory power with his great hairy chest and his long dog's nose, all this exhibits his "possibilities". And so with the ostrich, the crow, the jackal and every animal. They are born in conditions that demand such habits and characteristics, without which there would be no dog-headed baboon, no ostrich, no crow, no jackal.'

Ashamed of himself, Auab thanked the Master. 'Now I understand,' he said. 'But what are the possibilities of the snake?'

'The snake is a primary creature, without limbs, that goes on its belly.

Its undulant movement comes from the flexibility of the vertebral column, essential element of its structure. Its other characteristics are the flat head, the forked tongue, the fangs and often its venom. Venom emphasises the fire-character, given by the marrow of its long spine. The snake is a thing that glides, like a piece of slime. It is the prototype or symbol of all that creeps, viscous, undulant; and is fiery or aquatic according to kind as represented in an image.'

'Can the symbol of a snake evoke the principle of the snake?'

'Certainly. The magic of analogues calls on the real cause and origin of the natural form, evoking it by the form itself and the essential gesture. You, Auab, did you notice the magician's gesture when he transformed his stick?'

'I saw his hand throw the stick on the ground.'

Her-Bak corrected this. 'He gave the stick an undulant movement that even made the shape of a snake on the ground.'

'You observed well, Her-Bak. And vice versa, when he wished to break the spell he pulled the snake violently by the tail into a straight line. These evocative actions are typical of the magic of analogues. A cause can only produce varied effects if the genesis of the effect is accidentally modified as it were on the way: as if pure water passed through different colouring matters, acquiring different tints but creating, by the fact that it is water, relationships or analogies between the waters thus variously tinted.'

Timidly Her-Bak put a question. 'Will the serpentine gesture by itself produce the phenomenon?'

The Symbolist smiled. 'It is likely that you would imitate it in vain. Natural forms must be used in circumstances favourable to the evocation of their cause: this calls for knowledge of the world of causes and the nature of their effects. That is why mastery in this kind of magic is not at all common.'

'Doesn't one see it in funeral rites and images?' asked Abushed, who saw various implications. 'Why are foodstuffs offered for the dead man's KA unless as an evocation? The people themselves practise this imitative magic in thousands of gestures I should be tempted to call sorcery.'

'One must be exact in this sphere,' said the Symbolist. 'Rites and images follow what is laid down by those who know . . . we'll discuss this further at the right moment. As to popular magic, these gestures are a routine adopted through fear. It is a remnant of a traditional knowledge deflected from its educative purpose for purposes of utility. We mustn't confuse mastery with mimicry, knowledge with superstitious ignorance.'

'All the same, are we to think such practices are effective?'

'True magic is the science of the right gesture, the right word, at the right moment. Any departure from this principle makes it ineffective.'

'Are there not kinds of sorcery that work in violation of natural law?'

'Anyone who does this can only turn things from their course temporarily. He will suffer for it sooner or later.'

'I have a horror of such magic,' said Abushed, 'But I have often seen a man disquieted by some malevolent gesture recite a formula to attract the beneficent influences of the day. Are such practices of any avail?'

'If you were still in the Peristyle I should answer, all depends on the purpose. Besides, if you believe in it you will get the effect. But to a disciple I will say this. Knowledge of analogies is profitable in itself like all the laws of harmony. One who acquires consciousness of it can mitigate certain inharmonious events. But it is too easy to slide into superstitions that bring on, through imagination, the very evil they claim to exorcise.'

'If I congratulate myself on a success,' asked Her-Bak, 'or a pleasure, or some advantage, is it wrong to wipe out the ill luck that might follow by using certain gestures or formulas?'

'Such gestures and formulas,' the Symbolist explained, 'are meant to make up for any doubt that would jeopardise fulfilment of a wish, or to neutralise the malefic influence of the envious. Such practices may be excused in the ignorant, who defend themselves instinctively: they fetter the man who would leave animality behind.'

.   .   .

Her-Bak asked for a formal ruling. 'Master, can you tell us whether there are malefic gestures or not?'

'I will give you the truth. Every gesture has repercussions, like a pebble thrown into water, a cry uttered among mountains. Its consequences, harmonious or otherwise, depend on coincidences of time and place, sympathies or antipathies that it arouses in nature. But man isn't destined to be the slave of mechanical reactions; he is to gain independence of them through consciousness and impersonality. The poor creature who is haunted by fear, ever on the look out for trouble, is enslaved; moreover, he creates what doesn't exist. For you, disciple, such an attitude would mean disaster. It prevents that dilatation of heart which is indispensable to understanding. It feeds personal anxiety and the timidity that sterilises.'

Thanking the Master, Her-Bak permitted himself a personal remark. 'Fear disgusts me. I don't understand it.'

The Symbolist explained: 'Its symbol, *sndj*, which depicts a goose, dead and trussed, signifies the paralysis of something winged, a power of movement of which the corpse, like the mummy, is deprived. Fear is a shrinking in the nerve centres, a contraction that can inhibit the life-stream, coagulate certain humours, paralyse normal activity. It disorganises the flow of vital elements, stopping some, changing the course of others. Recall the word *ndj*, which exposes the constituents of a thing, and you have an idea analogous with disorganisation.'

'Is this contraction always harmful?'

'There's no wisdom in your question, Her-Bak. Do you know one single natural function that is solely harmful in its action? If Seth didn't exist, would Horus? What is the curdled milk that nourishes you? What means the fear that is simulated in Pharaoh's presence? Just as rennet coagulates milk and breaks up its constituents, so the King's presence is understood to act on his subjects with such power that they faint through the seizure that roots them to the ground, suspends the life-stream and paralyses their faculties. This obligatory ritual is a symbolic act of homage to the overwhelming effect of the royal personality.'

'This throws light on the meaning of *sndj* and the King's power over his subjects, though I couldn't admit that fear and respect should be allies. But this doesn't apply to fear of the gods, as in the expression "fear of Mut" . . .'

'Suppose I command you to fear water,' returned the Symbolist. 'How would you take it? If you fall into water without knowing how to swim it will kill you. But water isn't wicked . . . it can't be anything but water. In respect that you can't live under water it will work against you, for it can't change its nature, which gives it the power proper to its character and which, unless it is overcome or changed by some other power, will be destructive. You see then that "to fear" doesn't mean "to have fear", but to take account in consciousness of the characteristic power of each natural force, each principle, each Neter.'

The Master fell silent and left the students to meditate his words.

. . .

Abushed addressed the two Masters, saying, 'As for me, though I'm seeing things today in a very new light, I'm troubled over the difficulty of distinguishing between reality and illusion.'

Upuat broke in. 'An old man who spends his life dreaming in the temples has often told me that all is illusion, not only mental and emotional phantasmagorias but everything that touches our sense whether the stars or our own bodies.'

'Upuat touches the bottom of the problem,' said the Symbolist.

'Excellent,' said the Mystic. 'The greatest illusion that can deflect a student is the belief that mysticism is dream-life, a search for the Neter in nebulous meditation on a remote sky. Mysticism is the way of communion with the Cause from which all causes flow. But this can only be done through the matter such causes produce and the man himself who is their synthesis and expression. That is why physical consciousness is indispensable for the achievement of knowledge: without it one tumbles fatally into imaginative evocation.'

'This kind of evocation,' added the Symbolist, 'which is the basis of deceptive visions and fantastical revelations, derives from the same mistake as Upuat's old man's. If all is illusion such imaginary projections are no more illusory than the illusion of things.'

'One illusion's as good as another,' said Abushed.

'If that were true,' said the Mystic, 'there would be no causality, no creative Word, no incarnation of it, since form, product of the Word's incarnation, would be illusion by reference to its reality. Whereas form, which only becomes through the Word, is necessarily the Word in one of its specificities: all our symbolic teaching stands on this. I must then allow that transitory form, illusory as far as the meaning we attach to it is concerned, is not illusory inasmuch as it incarnates an abstract principle or potential function.'

'As our senses are our means of examination,' said Abushed, 'the limit of error is infinite.'

The Master took advantage of this to make some essential points. 'If we observe a thing,' he said, 'the form our senses shew us is illusory because it depends on imperfect means of perception; but it is in itself a reality by reference to the causal Form or Idea. An example . . . if the Word incarnates in a star the star is real in respect that it is a product of the Word which couldn't in the circumstances take any other form. But our sensory understanding of the star is relative as we can only observe it by a process of comparison. The cerebral function intervenes and sees only the actual form without its relation with the Cause, which is the reality.'

Upuat summed up what he could understand. 'Then illusion due to our senses is no more than a suggestion that alters our consciousness of things. But natural form is real in its relation with its cause.'

'This is right,' said the Sage. 'It would be gross error to reject the form of the universe in a world of illusion on the ground that all is appearance.'

.   .   .

Abushed shewed impatience. 'Isn't there something futile about these meticulous definitions? Perception depends on personal sight and understanding: it will vary with each of us.'

The disciple who was learning geometry cut in with vehemence. 'How can truth be interpreted arbitrarily? It is absolute. It is Number. Number determines form . . . what is there that is arbitrary in that?'

'I don't accept absolutism,' said Abushed. 'A man little endowed for vision of the abstract has the right to think his opinion real, since he conceives it as such in sincerity.'

'Our Masters,' the young geometer replied, 'teach that Number is universal reality. Sincerity and opinion are relative . . . there is no equivalence between the two terms.'

Upuat came in as conciliator. 'There would be, when sincerity derived from a real and vital experience. If an opinion of an argumentative kind or personal feeling is in question, there is of course no equivalence.'

'A man can't be judge of his neighbour's intelligence,' Abushed maintained. 'His own vital experience is never his neighbour's.'

'Clearly,' the young geometer agreed. 'They differ as the properties of two numbers differ. But the law of harmony that governs them is the same, like that which governs your and your neighbour's place in nature. There's nothing arbitrary in these laws.'

The Sage reminded them that no discussion can throw light if it wanders from the real point. 'The essential elements of our life and reactions are not many,' he said, 'whereas cerebral interpretations are infinitely various, although arguments, not realities.'

'I am too well aware,' said Her-Bak, 'of the difficulty of knowing with the heart instead of arguing. But the Sages who bequeathed us their knowledge say there is no other way of understanding it: I should think myself stupid to go on arguing.'

Auab smiled at him. 'I don't need to understand,' he said. 'If I free myself from all that is myself I should know all that isn't.'

'You may,' the Mystic replied, 'if you don't forget that your body is the temple of knowledge.' He turned to Abushed. 'The pure mystical endowment, renouncing all other enquiry, can acquire by "transparency" an inner knowledge that it is in no way concerned to put into cerebral terms. But the case is very rare. In all others a rigorous discipline is necessary to prevent thought from recreating the world and the Neters in its own image. That is why we must teach *what is* in spite of opinion. But no one is obliged to accept the rigours of the temple: all that prattling in the Peristyle proves it. However, you will remark it, we never allow it to be written down for posterity.'

'I see the reason for strictness,' said Abushed, 'but it accounts for the monotony of the texts and the wearisome repetition of formulas.'

'Abushed, you have enough proofs already not to let yourself be deceived by appearances. If you take note of anomalies in the texts, the various arrangements of letters in each word, and even the colour of the signs, you will soon be deciphering riddles of unexpected interest in these banal formulas.'

'If I wasn't sure of it I shouldn't listen to what impatience whispers me, "Who will give me the key?" '

'Yourself, if one day you discover the secret of the letters.'

With regret Her-Bak saw the Masters getting ready to go. He made a request in the manner of one who petitions a Neter. 'O my Masters, if I didn't know what rigorous secrecy surrounds the *mdw-Neters* I should ask a question that lies heavy on my tongue . . .'

'Lighten your tongue,' said the Symbolist. 'Put your question.'

'It is this. I am looking for the relation between *za*, magic power, *sa*, back, and *saa*, Sage.'

'You have reason to hesitate. But as you have noticed this we will give what may help to understand it. The power *za* has nothing to do with the projection of thought or will, unless in a popular reading and by extension. This word gives the active power of the fire whose channel is the vertebral column . . . there are various centres of residence and radiation in our body. It may be Sethian fire, consuming, destructive, when it is constrained or switched to sex or brain. That is why the back is said to belong to Seth. But when this fire is subtilised it is vivifying, quickening. This is the true magic fire, triple in its nature, giver of life or death.'

'It is a power to be feared then! Is it in all men?'

'It is latent in them, but few know how to make use of it wisely, very few how to master it. It reaches its perfection in him when a man, being quickened, radiates it without effort of his own, like a life-giving sun. Such a man is *saa*, a wise man, in whom the Horus-fire masters the Seth-fire and subjects it to his service. The same fire as yet unevolved gives the characteristics and signature of the personality *sa* or *za* and in its spermatic capacity it transmits paternal characters to the son *sa* or *za*.'

'I notice,' said Her-Bak, 'that it is always the letter *s* or *z* written horizontally that gives the personal and Sethian character . . .'

'. . . and that of opposition. Just so. This letter specifies, separates and particularises, as for instance in *sep*, occasion, case, example, division. The vertical form of *s* is active and activates. It symbolises the vital fire, released, subtilised, the mastery of which makes human worth . . . that is why we put the symbol in the hands of certain nobles. You see now the true meaning of *s* in the royal formula *ank wdja snb*, which refers to the two aspects of the fire in perfect balance. This is also the reason for its appearing in the word *snb*, which means the same. Are you satisfied, disciple?'

Her-Bak thanked him, saying he hadn't expected such a response.

'I will add something,' the Mystic said. '*Sw* means "he", but in royal symbols *sw* refers to the king of the South, *bit* to the king of the North. Yet, to designate royalty *sw*, not *bit*, is used. You will see why if you recall what has been taught you. Pharaoh is earthly king, He, the personality *par excellence* whose power in action and the functional importance of whose gestures one always tries to affirm. If a king runs he is that which moves. If to shoot arrows he bends the bow better than no matter what archer, he is the principle of penetrative force. At the helm of the sacred bark he is that which steers. If his hand holds fast the bonds of his prisoners, if he obliges his enemies to serve him as footstool, putting them under his sandals, he is the victorious gesture that subdues hostile powers. He is everlastingly the Idea incarnate in action, personified in earthly existence. You may relate *swt* therefore with personality, earthly concretion, the white crown, Osirian perfection, purity, represented by whiteness. And it is the Neter Osiris, master of the renewal of earthly lives, who defines the phases of terrestrial royalty, each phase the loop that encloses a king's name.'

'What then does the bee in the symbol of the king of the North mean?' asked Her-Bak.

The Sage rose. '*Bit* refers to the Horus revelation.'

VII

THE COLOSSUS

'You can follow two paths in the mountains, Her-Bak,' said the Sage. 'The first winds round it with many a twist, exploring; the slope is gentle, the ascent easy, varied, amusing. This path avoids points of danger. It never attacks the Peak and halts at shelters known to be safe. The other is steep, takes each phase of the climb without detour, skirts precipices and reaches a summit that is only accessible to a man who can face naked sunlight and danger. Which path will you choose, Her-Bak?'

'The quick and straight one,' Her-Bak replied.

'Be watchful then. What is practicable on the roads of Earth is more difficult in the way of Maât. An error of direction is soon noticed when you are crossing the desert, but not always in the search after truth if you let go the guiding thread.'

'What have I to fear? Are you not Master and guide?'

'Experience will shew you, Her-Bak, that a Master can only point the way. As far as it is a question of rational judgment and acquiring the notions that constitute a basis of knowledge, a teacher can give the precise ideas that were inculcated in himself. Such work forms part of an easy, winding road. I say easy because it brings into play faculties that are normal, belong to the lower mind and don't exact the use of faculties that are subtler and generally asleep. Normal mental faculties depend on the vitality of equivalent parts of the brain and the sharpness of sensory impressions. They work on one another by the analysis and comparison of recorded ideas. I say winding because the play of thought that results makes use of arguments based on such ideas . . . fallible because of their relativity . . . and sanctions every detour the various aspects of a problem may require. It is a winding and easy road compared with the rigour of an enquiry into causes, which for one thing depends on the awakening of subtler faculties and for another is governed by traditional knowledge of universal and irreducible law. It is a great temptation for the seeker to interpret what he perceives according to preconceived opinions and judgments, to lose himself in details and to call what for the moment is in-accessible to his understanding absurd. It is difficult to turn one's back on rational thinking. You are not afraid of the abyss? Instinct will seek the aid of a stick. You are not afraid of a lonely road? Other men's opinions will make you hesitate sometimes. You will be tested in your-self. Your utilitarian sense, your arrogant dialectic, will demand tangible fact and logical proof when your heart would have no doubts.'

Her-Bak sought the cause of the Sage's insistence. 'Your warning will be my safety,' he said. 'I shall take care not to turn aside, either through obstinacy or through cowardice.'

'May your own Neter underwrite your will in your whole being.'

.   .   .

'My own Neter? Again you raise my most agonising problem.'

'It is the problem of Man, Her-Bak. It is the problem of the King, who is Man's prototype. It is the essential problem of Egypt. Have you never been surprised at the importance ascribed to the gigantic statues of certain Pharaohs? Why did a Master of Wisdom such as Amenhotep son of Hapu deem the making of his colossus a capital work? To under-stand this you must study the connexion between the Pharaonic principle with the principle of the Neter and of man. You have noticed that Pharaoh is often spoken of as Neter in royal protocols? What in your view is the difference between Neter, king and man?'

After long reflection Her-Bak replied, 'I see three differences . . . in body, power and perfection. The first refers to the physical body . . . man and king have a body, the Neter hasn't.'

'Why do our images give the Neters a body if they have none?'

'I asked that question and I was told they are given bodies that the gods may have forms nearer those of men.'

'That is the usual answer, valid for images, statues and even temples. There's a part-truth in it as far as magic is concerned; enough, generally, for believers.'

'Not enough for me,' returned the disciple. 'I want to find in the Neter that which in the Neter and in myself is greater than an image.'

'Your desire brings you nearer the reality. But the reality must become self-evident or you fall into the opposite of the common error. Idolatry and spiritualism are two poles of the human illusion that dualises every-thing, even the divine axis of the world, in order to define, compare, condemn. Whether a man puts his faith in matter or in the power of a divine image it's matter that he worships, giving to the effect the importance of the cause. If he only thinks of spirit and worships it as apart from matter he commits Seth's sin and denies the creator incarnate in the creature. The Neters are the functional principles of nature. Theology will unfold their hierarchy for you, from the forces that are

F

knowable through the physical phenomena that are their effects, to the generative power-functions of matter, and finally, at the peak, the supreme agents or causes that determine the functions. Our sense and cerebral intelligence can't grasp them in the abstract; but sense and cerebral intelligence can study the evidence of their essential quality throughout the scale of creatures. It is for the part of witness that we choose animals typical of essential functions. As humanity is the sum of such functions, we present the king as prototype of Man, king of earthly creatures in various phases of evolution . . .'

'. . . with a difference in power,' interrupted Her-Bak, 'for power seems total in the Neter, great in the king and feeble in man.'

'Power originates action,' said the Sage. 'It is therefore immanent in the Neter-nature. But it comprises two elements, natural force and its potential, which can be modified by other Neter-powers and conditioned by the creature, thing or situation in which it is active. That is to say, these may be more or less attractive to the force in question. Thus man, according to his disposition, can be magnetic or refractory to it. As for the king, he holds powers conferred on him by Heaven and by men, so that the opposite is possible . . . men can eliminate or overthrow the king.'

Her-Bak felt confusion. 'Some other meaning escapes me, for this doesn't go at all with what is written, "Do homage to the king that lives in you, who is a fullness in the heart, a sun seen in its brightness, generator of human evolution." But no doubt this refers to the difference in perfection that distinguishes Neter from king, king from common man.'

'Weigh your words, Her-Bak. A Neter is a principle, agent or function in nature and cannot be more or less perfect. But you can compare king and man.'

'If king and Neter can't be compared in point of perfection, how can the king be called Neter?'

'Precisely as representative of a principle, the principle of Man, royal type of the human in the phase of becoming that is his time and country. It is always the story of becoming that dominates our teaching and you should study the scale of creatures to which it gives rise—from stone to man—as incarnate functions that have their sum and completion in Humanity. But listen. In itself a grain of wheat is all wheat, the plant that produced it, the plant to be. It is the perfection of wheat and sums up the idea of wheat. Seed then is the perfection of its species, the physical aim of its existence, which is victory over the death of its kind. Seed is the sum of it. But a species, in nature, is only a state of transition. In the original cause perfection is the aim: species are phases of generation in the return to it. Every species is a halt in the becoming of an organic function, which finds itself corporified before having attained its final aim, which is to play its part in the human organism. The organic function, thus arrested, produces creatures with its functional characteristics that participate in the general laws of life, assimilation, growth, reproduction. But don't forget that in the abstract creation, before there was specificity, man was the sum of all functions. If in the course of earthly becoming a thousand accidents happen, with changes of shape through adaptation, the totality still constitutes a step in nature towards its "end", man, and finds its place in him, marked and signed. Man, synthesis of all the functional possibilities in nature, is therefore like nature's own seed. That is why in his proportions, the variations in his rate of growth, he sums the proportions, movement and growth of the celestial bodies. He can but be a measure of his own universe.'

'Is there then a science that includes all others, a science of man?' asked Her-Bak.

'Yes, Her-Bak. A science of Man, measure of Cosmos and key to it.'

.   .   .

The disciple listened while these words re-echoed in the silence. Then, 'If man is the synthesis of nature is he its king?' he asked.

'Seed and summit of creatures living on Earth, he is nature's king as Pharaoh is king of the people and country whose leaven, *heqa*, he is.'

'I didn't know that *heqa*, a sceptre or governor, also meant leaven.'

'Don't be stupid, Her-Bak. Learn the simple meaning of the symbol . . . isn't *heqa* a crook that grips like the shepherd's and keeps the sheep in the flock? Isn't this the part of a leaven that takes the dough and changes it to its own nature? And *heq* enters into the formation of *henq.t*, beer, the fermentation of which makes a powerful yeast. Just so a king is the leaven of his people, according to his country and time. Study of his name, *per âa*, will shew you its real meaning. *Per*, house, place, contains the idea of going out, appearing, manifesting. *Per* gives place as defined by what it contains and what it should reveal. A house, for instance, has the character of the man who lives in it, as the body or house of the KA has the KA's. The hieroglyph of *per* is a rectangle in which an opening indicates the possibility of entry and departure. The movement of departure is given by the addition of the letter *r*. *Per.r* means to go out, shew oneself, the manifestation of what was within. The same word with the addition of *t*, *pert*, means a visible product, grain, seed, issued from the place that contained them. Now study the words formed from this root: *kheper*, the state of gestation or becoming of the germ; *neper*, the ripe grain, living, vigorous; *nepri*, its Neter or active power; *pert*, the visible product. There is therefore an intention to identify the visible product, the process of manifestation and the place or house out of which the product came, as shewn by the same hieroglyph and the same root.

'This leads to the conclusion that Pharaoh's name, *per âa*, identifies the king with the place in which he is the active principle. Moreover, *âa* means grandeur in the sense of the extreme limit of possibility in the thing thus qualified. In this case then it refers to the highest measure of human power, perpetuated in a succession of kings of the same great house. Each Pharaoh is a moment in this continuity. But note that he is "made" of all the *pert* his kingdom affords him; products of his subjects' activity, products of earth that are its image. He participates in them all, quickens and makes them prosper, as a leaven gives life to the dough; thus making a continuous flow between king and kingdom.'

'Does this apply to the kings of other countries?'

'What do you think, Her-Bak? Can the temporary leader of a people be other than an expression of the tendencies of the time? But a leaven can regenerate or destroy according to the quality of such tendencies and the wisdom used in their management. In the succession of our kings, selection and training of the heir make such expression the more effectual that the royal principle may persist and be renewed in accordance with the character of the time. If an age has its character Pharaoh can be called its Neter, in principle.'

'The royal principle has been taken as far as it will go,' said Her-Bak, 'I see why his statue must shew each Pharaoh's character.'

'The statue expresses in fact connexions of measure, nature and function with the phase Pharaoh represents. The ideal royal statue is the Colossus, which shews Pharaoh as witness to such a phase and symbolises Man, image and measure of cosmos.'

'Master, I see the importance of a statue if its details and proportions speak of such a reality.'

'A reality on which all our symbology is based. In ancient times our Sages were careful in the use of it so as not to profane the vital secret of universal correlation. In times of decadence words and details multiply, revealing certain factors that were held back until then: the conscientious student will find confirmation of this at every step. But our architecture has kept without swerving to the rigorous teaching of universal law. The Colossus remains the greatest lesson for man.'

.   .   .

MAN

'There is no question at this moment,' the Sage said, 'of studying the human body in detail. I will only mention essential points that by symbol and name are a teaching in themselves.

'It is profitable to note, first, that measures of length are based on the arms and hands, with the finger as unit. Esoterically man is seen as a five-pointed star. The highest point is the trunk and head; the lateral points are the arms; the two lower are the legs that touch earth. Arms and hands serve as measures: the forearm, *â* which with the hand gives the cubit, is also the symbol of individuality. The hands do, give or receive; but the right hand is active, the left passive: if we befigure someone with two right or two left hands it is to specify an active or a passive character. The back, supported by the vertebral column, is called *iat*, like anything with an axis and two poles. The north pole, the head, cranium and all, is called *tep*, the south pole, heel and sole of the foot, *tb.t.* The twelve ribs, which develop the chest like a sphere with two spirals, are called *spr*. Note that this framework which swells and collapses on inspiration and expiration has the same name as the function *spr*, which means to aspire, strain towards, implore. The root *men*, which has in it the idea of base, foundation, stability, gives their names to the thigh, *men.t*, base and stability of the trunk, and to the breasts, nutritive base of a child's life. If you would understand the process of formation, nutrition and transformation in our flesh, study the visceral organs of generation and nutrition in the belly, *khat*, bearing in mind that *khet* means wood, a thing or a fire. *Khat* is also the word for a corpse.

'The organs of animation and renewal are in the rib-cage that contains the *hati*, the heart-and-lung group, inseparable as to function. The heart of flesh, *âb*, is a dancer, *âb*, whose movement of contraction and dilatation propels vital activity and is the motor of animal life. It governs the rhythm of the blood-stream. But the heart couldn't do this without the help of a twofold organ, the lungs, where fire and air carried by the breath, *nef*, and the blood, *senef*, meet. As fire can't live without air the heart of flesh needs the lungs, *sma*, to give the blood life and unite air with fire.'

Her-Bak drew the symbol of union, *sma*, on the ground, 'Is the part played by the lungs the reason for their name, *sma*?'

'If you give the word its real meaning. *Sma* means to join, in order to give them life, two separate elements of the same origin, so that each takes the other's qualities, without fusion, and is the better for it.'

'I understand the symbol *sma tawi*, union of the Two-Lands,' said Her-Bak. 'Flowers of the North entwine with flowers of the South, yet they live independently.'

'Like the Two-Lands,' agreed the Sage. 'There is unity without fusion by alliance within the central government. *Hati* then is the triad that provides a vital, organic drive. The symbol of *hati* is the forepart of a lion, shewing the heart of this solar animal and its powerful chest or breath-capacity. Its head, with characteristic solar mane, completes the symbolism. The lungs, inhaling, are quickened by Amon's breath, while the heart obeys Râ and his Horus-Word *her*. The whole life of the human being, thus unfolding, nourished and quickened, is reflected in the face, *her*. The face mirrors the Word, *her*, whose five modes of expression are the five senses. It is said that celestial Hathor is the "house of the Horus-Word", as her name, *het her*, tells us. That is why our images often shew Hathor's form isolated.'

.   .   .

'Are you speaking of that strange face with cow's ears?' asked Her-Bak. 'How is this symbol to be read?'

'Very easily, by the cow's nature. The cow is the passive mammifer *par excellence*. And the ear is essentially passive: the clarity of its hearing is proportional to its passivity, just as neutrality is the condition of under-standing for the inner ear. The ear is called *mesdjer*, from the root *mes*, to be born, or born, and *djer*, limit, or to bind. This symbolises its two essential functions: *djer* alludes to the fact that our sense of orientation, of direction in the space in which we find ourselves, resides in the internal organ. It is this centre that gives us our sense of balance. The meaning of *mesdjer*, to be born and to bind, draws attention to the way in which the ear exercises the sense of hearing: it unites the sounds or "words" which the two ears hear separately. It is their receptivity to the Word that suggested their appellation "the living", and it puts them in relation with Hathor, mother of Horus.'

'The ear must have some relation with Ptah,' said Her-Bak. 'I have seen steles with a prayer to Ptah on which ears were engraved.'

'Ptah is incorporate fire, conceived in a terrestrial "ear", in passive, inert matter, of which it becomes the activity, creator of bodily form. Hathor, the heavenly cow, is the divine passivity that perpetually receives and conceives all forms of the Word. She is the cosmic aspect of passivity of which Mut is the terrestrial aspect. Now you can understand the symbol of the passive ear.'

'Hasn't the eye too a passive role?' Her-Bak asked.

'The eye has a twofold function. It receives light and gives out energy. The eyes are essentially dual: their sight is dualised and "crossed" in the brain. That is why we symbolise sight, *maa*, by two eyes and the "scythe" that separates them. Their character is twofold as well; the right eye is solar, the left lunar. The word for an eye is *àr.t*, whose root *àr* means to do in the sense of to create, to work up. Don't confuse it with *dy* or *rdy*, to do in the sense of to execute.

'The word for the sense of smell is *khnem*. Smell is *seti*, the same word as that for the seed which creates form out of receptive matter. The function of smelling, *khnem*, has the same name as Khnum, the potter-Neter who gives form to fecundated matter. As to the sense of taste, its Neter is called *hw*, which signifies both the nutritive principle in food-stuffs and the principle of taste. The mouth's function is to discern flavours; salts are only active in solution and to distinguish the flavours of material substances requires humidity. The tongue is the fleshly organ that takes food, masticates it with the help of the teeth and tastes its flavour; it is also the site of a most subtle sense of touch. And it is in contact with organs of nutrition of which it is the mirror. The word for it, *nes*, deserves study, for the letters *n* and *s* designate two aspects of the fire that quickens the world.'

.   .   .

'Please explain this that is so important,' Her-Bak entreated.

'The *mdw-Neters* are there to teach you to understand them. I will add this to help you. Pronunciation of the two letters is effected by the tip of the tongue, with the breath of the nostrils for *n* and of the mouth for *s*. Now *ns* is cosmic Man's double source of energy. *n* shews itself above all in the blood and its qualities; *s* in the marrow and all that derives from it. Notice that the inversion of these two letters gives the root *sen*, which means "two".'

Her-Bak saw the point. 'As they were chosen to form the word "two", one may suppose they express what is most characteristically dual.'

'The conclusion is sound. Don't forget this. What you must keep in mind if you are to follow our Masters' thinking is that all organs work together in the functioning of the whole, under the direction of heart and tongue. As the texts say, "All the eyes see, the ears hear, the nose smells, comes to the heart, which synthesises it into living consciousness. All that is thus conceived will be repeated by the tongue and worked on by *hati*." In this way the manifestation of things comes about, in the mode of creation and in circular fashion. If you can hear the meanings of "heart", "*hati*", "tongue" in yourself you will understand the connexion of human and cosmic organs, and the cosmic functions which human functions illustrate. At the same time you can study the relations between our senses and the world's constitutive elements. You have just seen that taste is the sense of the liquid, the water element; that sight is the sense of the radiant, the fire element; that smell is the sense of the vaporous, the air element; that touch is the sense of the corporal, the earth element. This is the common explanation of the obvious relations between the sense organs and states of matter, the practical, realistic point of view. But there is another, less obvious because of a subtler, a causal order, which takes into account the generative quality of each sense and its principial origin. The passivity of Hathor who generates the Word is the source of the quality of audibility. But this "celestial face" contains also the other four generative principles, fire-light that causes visibility, essential air that causes tangibility, essential water that causes sapidity, essential earth that causes odorability. You will notice that this differs from what I first said about the elemental relations between touch and smell. We are speaking now of the secret qualities of air and earth considered as factors in genesis: it is this that makes them secret, or not usually discussed. As to Earth, compare what has just been said about Khnum and smell. As to Air, cause of tangibility, remember that it is the *Air-Neter Shu* who by separating heaven and earth gives them both tangible existence in duality.'

'Since the organs of sense are in the face,' said Her-Bak, 'the face is a mirror in which all we can perceive is reflected.'

'Just so. This is why the word *her*, face, denotes also the chief, *heri*, whose part is to keep in contact with the external world by his faculties of perception, to see, hear and observe. To the governed he presents the face of authority, the supreme authority to whom he gives information and warning. Never forget that the inner meaning of *her* is "the sense of the presence". When you say *her àb*, meaning "in", "at the heart of", you are saying precisely "what is present in the heart of . . ." *Her sa*, behind, means "present behind"; and it is the same with other phrases that use *her* in this sense.'

'It is the presence that the exercise of the facial senses reveals,' the disciple remarked. 'But why is the sky sign so often added to the chief's title?'

'Because this sign, called *her* in such a case, indicates "above" or "higher". A man's head drawn in profile and containing the brain symbolises another phase of authority. It is the summit of the human body, *tep*, which is upside down in the word *pet*, heaven, world of ideas that reflects the world of archetypes. The head is the centre where relation, comparison, organisation take place and command is exercised. The chief, *tep*, isn't necessarily in direct touch with those he directs, which is why you will usually find the two words *heri tep* coupled, for most head men or chiefs in our kingdom are obliged to double the functions of observation and command in order to ensure the carrying out of the law.'

'Master,' said Her-Bak, 'you have taught that the brain has a secondary role by reference to intuition. How is it that in the imagery of some funerary texts the head only is shewn, sometimes emerging from a mound or plant, as if it were the dead man's surviving element?'

'Your interpretation is incomplete, through ignorance of certain constituents of the being. Pending fuller instruction, remember that the human head contains not only the organs of thought and the cerebral centres of every bodily function, but physical centres, seats of higher states of which we will speak later, that when awakened are in touch with the spiritual heart. It is a complete little world where all "states of being" and all activities possible to man are found, as it were in posts of command. And finally, it is in the head that there is enacted the highest mystery of sublimation into subtle energies of physical elements that proceed from the body, just as the corporal senses, which have their organs in the face, are transformed into "spiritual senses" there. The head then represents the highest gestation of human functions and in the case you mention symbolises a similar gestation after death.'

.   .   .

The disciple listened closely, fearing the possibility of misunderstanding. 'So important a teaching,' he said, 'should leave no room for doubt. Could you enlighten me on one point? If the intelligence of the heart is to conceive of knowledge as a combined product of perceptions I can't see, in spite of all you have just said, why the head, *tep*, symbolises the chief who co-ordinates and commands.'

'Your question certainly calls for an answer,' said the Sage. 'An unfinished teaching could mislead you. Your idea of a chief is wrong. A chief, *heri*, *tep*, or *heri tep*, is neither king, the leaven of his people, nor the spiritual quickener of king and kingdom. I will tell you, at the right time, what you must know about this dual power; but from now on look for its image in man, in whom all stages of consciousness, were it only in embryo, are found. As the moon reflects Râ's burning light in light that is cold and thin, so the heart's vision is reflected in the brain. But whereas the heart synthesises perceptions into vital consciousness the brain separates, localises them, as well as performing other functions of comparison and co-ordination that are indispensable if a chief is to form rational judgments. That is why the word for brain, *ais*, is an inversion of *sia*, the consciousness of the heart.'

'I thought the cerebral organ was called *âmm*.'

'If you would understand the nature of things you should study attentively the name that is given them and the reason for it. The word for the head viscera is *ais*, the same as that for the belly viscera. This is in no way surprising if you notice that both have multiple convolutions. The functional analogy is as real as the look of it: the brain, *ais*, handles sense-impressions as the intestines handle food prepared in the stomach. The breaking-down and localisation of various substances in the alimentary mass takes place in parts of the intestine specialised for the purpose. Similarly, various regions in the cerebral convolutions, each according to its function, take in sensory perceptions, which, isolated and localised, are compared, examined, in other functional regions of the brain and projected from the material organ as ideas. The parts of the head viscera, then, work like those of the belly viscera. They select constituents of what comes in according to their "functional affinities". But here we must distinguish material and therefore quantitative functions from functions of a more abstract and qualitative kind. It is here that the wisdom in our language gives you a vital glimpse of what speculation could never discern and express.

'Compare the word *ais*, name of the upper and lower viscera, with *âmm*, which refers to a function belonging as much to the body as to the thinking personality: the function of ingesting, absorbing, on the one hand foodstuffs, on the other perceptions. I am speaking now of an immaterial function that causes the physical activity of an organ that swallows and incorporates because of it. This applies to the animal that devours its prey, to the brain that absorbs sense-perceptions, and to Ammit, swallower of the dead, who is no other than nature taking back into herself those parts of a corpse that belong to her. *Âm* is the root that signifies this function. *Âmm*, by the double *m*, gives the idea of reabsorption into oneself, monopolisation. *Â* suggests individual limitation. In point of fact, nature, belly and brain absorb in proportion to their capacity.

'Now consider *ais* as a material organ. *Sia* is the immaterial fruit of perceptions assimilated by the intelligence of the heart. Thoughts, product of the cerebral organ *ais*, proceed on the one hand from a contribution from without, ideas put forth by other brains and taken in by the mental faculty of absorption *âmm*, on the other from personal experience, sensorial or intuitive perceptions changed by comparison, dissociation or association of ideas received and recorded. Such personal thoughts then become forms that the brain *ais* puts out and the *âmm* function of other brains may receive, without intervention of word or writing, by evocation therefore.

'Understand, Her-Bak, that as the sun's sphere of radiation is larger than the physical globe, *àten*, a sphere of heat, light and various wave-movements, your functional thought-body, *âmm*, is larger than your brain, *ais*: it is because of this that you can recall memories and ideas written in *âmm* at the instance of the corresponding centres of *ais*, which are only relaying stations.'

. . .

Her-Bak strove to master the positive symbolism of the hieroglyphs and the meaning of the roots. 'This difficult lesson,' he said, 'was indispensable if I was to learn how a play of letters can teach without theory, by symbolic evocation, the connexion between functional causes at work in the human body and the organic functions that are an expression of them.'

'Your effort has borne fruit,' said the Sage. 'You have understood the aim of my discourse, which should serve as example when you are trying to decipher our teaching. But you must still concentrate on learning to extract the marrow from a theme. What have you actually gathered?'

'If I have really understood,' Her-Bak said, 'the organic spheres of the brain *ais* and the immaterial function *âmm* work together in the production of thoughts that are written into *âmm* and *ais* can recover them at will.'

'Exactly. But success will be proportional to the vigour and equilibrium of the head viscera: memory will be good or bad. This exhibits the relativity and fallibility of ideas so recorded, since they proceed from co-ordinations of appearances that are more or less complete. Transcription by thought of knowledge gained by the heart is another thing. Consciousness of this order is a putting of something perceived in relation with what corresponds with it in ourselves. In contrast with such reality thoughts that derive from an association of ideas external to your true being are excrement. The world, or state, *âmm* is a state of perpetual absorption of all that is measurable and quantitatively assimilable in nature, whether material food or rational concept. It is nature's greed. *Sia* is the world, or state, in which transmutation of the separative, analysing, Seth-activity into the synthesising Horus-activity facilitates discrimination between the personal and particular, *i*, and the universal, *a*. This is the Sage's critical sense. Once more then we find that the concrete, *ais*, can lead to the abstract, *sia*, whose fruit is immortal.

'But that what I say may awaken a vital logic in you and not merely be turned into set ideas, you must learn to distinguish between those two modes of thinking, taking advantage of the more complex to record enlightening details but avoiding an analysis of dissected factors that would destroy vital unity and obscure the simple, original idea.'

.   .   .

Her-Bak couldn't hide his perplexity. 'Master, could you explain in what sense I'm to think of thought as useless for getting knowledge?'

'Nothing in man is useless to him, but one must give each factor its true part. Thought should translate what consciousness has written in your whole body. To do the opposite is the way to error. If you write into consciousness what you have worked up by argument the result will be imaginings and arbitrary systems. You can invent nothing. You must assimilate what really is. This is to reverse the mode of thinking in which brain is king. Instinct, animal consciousness such as that of ant or bee, knows without thinking what correlations of an invisible kind there are in nature though unable to co-ordinate ideas. But man, endowed with reason, who believes in incarnate spirit and gives his higher consciousness precedence over thought, goes beyond animal instinct and develops intuition. I call you to the true path, Her-Bak. I speak living man to living man. I make no distinction between spirit and body, for all your body is required if you are to receive this teaching. You know nothing about the Neter, little about the king; you are man, man is your cosmos, by man you will know everything if you turn your back on Seth and his science. But for that you must learn what puts man above animal, even the human animal, the earthly man who hasn't yet had the first quickening. It is this first quickening as well as the quality of his individual KA that distinguishes him from the higher beasts. Man can receive two quickenings: one reaches its realisation in the extreme possibilities of nature, the other begins his return into the Cause.'

'If the first reaches the limit of possibility in nature,' said Her-Bak, 'then nature can make nothing more perfect than man?'

'Precisely. Man, born of woman, Man in himself, is the most perfect of creatures that carry the seed of their own reproduction on Earth.'

'Then the second quickening should carry man beyond nature?'

'Beyond and this side of it, for the quickening principle that is his divine KA is the very essence of the Unpronounceable, independent of nature and the Neters, which only affect the lower KAS.'

'Is nature dependent on the Unpronounceable?'

'Necessarily, or there would be two absolutes. But nature must follow the cycles of becoming of which the divine KA is independent.'

'You said "man born of woman". Is there a man not born of woman?'

'It is always a woman that gives the earthly body. While she carries it and nourishes it with her own substance the first quickening of the body takes place, at the critical moments of the fortieth day and the fourth month. In a man's life outside his mother's womb there is a continuing birth of the individual KA's consciousness; and it is also at the fourth period of its earth-age that a quickening takes place. Then for the king of earthly creatures there begins the possibility of a reign which surpasses that of earth-man through the growth of his higher consciousness, which he should nourish in himself as his mother nourished his body. So doing, he frees himself from the laws of Earth; and that the more as the influence of his divine KA grows preponderant. Now you have the true king, who is the seed of his incorruptible being, the human Horus woven by his KA in the man who has sought to know it. His kingdom is not of this Earth, for such a man, as you suppose, is beyond Earth-nature.'

'Where is this king's throne?'

'In a man's heart. This is no empty word, nor myth, nor image. It is positive reality. Do you think you know your heart?'

'I know it makes my body live, but I don't know it.'

'The heart that gives your body life is a vessel of flesh, blood-distributor, *àb*, the eternal thirst whose rhythm governs your existence. It imposes this rhythm on your whole organism, as emanations from the sun Râ impinge on the "wanderers", the planets, that live in its orbit. Râ, heart of our solar system, like the heart that is the sun in our body, could never perform its life-giving part if its physical form was its sole reality, destructible because corruptible. But our texts always speak of the "indestructible Sun". When we adjure a dead man not to lose his heart, *àb* or *hati*, in the other world, we obviously don't have in mind the heart of flesh that is shut up in the tomb. The heart, like the sun, is the

centre of a world or system. It has, like the sun, two aspects, one visible
and corporal, the other only perceptible by its effects. Aten, the solar
disc, is but the physical body of the real star, centre of spheres of light,
warmth and various powers. The true solar heart is the source of our
world's life. The heart of flesh, *àb*, is the body of that sun of life and fire
which is the radiant centre of the soul, BA, whose lower aspect moves in
the blood. Our true solar heart, our spiritual KA's centre of attraction,
is the meeting-place of everything in us that desires and accepts its
impulses. It can steady and quicken the heart of flesh, which beats with
its life: then the one heart becomes a heart of fire, a centre of light, a
source of life that has all power to subjugate the animal in us.'

         .   .   .

Her-Bak meditated these words, which gave his life purpose. But
the Master knew that vision, if it is to be effective, must connect with
something practical. 'I have shewn you the goal,' he said. 'What matters
now is the means. Can you find it in what I said about the *mdw-Neters?*'

'If I have really taken your meaning,' Her-Bak replied, 'I think I may
conclude that a man has two means of understanding and co-ordination,
the comparative intelligence *ais* and the intuitive intelligence *sia*.'

'It is as you put it. Our Masters attached such importance to this that
they devised a formula . . ."*hw* is in the mouth and *sia* in the heart". You
know that *hw*, Neter of taste, is the principle of the discernment of
flavours, material therefore. If you remember the lesson on the *mdw-
Neters* you will know that the double letter *ai* symbolises two aspects of
original Activity: *i* gives the Me, *a* the not-Me, the Self. *Sia* is discrimination of the Me and the Self. It is therefore the principle of Wisdom,
knowledge of all things. It is Understanding, which gives vital consciousness. As the comparative intelligence *ais* is conditioned by the strength
and precision of the cerebral faculties, its conclusions are relative. Into
the play between *ais* and *sia* comes the personality, which may accept
sia-knowledge in thankfulness or make difficulties . . . you have the
emotional principle there. If emotion isn't suppressed, or diverted by some
rational interpretation, it will play a helpful part; it will manifest organic-
ally the consciousness of what is revealed. It acts on the heart through the
solar plexus and awakens the solar light . . . hence the phrase "intelligence
of the heart". Mastery of these faculties, with total submission of thought
to heart-knowledge, is *saa*, from which *i*, the Me-principle, has been
eliminated. It is the principle of Wisdom.'

Her-Bak didn't know how to express his gratitude. 'There is then a way to knowledge,' he murmured, 'and a man may choose it. I see my path.'

The Master took the disciple's hands. 'Today is your "third day", Her-Bak.'

With fire in his heart Her-Bak accepted this as a gift from the Neter and felt new certainty. 'Now you are on the road,' said the Master, 'there's an easy way of keeping it. It is to accept without arrogant criticism the reality of a tradition passed mouth-to-ear, guardian of our secrets. Certain precepts will solve many an enigma for you if you learn to read and interpret in the light of the thought that formulated them. Listen then and see if this doesn't give you the proof and reality of what I have said about the heart. "He whom God loves listens. He who listens not is against his Neter and the enemy of heart-knowledge. It is the heart that decides whether its master shall listen or not. What one wishes a man by the formula Life-Health-Strength is perfection of heart. A man's heart is his own Neter." Now do you know your Neter, Her-Bak?'

VIII

THE SKY

The Sage led Her-Bak to a door symbolic of a more advanced teaching. Entering, he said, 'A year has passed since you passed this door. Have you passed the same threshold?'

'Of course. It's the same door.'

'Do you find yourself in the same place?'

'It couldn't be otherwise,' answered the disciple, surprised.

'And yet it isn't the same place. A year has gone by, a cycle has closed, another has begun. Time has changed the place, for nothing stands still. You think you are still the same Her-Bak?'

Joy lighted his answer, 'Your teaching has changed my mentality and transmuted my worst resistances into living force.'

'Not only the teaching. The method of concentration and meditation you have used since your admission has developed your understanding. You have learnt how to translate in your thoughts what your heart perceives. Your own experience has proved the efficacy of our symbolic system both to teach and to veil the mysteries of nature. You have been given elementary directions for the study of man in yourself and in society. Today we shall widen your horizon. What is Nut?'

'The sky that contains the stars.'

'What is *pt*?'

'It is . . . that which contains the stars.'

'Why two words for the same thing?'

Her-Bak reflected, hesitated. 'I have seen Nut's image holding the sign of the sky with lifted arms: perhaps the sky *pt* is beyond Nut's . . .'

'Like a lid? Is this worthy of a disciple, Her-Bak? You no longer have excuse for such feebleness of expression. Are you any better equipped to study the word *sba*, a star?'

'What am I to say? You have taught me to look for the fact in nature and symbol, to mistrust fantastic supposition. I have spent all my time studying vegetable, animal, my own body. Be indulgent, Master, if I haven't had one single hour to study the stars!'

The Master's reply dismayed Her-Bak. 'I don't wish to add to your labours. The sky is far away . . . let us put off the journey.'

The student saw but one thing, an opportunity lost through his own fault. Deploring his caprice, he recalled an earlier lesson. 'You told me,' he said, 'that *sba* means three things that seem different . . . star, door, teaching. I know there's always a reason for such similitudes. I see that a door, an opening, may symbolise instruction. But what connexion have these two things with a star?'

The Sage made no reply. Her-Bak pursued his thoughts. 'A star is inscribed in these three words . . . then doesn't *sba*, to instruct, mean to give light? And isn't the door, *sba*, that through which one passes? Could *sba*, a star, have an analogous meaning: that through which something passes, light?'

'In this way,' said the Sage, 'you could find your answer, in the letters of the word. Use it to try and find out the meaning of the sky Nut and the sky *pt*. Reflect on it all day. If your meditation opens your ears we will answer your questions this evening.'

.   .   .

When it was full night the Sage made Her-Bak climb a narrow stone stairway that gave access to the terraces. Along a passage that opened half way up they entered a cave-like chamber with paved floor, monolithic blocks in the ceiling, rough-hewn walls . . . a crushing atmosphere in which it was a relief to get a glimpse of the sky through a slit.

The Sage seated himself. The disciple did likewise, mute. 'It is for you to speak,' said the Master. 'Say what is in your heart. Let us hear what thoughts have come to you.'

Her-Bak sighed. 'More questions than answers. First I meditated the symbols of the words Nut and *pt*. I noticed that Nut is depicted by a vase supported by the sky-sign, while *pt* is written with the letters *p* and *t* placed over it. I said, then Nut's symbol is an urn, her image a woman clothed in waves. The sky-sign denotes an idea, not a thing. An urn is that which contains. Urn and woman give Nut this character. But a woman gestates the seed she contains and bears children: thus also with Nut? As regards *p* and *t* in *pt*, I don't see the meaning, nor the exact significance of their symbols, so I can't explain.'

'Your reading as to Nut is correct,' said the Sage. 'As to *pt*, it is the home of the Neters.'

'I'm still not satisfied,' said the student. 'Are Nut and *pt* different skies? Sometimes the sky-sign sustains an urn, sometimes Nut lifts it. Which is above which?'

'Take care, Her-Bak. You confuse physical image with symbol. I will try to make you understand by separating inseparable ideas.

G

'There is in this universe a unity, a coincidence, a superposition of factors, that our thought is impotent to conceive without dividing them. If you wish to describe what is like a volume, cube or sphere that contains everything in terms of reason, you will have to cut it into slices, after which you will only see surfaces, anatomised parts. It is for you, disciple, to exercise your consciousness and use our methods, using the symbols to explain to yourself what you have perceived.'

Her-Bak silenced a swarm of arguments. A simple image stood out. 'I see my body,' he said, 'as an envelope containing organs that transform foodstuffs. I see vessels containing humours, blood, liquids of various kinds, that circulate. I see channels filled with air that renews the blood. I can call all these containers urns . . . Nut's urn or body? But none of them would function without the energy that gives everything movement and strength . . .'

'. . . call it generative fire.'

'Yes, Master, but it isn't visible. One can only judge of it by its effects. It's as if the life of each vessel depended on a state of affairs in another world. Without it they would be inert; yet if they didn't function there would be no energy. Which world comes first, that of the vessels or that of the unseen force? To know the answer you would have to experience the functioning of all parts together without separating them. I shall never do this by thinking: I should have to look at each by itself and in relation to the rest.'

The Sage agreed. 'What you say is excellent. As observer you can take three positions. First, place yourself above, in the world of abstractions, and try to conceive of the play of causal forces and creative ideas. Second, place yourself within what is in process of becoming, live with it. Third, place yourself as man, final product of creation, face to face with it and study each of its elements. The test of your insight will consist in your not confusing the three states, which compose a unity. As to the first position, creation is continuous: what you may come to know of the abstract world exists and brings abouts the gestation that gives quantity. As to the second, you are in gestation yourself. As to the third, you are also a product of this, you, conscious man who observes. What do you see, conscious man? You see stars in the sky; we shew you their journey in the framework of Nut's body whose feet and hands are the two horizons, both the visible and those that limit our understanding. For symbol we take a woman's body, and sometimes we give her robe the characteristic of water, precisely to signify gestation. Her children are the stars, each a personality with its own life. And in Nut's body gestation too is continuous; there is simultaneity in all its functions. You have expressed this in your image of the human body. Return again into yourself and try to experience the synthesis of these worlds, each of which manifests its own function while sharing in the life of the whole ...

'The vessel of flesh that contains the organs of nutrition isn't the whole of your body. Every organ that contributes to the transformation of foodstuffs into your own substance is a vessel of flesh and each particle of it has the same nature as the vessel. The water-vessel isn't simply a system of vessels that carry liquids: every liquid in the body is itself a vessel with specific qualities. The air-vessel isn't only a tree that distributes air in the chest: blood is a vessel that conveys the life-giving properties of air to the smallest parts of the body. By means of it and throughout the external envelope these properties are absorbed by humours that become vessels each according to its role.

'Now in each vessel, or world, or state of substance whether solid, fluid or aerial, the other two collaborate after their nature. We may speak of flesh, humours, air, but the three are allied in common activity, living, simultaneous. Thus it is in Nut's body, which symbolises the generation and gestation of all heavenly bodies. It is the cyclical movement of these bodies and vessels, the whole harmonious order on which they depend, that constitutes the geometrical and astronomical aspects of *pt*. If you could perceive the inextricable criss-cross of waves, emanations, radiations and courses you would see what I mean. *Pt* is the "place" and fire thanks to which Nut gestates ideas that belong to the sky *pt*. But if you would localise this "place" you will find yourself as helpless as if you tried to localise the vital fire in your body. For although you may know about organs of emission and transfer, it isn't just a part of the body that is deprived of the fire without which it decays and dies, as when the soul leaves the body. It is the soul of the sky that gives Nut her life.'

'All this,' murmured Her-Bak, 'chimes with what my heart tells me.'

'Then you will understand that *pt* is the space where Numbers live and impose their being in great and small cycles and all the time. Just as no part of your body is independent of its Fire, so no substance in cosmos, no star, is independent of *pt*.'

       .   .   .

'When it is said,' asked Her-Bak, having reflected, ' "That which is in Heaven, on Earth and in the Dwat", what is to be understood as to those places?'

'They are three states of one Spirit, from beginning to end of its metamorphoses. Again strict definition is impossible; but it may be said that Heaven is the world of Spirit, of the causal hierarchies, the archetypal world; the Dwat is the world of form-principles, the ectypal world, the world of forms that define spirit in substance; Earth is the world of types, bodies, spirit incorporate. The Dwat is much less a place than a state: you yourself, when asleep, live in the Dwat without knowing it. It comprises regions that correspond with different states of consciousness and, in relation to Earth, different times. As in nature there are two moments when dark and light meet, when light hides in darkness and when it emerges, so there are two phases of the Dwat that correspond with two opposite phases of transition and the states that proceed from it. The image *aker*, two lions, or sometimes a double forepart of a lion, symbolises two extreme times in the Dwat. One of the lions is "yesterday" and looks west, the other is "tomorrow" and looks east. Both turn their back on "yesterday's" sun, which is below the horizon. It is night. The sun is travelling in the Dwat. They are the keepers who open and shut the gate into the shadow-world. That is why we use the lion in the theme of the bolt, the part that slides east and west in the fastening of a door.'

'Haven't I seen bulls instead of lions?'

'Their role as keeper is the same. It is their nature that differs. But for you these symbols are still dumb images, Her-Bak. It is difficult to speak in concrete terms of what isn't perceptible to sense. If at the right time I can awaken in you a consciousness of the states that make up a living man, *akh*, BA, KA, we will return to the subject. Just now you must gain contact with the visible heavens, where there is no woman Nut nor sign *pt*. Yet these symbols will set the direction of your search for those "places" in the sky where Nut's vital functions are incarnate and for the secret of *pt* in functions that are geometrical.'

.   .   .

The Sage and his disciple climbed the stair that led to the astronomers' terraces. Observers, absorbed in their work, paid no attention to them. Some, at fixed posts, plotted the voyage of the stars to the meridian; a few beginners were learning to take sights and work the sectors, view-finders and circles. The Sage introduced Her-Bak to the Master Astro-nomer, saying, 'I entrust my disciple to you that you may instruct him in the laws of the sky, in the measure that he can profit from a first lesson. Today, I ask you to give him no more than the preliminaries on which this science of truth is founded, that later he may be able to shew by his own efforts how much he deserves to learn from you.'

The Astronomer bowed. 'Master of Masters, your wishes are commands. But I am responsible for the secrets that are bequeathed to me: let the disciple be judged by his own mouth. Her-Bak, look west . . . now turn slowly to the east, watching the sky. What do you see?'

'As I turn I keep on seeing new stars.'

'If you stand still all night what will you see?'

'I shall see the stars passing before me.'

'What moves? The stars or yourself watching them?'

'If I stand still it must be the stars that move.' Her-Bak paused. 'Unless Earth turns as I have just done. Is this possible?'

The Astronomer smiled at his bewilderment. He gave the disciple time to think, then asked, 'If the stars move, if Sun and Moon travel, why should Earth alone in cosmos stand still? The idea repels you?'

'It would be strange,' Her-Bak replied, 'if one had to imagine that Earth, that seemed still in a shifting sky, was on the move. But everything I learn proves that my senses are subject to illusion . . . I don't dare deny that such movement takes place if you tell me it is so.'

The Astronomer watched Her-Bak benevolently. 'I will make no statement,' he said. 'Your experience of illusion is enough to make you careful. What matters to Earth's inhabitants is that they should know of their vital connexions with the sky. As to the movement of the stars, it is better to note what you see than to imagine what may deflect you from the real meaning. Then we will place ourselves at the centre of the sky we are watching, where all star-movement is seen by reference to ourselves.'

'But there are no roads in the sky,' objected Her-Bak. 'And all stars are alike . . . how can one recognise them?'

'The starry sky,' replied the Astronomer, 'seems to us to be in perpetual movement; but it has been observed that it doesn't go in a straight line in a given direction but seems to move like a disc turning about a point. This point isn't exactly in the middle of our sky; it is a star, or region, around which the Indestructibles circulate. Star-groups describe about this point a circuit that brings them back to the same spot at the end of a year. The Indestructibles never leave our sky; the rest move in the same direction, but they disappear, each in turn, at the horizon. Those you see tonight will return in a year at the same time to the same place, except five wandering planets of which we shall speak presently. That is why the word for a year is *ren-pt*, "name-of-the-cycle", or circuit, of the sky.

'However, in spite of these movements it has been observed that the totality of the star-picture is made up of groups. One very ancient teaching gave their names, defined their character and enabled us to place them. It was noticed also that a grand procession of stars sails across the sky like boats on a wide river from east to west . . . we call this the band of the zodiac. The Ancients, seeing that the stars in it reappeared at the same place at the end of a year, divided them into thirty-six sectors and the stars belonging to them were called *bakw*, decanates . . . you know that each reigns in our sky for ten days.'

'Has the word *bakw* any connexion with *bak*, a servitor or producer?'

'Without question, since the *bakw* do the will of their master, Amon-Râ. For it is he, the Sun, who throughout his course is master and life-giver in the twelve regions he visits. That is why we depict him sailing in his boats, one for the day, another for the night, accompanied by different stars according to the hour. But I must draw your attention to the symbolism relating to this celestial stream, which we use with triple intention. First, to evoke an image of the flowing waves that constitute Nut's heaven, body or robe, waves across which the stars shape their course. Then, our Sages wished to indicate by means of the symbol the zone or band in which the decanates and planets, the five great travellers, circulate, though at different speeds. Finally, it suggests the idea of a cycle; and this allows us, by means of comparison, as it were to fix the different regions of the sky.'

.   .   .

'If you watch the celestial movement from east to west you will notice that the Indestructibles, neighbours of the fixed point, take the shortest road in the same time. My simile of the disc is therefore no more than an explanatory device without reality, for if it were really so the southern stars would take a longer road, and move faster, than those of the great stream. Thus, the changes of position appear to us as if we were at the centre of a hollow sphere that turns round us. It is by differences in speed that we distinguish the planets, which traverse the whole sky between the banks of the stream in a time different from that of the decanates, a time that constitutes for each its own cycle. Two of them accompany the sun very close, it may be before, it may be after, in the eyes of the terrestrial observer. They wax and wane like the moon, but with long periods. The first, closest to Râ, is called Sobeg, Mercury, and sometimes Sobek. When too close to the sun it is "burnt" and its nature becomes solar-Sethian, Sobek. Otherwise it is lunar and is called Sobeg. Thoth often symbolises the second function. The sun's second companion, Venus, also fulfils a dual function, according as she is present at Râ's setting or rising.

At his rising she precedes him: she is called *dwaw* and is identified with the phoenix, bird that carries the soul of Osiris.'

'Notice the name *dwaw*,' said the Sage, 'and the time of activity, dawn, which corresponds with a state of region of the Dwat.'

'When light begins to conquer the dark,' murmured Her-Bak.

'You understand why we see *dwaw* as the carrier of souls that are ready to emerge from darkness. The other name of this star, the evening star, is *wâti*. Its Neter is Isis and it brings food to the Sun, a viaticum for his journey through the night.'

'Does *wâti* mean unique?' Her-Bak asked.

'It's a play of words on a most secret meaning.'

'How shall I write all these new things in my memory?'

'By one only procedure. Watch our images come to life.'

The Astronomer went on with his exposition. 'The other three planets are great travellers. We see them crossing the sky at different speeds; but they don't quit the banks of the Great Stream and keep to it sometimes in the reverse direction. Their light is constant, neither growing nor diminishing perceptibly. They appear in the sky day or night.'

'How can one know that when by day they're invisible?'

'It's easy to follow their course by reference to other stars. If we can predict their return we must necessarily know their route. The first of the three, Mars, is called the star of the East, or Red Horus, sometimes Horus of the Horizon. The second, Jupiter, has several names that indicate various attributes, the chief being Star of the South. This isn't the time to discuss the whole science of the planets: I will give you now only the deeper meaning of their names. The name given to the Star of the South, *her-wp-sheta*, means "Horus who opens the secret land". The third, Saturn, is called "Star of the West that crosses the sky" and "Horus Bull of the Sky". You must remember that these names refer to the influence of these stars on Earth. Clearly, the Star of the West doesn't belong to the west any more than to the east; but west is that side of the horizon where the Sun goes down, leaving a reign of darkness . . . there is illusion here to Saturn, who rules over shadowy places, hidden, subterranean life, Amenti, the West and world of the dead, the end of things. The name Bull of Heaven shews Saturn's kinship with the moon, which often bears the same name. We shall see why.

"The name Red Horus for the star of the East indicates its colourful, ardent, active and combatant nature. Similarly, Horus *wp-sheta*, *sba resy*, Star of the South, Jupiter, is connected by this name with the white crown and the character of fulfilment which belongs to that region. If you remember that the opening of the mouth, *wp-ra*, and of the eyes, signifies reanimation, you will deduce that the word *wp-sheta* relates to the mysterious quickening of Earth, which is one of the functions of Amon whose name also means hidden, secret. For Amon reigns over the invisible, while Râ is Neter of the visible world. You will see a relationship in the movements of Jupiter and the Sun. The Sun travels the stream of thirty-six decanates in twelve months, Jupiter in twelve years, crossing three decanates in a year. There is thus a numerical connexion between the Sun and this Amonian star, as there is between Râ and Amon.'

'And the great Amon-Râ?' asked Her-Bak, with hesitation.

The Sage intervened. 'You haven't yet understood the Neters . . . let things come at the right time. What is profitable for you now is to notice that a similar parallel exists between the Moon and the Star of the West. Saturn travels the stream of decanates in roughly as many years as the Moon takes days to accomplish the monthly cycle, about twenty-nine. There is thus the same connexion between Saturn and the Moon as between Jupiter and Râ. And as the Moon rules the period of gestation on Earth, Saturn is in effect Master of Time for us. This shews a connexion between the Neter Thoth and these two stars, for Thoth sometimes has lunar character and his name *djehwty* is very near *djehty*, lead, Saturn's metal.'

'Would Thoth be Saturn's Neter as well?'

'Exactly that, in his function as measurer of lunar periods. Don't forget that Thoth and Seshat count the years on a frond of the palm tree that puts out a new branch each moon. This will make it clear to you why *djehwty*, measurer of lunar periods, is identified with *djehty*, lead, which is Saturn's nature. Saturn, Star of the West, is also Master of lunar periods.'

'Every word you speak,' said Her-Bak, 'shews what knowledge is to be gained by study of the *mdw-Neters*. You are giving me a stiff programme. But how can one Neter symbolise several stars?'

'You will find out,' said the Sage, 'when you study the forms and symbols Thoth takes according to function.'

'Then who is the Moon's Neter? Sometimes they say Thoth, sometimes Khonsu, sometimes Osiris. Yet they say Nekhbet is the Moon too.'

'Come, Her-Bak. Has the Sun but one name?'

'Several. Khepri in the morning, Râ during the day, Tum in the evening.'

The Astronomer corrected this. 'Kepri is sometimes the Sun's name at evening. It may happen that Tum is his name in the morning. Is he not also called Râ-Horakhti and Amon-Râ? What is there that is surprising in having different names for the Moon?'

'If I have understood,' said Her-Bak, 'the names are functions.'

'A judicious remark. Notice also the obvious differences between the two luminaries. The Sun lights the sky by day, the Moon lights it by night. The Moon is only a mirror. As such she changes aspect continually throughout her monthly cycle, from crescent to full Moon and back. The name Nekhbet denotes one of these aspects of her relation with Râ. But her journey through the sky puts her, as it puts us, in relation with other stars. The complex functional characteristics that result are symbolised by several Neters that bear her crescent though none is in fact the Moon's Neter. Still, for reasons I won't go into, Osiris-Iah is in actual fact one of her true aspects. Don't expect more today than the elementary notions that will put you on the right path. This subject is never written about. Our teaching is strictly oral and figurative. It fathoms cosmic law and its natural outworking in the process of evolution. It is the basis of orientation of our temples, the proportions of our monuments, the organisation of the kingdom: you will find the hidden significance of the gods in it. By means of these ideas you will get proofs of its reality; but you will find no detailed account of it in the texts.'

.   .   .

'I'm beginning to understand the need of secrecy,' said Her-Bak. 'Everything in the universe hangs together and what seems the smallest thing may reveal the greatest.'

'Don't talk in a vacuum,' said the Sage. 'What are the greatest things?'

'Master, they are the most sacred.'

'What are the most sacred things?'

Her-Bak didn't hesitate long. 'Everything, I think, that pertains to the secret of life.'

'In the disciple I salute the Master,' the Astronomer said, 'but does the disciple know what life is?'

'A pity,' sighed Her-Bak, 'my Master has told me and I am incapable of repeating what he said. But I see the connexion with what I have just been learning.'

'Your answer satisfies me. As you have a sense of the sacred you may ask me what you want to know first of all.'

'Why don't the heavenly bodies tumble on each other?' Her-Bak asked.

'We have to see the celestial world,' replied the Astronomer, 'as a great body of which we are a minute particle. It has a heart, a liver, lungs, all the organs necessary to man. We see but a minimal part of it.

It is discontinuous as to its component quantities or stars, continuous as to the vital interdependence of its parts. Every individual in it sustains his own life and integrity by his reactive power, which keeps him in place and rhythm in the general movement. If it is extinguished the exchange of complementary humours is suspended and there is cataclysm, in the body or in the universe to which this "organ" belongs.'

'Then Nut's symbol is more than an image?' Her-Bak asked. 'It sets forth a truth that is imperceptible to our sense?'

'Remember that the whole universe is alive and that as the source of everything whatever is one life itself is one, despite appearance.'

'I shall try to feel what I can't see,' said Her-Bak. 'Will you be good enough to speak of the stars that are most important to Earth?'

'Before all other is Sopdit, Sirius-Sothis. As her name tells us, she is the great "Provider". It is she who regulates the flow of the divine Nile ... I repeat, the "divine" Nile. She is the vital centre of our world and its "cold pole". She is weight; that is, the energy that animates our universe. Her appearances measure our greatest ages. But tell me, Her-Bak, what do you know about the Sun?'

'They say that Nut swallows him every night and gives him back to the world every morning: this image seems gross to me. I've heard Nut called the sow that eats her litter ... a figure of speech that revolts me. If one must consider a fact, why not shew it as it is in the sky without recourse to these banal images? It makes me want to shut my eyes and look for the abstract causes that regulate the phenomena.'

'A very salutary result, Her-Bak, and one that justifies our system of teaching. If we only shewed what was visible it would be deceptive, for you never see the sky in its entirety. One would have to set forth its governing laws by means of abstract ideas; but reason would at once seek the support of concrete fact and this, necessarily incomplete, would fail to disclose the life of the universe. Concrete images stimulate search for the abstract, by way of compensation, while abstract ideas urge us to focus them in concrete images. If the image isn't vital and true the enquirer will be misled, whether in mysticism or philosophy. It is to avoid this that we describe principles and functions in words and images that are brutally concrete. The profane will be deceived; but the child of science, for whom this is meant, will look for the meaning, through reaction. If the Nut allegory speaks of giving the Sun back to the world it's because in spite of the seeming absurdity there is in fact a gestation. Try to find out what it is.'

'How is this possible? The Sun, reborn daily, is still the same Sun.'

'Not exactly the same. But to understand this you must meditate
again on the simultaneity of functions. Every seed produces an individual
of its own kind which will reproduce itself with its own seed. But
clearly when the new seed produces a new individual it won't be identical
with its predecessor, or there would be neither adaptation nor degeneration. As to celestial revolutions such as the Sun's daily reappearance, we
can say likewise that although one day resembles another it isn't identical.
Add the stellar conjunctions, which are constantly changing. Thus, a
Sun is new every day through the daily difference in its situation, in its
own and other courses that are run in co-ordination such as the lunar
cycle, the periodical conjunctions of lunar and solar cycles, right up to
the periods of Sothis. And these revolutions are repeated without ever
becoming identical, since each is in correlation with revolutions still
vaster. It is in this way that we measure the phases of time, from the
smallest up to the cosmic year. If we have daily seasons we have monthly
and annual seasons and so on to the measures of Sothis and cosmic time.'

'Was I blind until now? Your words bring new vision. Henceforth I
shall see the Sun as born every day, growing, ageing, going back every
night into Nut's body and fecundating it to be reborn of her next day.'

The Astronomer congratulated Her-Bak. 'This manner of thinking,
that seemed childish to you, will in time yield unexpected fruits. And if
some too cautious reasoner mocks your belief tell him he will never
know the most precious secrets. If we still have this knowledge it is
because we have held to the thought of the Sages our Masters for
thousands of years. They saw in the stars as they appeared the living
functions of an organic universe in which all bodies whether of stars or
beings are but stopping places for souls on their way through multiple
transformations. This is what the legend means when it says that each
star is a soul. This is the meaning of the five-pointed star, symbol of Man.'

Her-Bak wrote each word in his heart. He tried to get yet more light.
'I understand the principle of renaissance, but I didn't think the Sun was
dependent on the Moon.'

'He isn't, not in the least. But he creates a relationship with her that is
important for Earth. All Earthly life depends directly on these two: from
this point of view it is impossible to think of one without the other.'

'Isn't Râ master of the sky?'

'It is written, "Râ is master of the sky because he has two eyes, the
Sun and the Moon".'

'How can Râ have two eyes, himself, Râ, and the Moon?'

The Sage rose, unrolled a papyrus and answered. 'The saying reveals a fundamental truth. The Sun whose globe, *àten*, we see is only the eye of divine Râ, worshipful Master of the sky, of whom it is written here, "He is far away, on high. He watches the Neters and the Neters cannot meet his eyes. He speaks truth when he says, 'I created heaven and earth. I put the souls of the Neters into them.' " He is shewn riding on Nut's back as if he were the power in it, the fire that rules her. "Râ is Master of Heaven, it is He that makes day. He lights our universe and contains its stars. And Nut is nature who bears children and takes them back into herself. The Neters are in nature. Râ is not in nature but nature proceeds from him. And as nature Nut is time, which is but the interval between seed and fruit." '

Her-Bak still heard these words while the Master was rolling up the papyrus. Master and Sage exchanged a few words and Her-Bak spoke, as to himself, linking the ideas that had been given him. 'Nut, as nature, is time . . . this is the Nut who bears children. Saturn, Star of the West, Bull of Heaven like the Moon, is Master of lunar time. Lunar time is not solar time, but there are conjunctions. The circuit of Nut's stream divides into thirty-six parts, three decanates to each of the twelve months, the length of the solar cycle. The year divides into seasons, three seasons of four months. Is number three the number of Time?'

The Astronomer glanced at the Sage, who said, 'This is the real meaning of *ter*, time measured, that is to say the principle of the division of time. It is a ternary principle, though the ternary constitutes a unity . . . we can never comprehend a unity that isn't composed of three elements as a prime surface is defined by three sides. The ternary principle is related to the divisions of the sky which the Sun crosses in his annual course. The twelve months of the year, each of which comprises three decanates, cut the celestial journey into twelve sections or regions which are like houses where Râ's visit lasts one month. But for half a year, during his passage through six of them, the Sun shifts northward; during the other half he turns again south. Thus the dual movement divides his journey into two half circuits: the northern and southern sky are as different in character as *hat* and *peh*, the front and back of a lion. If you divide a fruit in two, cutting its axis through the middle, the tail half is the northern sky, the other that bore the flower is the southern: this differentiates the two halves. Thus it is with the *aterti*, the two *aters*, *ater* of the north, *ater* of the south, of which Egypt's north and south are mirrors. Each *ater* is a half circuit of the Great Stream, *aterw*, of the sky. They are palaces that contain the "houses", temples for north and south with an equal number of chapels, for the Sun's journey.'

'Master, you shew me all heaven,' Her-Bak exclaimed.

'No. These are only some fundamental principles to guide your studies. Don't make the mistake of analysing them, or you'll lose your sense of the vital facts that are their reality. It isn't without reasons that we refuse the influence of foreign schools which define these ideas.'

.   .   .

The Astronomer rose. 'The hours pass. Let us leave theory and look at its uses in our method of measuring time.'

Her-Bak was led to a chamber with thick walls, isolated, where every precaution had been taken to maintain a constant temperature. Water dripped from graduated vessels on stone tables. 'Look at the spiral design on the inside of the vessel,' said the Astronomer, pointing to a clepsydra or water-clock. 'Circular and horizontal markings tell the time by the water-level. Vertical markings shew fractions by a regular division that takes account of shape and volume, so that the time can be read at each minute down to its smallest unit of measurement by the water-level on each circuit of the spiral. But for watching the stars we use more precise instruments. We have emphasised the sky's dual aspect, living and geometrical. The geometrical presents a strict logic that calls for mechanical aids.'

Her-Bak examined the clepsydra. 'The symbol of a vessel that tells time is very fine,' he said, 'because an hour, *wnwt*, is a twelfth part of Nut's body, by night as by day: Nut . . . *nw*, vessel, of the *wnwt*, the hours. I should never have seen this correlation when I was in the Peristyle. And my teachers would have found this word-play ridiculous.'

'Routine and prejudice distort vision. Each man thinks his own horizon is the limit of the world. But you, Her-Bak . . . do you know what an hour is?'

'It's the twelfth part of . . .'

'That's no secret. I'm asking you for the vital meaning of the word.'

Her-Bak was dumb. The Astronomer laughed at him. 'It's a good thing to know one is ignorant. Our whole life depends on the movement of the sky. Do we not distinguish the annual influences of the Sun and monthly influences of the Moon throughout nature? And there are influences of longer duration caused by star-conjunctions and the Sun's position among the constellations. There are shorter periods, the twelve parts of the day and of the night, the hours, of equal duration in ordinary life; but their real duration is unequal, according to the Sun's position in the sky. The experience of several thousands of years has given us knowledge of the indisputable influence of the constellations of the Great Stream and nearer stars. The combined influences of these blind forces affect man's disposition and character, according to the individual. That is why men find themselves in harmony or disharmony with events according to the time of their happening. This is the meaning of our phrase "at his hour". We take account of it in the distribution of posts and functions: every priest and official is classified by the facts of his astrological character. The destiny of the Pharaohs themselves is watched from the beginning in the light of this exact science. We will come back to the subject. Tonight you have been given several clues that have been withheld from many seekers.'

'Why tonight, Master?' asked Her-Bak, troubled.

'Because it is the time to speak. Happy is the man for whom it is the time to hear.'

IX

FREE WILL AND FATE

Her-Bak watched the sky. For months he lived more by night than by day. One who 'knows what pertains to the stars' will think it a duty to bring out the gifts of so exceptional a student, one who shews such keenness in the search for truth, accepting no compromise. The Astronomer therefore was able to carry out a stiff programme, to train Her-Bak in exact observation, in the precise calculation of the stars' courses, in the interpretation of phenomena and all the while, in spite of such rational exercises, to practise him in the intuitive perception of invisible causes. He habituated Her-Bak to 'live' the celestial movements while remaining in touch with nature; to rid himself of obsession with allegories as with appearance.

A day came when the disciple noted for himself the effect of certain stellar situations on human disposition and activity. This gave the Master profound satisfaction and in agreement with the Sage he revealed to Her-Bak little by little the meaning of certain configurations: thus, the legend of the seven Hathors who attend births, bringing the new-born good or bad fortune, became for the attentive pupil a parable shewing how forces that flow from the conjunctions of Earth and Heaven affect men for better or worse. He saw it as a law of Necessity, exhibited in the connexion of the star-pattern in the band of the Zodiac with the hour of a man's birth. Patient and profound examination of a large number of cases, in nature and those registered in the temple, changed hypothesis into conviction. Time passed. Her-Bak taught himself, and grew melancholy.

.   .   .

The Sage, watching him, knew the reason for this. He allowed it to reach a maximum and precipitated a crisis.

An eclipse of the moon drew a number of observers to the terrace. The Sage and Her-Bak, sitting apart with the Astronomer, listened while he described the progress of this phenomenon, dwelling on its disagreeable influence over man and vegetable. A profound sadness, growing with the moon's reddening gleam, completed the disciple's despair. 'Fate! What a frightful burden!' he exclaimed. 'What negation of personal

effort! If our whole destiny is settled by the stars we can change nothing
. . . why fight against oneself? It is useless to try and push on at the cost
of such sacrifices with a process that can only work out in its own time.'

Serenely the Sage watched the moon. 'You are right, my son. Nature's
fate and the animal's is fixed by the stars . . . what advantage is there for
them in knowing how it works? A disappointing enquiry. A useless
luxury. You have seen through it. Then abandon such wearisome labour.
Set up house, feed and clothe a wife. Make your life a long day of happiness . . . if the stars permit.'

Despair gripped Her-Bak's heart. A sob choked him. Tears he tried in
vain to keep back blinded him. The eclipse was now total and a sound
of chanting to the beat of tabors and sistrums came sorrowfully through
the night. He rose and shook his fists at the moon and the invisible singers.
'What use are these shows? Can they hasten by one moment the return
of light? All is written in the stars. All is in vain.'

The Sage signed the Astronomer not to intervene. 'If you're sure of
this, Her-Bak, follow your harpist's advice. Seek less costly pleasures, for
it is useless to go against the heart.'

'Heart or reason, no matter! They are ruled by the stars. My instincts,
my nature, my body . . . all is determined by number, by the stars, forces
whose plaything I am. Why give us the illusion that our heart is master?
My heart is a puppet, a slave, like all else, of fate.'

.   .   .

The Sage waited for the storm of primordial grief to abate. Then he
lifted his grave voice and Her-Bak seated himself, trembling. 'My son,
there is error in what you have just said. Your heart, seat of enlightenment,
sia . . . is it not here that your divine KA dwells? But your KA isn't fate's
slave, for it is no part of nature. All else on Earth or in Heaven, even the
solar disc that lights us, is part of nature, but the spirit-soul, like divine
Râ, is not. If the spark becomes conscious in your humanity it grows
into a vital germ and through this, if you let it govern the animal-human
in you, you will be master of your fate. The soul is not subject to the stars.'

'But all my being suffers their influences!'

'As you have just suffered the depressing experience of an eclipse, for
the instinctive self is subject to them. But as soon as animal man begins
to obey his higher self he only feels them as inclinations, no longer
compulsions. The soul is free and can alter its course. But I repeat, the
condition of independence is submission to the immortal consciousness.'

Her-Bak refused to accept hope without certainty. 'If my soul didn't

suffer the influence of the eclipse, yet my lower self rejected the higher . . .
the result is the same.'

'No. You obeyed it when it urged you to examine your doubts. That
is where free choice lies. Your body will always feel the influence of
the stars: you will free yourself when you learn to be neutral and follow
the instructions of your heart without letting things perturb you.
This is the way of Maât. The wonders that are spoken of it, the promises
that are made, would be empty words had they no relation to this fact,
that it liberates the man who is conscious of such liberty from Fate.'

Her-Bak submitted a point. 'Doesn't liberty come about by itself little
by little without intervention of man's will, as change comes about in
species?'

'It's a remarkable achievement,' responded the Sage, 'to formulate
two resounding errors in one sentence. Freedom is the fruit of personal
effort to go beyond nature. As to the development of species, there is
no such thing as physical evolution: there is no progress except in the
acquisition of consciousness. The existence of species merely seems like
a pattern of advance, periodic and regular, with its renewings that have
similar but not identical characteristics. Every month, every decade, sees
the birth of insects that hatch at the appointed hour: the same law tells
a bird to prepare a nest when the time to lay eggs approaches. As well
as this sequence, verifiable because short-term, we must also recognise
the existence of long-term phenomena that are less easily checked: I am
speaking of geneses that produce hitherto unknown creatures. One sees
in certain epochs the appearance of animals, plants and minerals for
which no seed is known to have existed, abnormal births following vast
movements as if Earth had changed its place in the sky. This is in effect
the case. The cause of such apparently sporadic phenomena lies in the
universal harmony; changes in the heavens that give fresh character to
an epoch are also the creative cause of such variations. When a new age
begins types that were a product of the precedent era subsist until
degeneration of seminal power by exhaustion of the primitive urge, then
vanish. Don't let yourself be taken in by so-called accidents that together
make a logically seductive picture. Judge by cause, not effect. The cause
will be found in the principles of generation.'

'Am I to think,' Her-Bak asked, 'that we needn't see the products of
nature as an uninterrupted sequence of things that spring from one
another by natural transformation?'

'Such a theory would assume a physical perfection of species through
gradual evolution. This would be wrong.'

H

'You told me,' said Her-Bak, 'that there is in nature a variety of organs that make a whole in man. Is there also, in the animal kingdom, an evolution that achieves such a whole in the mammifer? Now you seem to deny it.'

'You confuse evolution with adaptation and sequence,' the Sage replied. 'I have said as well that every organ incarnates a principial function which becomes self-conscious in matter. In the act of creation all possibilities, functions, organs and species are contained as Ideas. Their incorporation happens in accordance with stellar times or cycles and looks like a series of accidents. Thus, man is not a synthesis of embodied species or functions but of cosmic states; a synthesis that can only take flesh when nature has embodied all organs or expressions of function ideally completed. He is a complete expression of his universe, an effect of a synthesis in the heavens.

'But in man's primordial state there is no opposition, no duality, consequently no death. He is a complete image of the All and this must lie in the purpose of the creative Cause. But there is also in man's paradisal unity a *possibility* of scission, as in the creation of Heaven and Earth: there is then a fall. But scission isn't a necessity. In the complete man there would be simultaneity of states and, again without division, he would have identity with the Cause, whereas as Man fallen we are conscious of such states as separate and in phases. Creation then is the principle of the fall, while perfection as willed by the Cause, and without all that is consequent on the fall, is no longer creation in the same sense but a manifestation or incarnation of unity.

'Species are a shaping of numbers and functions contained as ideas in the principial creation, possibilities that is, made real in a kind of succession outside time, which seems absurd to the cerebral intelligence. The principial creation should be regarded then as a virtual creation that will appear effective to us in corporeality. We can say now that once they have appeared on Earth species only evolve in consciousness, but they can adapt themselves to the conditions of existence and the necessities of the time. As to the mystery of their appearance on Earth, listen carefully to my answer and try to give the words their true meaning: each Neter, when the time comes, calls into life the particular, and the assemblages of particulars, that belong to him.

'This produces the appearance of a continuous process of evolution. If there were such a thing we should also be able to watch the change of mammifer into man and the growth of human intelligence out of ignorance into the highest range of consciousness so far experienced. And the further we look back the more clearly we see evidence of a

state of high "knowing" that as we go back was more and more a state
of receptive intellect or intuition. The nearer we return to the humanity
of our day the more it degenerates, with the progressive complexity of
rationalism, into analytic materialism and loses the art of vital synthesis
that belonged to the ancient Masters. This sacred science has always
known of certain cosmic factors that human thought only rejects because
they are outside the range of its cerebral faculties. Indisputable evidence
of such Knowledge proves that there existed in very remote times a
higher humanity now degenerate in races that are exhausted, unable to
advance otherwise than in the mode of animal evolution. There is no
possibility of growing from brute animal into reasonable man: there must
therefore be a special inspiration or quickening that separates the human
from the animal kingdom absolutely.'

.   .   .

'Was it this quickening,' asked Her-Bak, 'that gave man intuitive or
infused knowledge, or did he acquire it consequently? Is there an evolution
of consciousness in humanity or degeneration?'
'Again you confuse two problems, that of consciousness in itself and
that of evolution of races. We shall study consciousness later. Today I
will only say you must distinguish innate consciousness from consciousness
that is acquired. The first is implanted in the new-born through circumstances to do with heredity and personal incarnation. This, the intelligence
of the heart, is intuition latent and it can be awakened by training.
Acquired consciousness arises out of innate consciousness ceaselessly felt
and confirmed in sensory experience. As to the races of men, successive
epochs of terrestrial humanity, though they may co-exist, have each
embodied and developed one of the psychic faculties the sum of which
makes higher man. Realisation of the faculty particular to a given race
brings it to its peak, then, when a fresh human season starts the flowering
of the faculty next in succession, to its decadence. Take the black race.
It began with the consciousness of instinctive nature. It worshipped natural
forces and developed psychic vision. Its failure, which is due to the ignorance of the mass, consists in believing that consciousness of this order
is its perfection. But its Sages are not deceived. Today you notice among
ourselves the early symptoms of an analogous miscomprehension in the
use of the rational faculty. Mental power, now due to be developed, will
lead man to an insolent confidence in the superiority of rational thinking
and such an abuse will bring disaster to those who haven't understood the
scale of consciousness. Man's highest achievement is the acquisition of

intuitive-spiritual gifts, which should take cerebral gifts into their service. The Sages of a given race are those men who consciously make use of faculties already acquired and develop the specific gifts of their own race, aware that their importance in the scale of consciousness is relative, without ceasing to cultivate subtler modes of knowing. Each race carries its innate consciousness in itself and the impulse needful for the flowering of its particular endowment. The consciousness it acquires is its own too; but the experience of its *élite* enriches the consciousness of humanity and makes for its overall progress. Such a race, when this experience is exhausted, may degenerate; but progress made is established in cosmic man. In this way consciousness evolves race by race though each degenerates.'

'Haven't there been at all times men who developed all faculties?' asked Her-Bak.

'Those who brought what was needful into incarnation. These are but individual cases.'

'And there is no continuous physical evolution of humanity?'

'Evolution of consciousness brings growth in general sensibility. The effort to achieve it is of a vital kind that provokes reaction in the centres and nervous system, in the sexual disposition as well. This brings free will into play, without which there is no freedom. Such growth in consciousness doesn't depend on the will of the intellect or its possibilities but on the intensity of the inner urge; but such intensity, which distinguishes an *élite*, is born of disquiet, a conflict caused by shock when intuitive consciousness experiences a reality that challenges what isn't real in ourselves. Such a shock, so fruitful, is the result of events that leave their mark in the soul. That is why we seek the challenge of brute reality rather than a sensual or cerebral refinement that sterilises.'

'I understand this by my own revulsions,' said Her-Bak.

'Don't revolt if you wish to profit,' advised the Sage. 'Accept emotional shock, hurtful experiences. Don't resist them. They are your most useful means of advancement. You would know how humanity progresses, Her-Bak? There is no mass advance from race to race, any more than from species to species; but there is selection of individuals who will be the seed of the race to follow. Nature pursues her course by phases, with a tendency to degeneration through inertia. Humanity, left to itself gains consciousness too slowly, for natural man avoids educative suffering. Yet from time to time there is a prodigious leap. Suddenly, in an exhausted world, an exceptional being arises, at a time and in a place favourable to his development. Such a one is the manifestation of a higher consciousness that incarnates voluntarily, a Presence that awakens others who are so predisposed. In this way, at times that can be foreseen, new *élites* are formed that increase the gain in human consciousness.'

Her-Bak listened with growing interest: the conclusion seemed clear to him. 'Such no doubt was the origin of our wisdom.'

'Yes. And now you will understand what so perplexes teachers in the Peristyle. They don't see that the beginnings of our history witness to the co-existence of primitive life and high knowledge.'

'Master, what peace would come with the solution of this riddle.'

'Try to see where this leads. The man who is outstanding in his time is always one who has faculties that others of his time haven't yet developed. He is the precursor of an age that is on its way to realisation and shews the path. The masses won't follow, but those who are sensitive to the new state of consciousness form a group and become the germ of a new race. Thus races succeed one another in a manner that can be foreseen. For if the exceptional man is a sporadic creation, precursor of what is to come, a group can only form if cosmic conditions encourage it. Such conditions will even constrain a group to look for a suitable country, whence migration.'

'Here again,' said Her-Bak, 'there is determinative action.'

'Necessarily. It is this that enables us to foresee such happenings. This is only possible to vision that sees a whole, advancing because it is living but obedient to determinative law.'

. . .

The disciple thought over the correspondence of law with fact in the past. 'This could be the history of Egypt's foundation,' he said.

'Yes. The beginning is in a very remote age. We stand now at the opening of its last phase.'

'This is terrifying. How can you speak of its last phase?'

'I mean the last phase of our initiatory mission. There is but one truth: its mode of expression follows the rhythm of each epoch. We must accept this rhythm until the coming of the future Envoy.'

'How can such things be known so far ahead, Master?'

'Foresight is easy if you have in front of your eyes the picture the Ancients drew, in which the facts of the past guarantee the facts of the future.'

'One can't feel glad about such a future.'

'There's nothing to be glad or to grieve over. Every man must act in the rhythm of his time . . . such is wisdom. We have obeyed. Our part was to reveal the science of the heart and of synthesis to the world. But periods of transition between successive ages are marked by trouble and indecision and only the knowledge of the Sages can mitigate disorder. That is why it matters that you should be instructed, Her-Bak. But you still seem to falter.'

'No longer! I have seen the principle and purpose of free will. I must never repeat the mistake I made. If only I could be shewn the programme. What is the practical purpose of instruction?'

'To detail within what is possible what the Ancients gave in concentrated form. To reveal in symbol and historical tale the positive bases of our knowledge, in a manner suited to the new mentality. Until the end of our time every moment must write its symbol, in the form and proportion of monuments, in the names of Pharaohs and men, in the smallest detail that may tell future generations the message and proof of our science. This is the part of every Sage until the final collapse, to watch over the fulfilment of necessary changes in accordance with Number and canons foreseen from the beginning.'

Her-Bak regarded his Master with wondering eyes. 'It is astonishing, the serenity that can foresee our fall as well as our greatness.'

'What matters our fall or our greatness if all is conformable with harmony? The Sage mustn't be attached to a land or a people, if he would guide impersonally. He studies in every race its inherent gifts, notes without judging what gains in consciousness have affected its vital reflexes and morals. He knows that in each an *élite* is formed that survives degeneration of the people, each valuable in itself. In every people he sees a fruit that is a product of the environment: heaven makes earth and country and this makes the man who lives there. He studies this sequence, inevitable for all that derives from nature. His work tends to create a harmonious environment and removes useless suffering for the masses. But he aids and protects the formation of an *élite*.'

Her-Bak kissed his Master's hands. 'This assumes a power that can master human passions.'

'It is the fruit of impersonal vision. Every disciple of wisdom must gain such mastery. You, child of Egypt, must be instructed in this so that you will make no mistake and grasp the mission of this marvellous land.

'For several thousand years the Egyptians were chosen to be witness of that indefectible wisdom which aids humanity. Other peoples have won great learning, but Egypt has kept in its integrity the fundamental principle and programme that was entrusted to her at the beginning. She has been faithful to the symbol of that sole stream that flows from the Black Earth and fertilises the Two-Lands. She has acted to the last detail her part as a concrete mirror that reflects abstract Harmony. She has transcribed the laws of Becoming for a section of humanity, during the time assigned her for the instruction of mankind, making her revelation as was appropriate. She has made a reality of the symbolic crucible to which neighbours bring their contribution to help form the future Horus-Sun. She has achieved her aim. But she has come now to the dangerous point where pupil thinks himself equal with master and puts letter before spirit, image before reality. For when a traditional knowledge takes the form of a religion, with its train of doctrines, rites, all-powerful priesthood, the purity of tradition changes to the advantage of compulsory beliefs and religious laws that serve the purposes of clerical authority. What were symbols become tales for the people, for whom divine Qualities become idols. Priests take the place of God and arrogate to themselves the right to govern men's consciences. The mystical power of a revelation becomes exhausted when through analysis and complexity religion deviates from the pure first state. It is in this way that we can explain the degeneracy of a priesthood, when it assumes a power that has lapsed, with the cult of sanctuaries Spirit no longer inhabits. I speak of cults, not of our Knowledge. Wisdom stands, imperishable, even when forms of religion have ceased to correspond with the inspiration of an epoch. An initiate is always responsible for what he has been given or acquired, and for what is yet to be revealed. The consciousness of a succession of initiates remains our endowment. Their wisdom is written for ever on our stones and walls and a time will come when men, disillusioned by sterile science, will return to the fundamental law.

'Egypt is immortal because she is the natural guardian of immortal wisdom. Her black earth emerges fertile from the waters that drown it. There is for no living people an hour of glory or disaster. Each country has its people, its soul, its character; each has a destiny that belongs to its genius, its KA. Each, at decisive hours, feels the power of its spiritual inheritance, the sum of the genius more or less wise of its fathers. And in spite of the vicissitudes of its life and the incoherence of its directives a people exhibits the characteristic signs of its primordial destiny, in such a way that what Sages prophesied is found valid at analogous conjunctures: do not such prophecies derive from knowledge of the concordance of one age with another? That is how we see that in a distant future Egypt will again be a centre and refuge of wisdom in a disabled world.'

Her-Bak followed this account of the superhuman law that governs history with deep respect. He understood the secret evidence of it and meditated in silence. At last he forced himself to envisage his country's destiny. 'Master, will you tell me what will become of the marvellous organisation our Sages established?'

'It will stand, with the acquired rhythm, and go on with its work until the new Revelation. We must guard our treasures, so as to preserve their message until the day when light is reborn.'

'When will that day come, Master?'

'When humanity, given over as of old to an accursed science, finds itself once more on the brink of catastrophe. But I am saying more than you understand, Her-Bak. Hasten. Train yourself to read as I have read, by yourself.'

Her-Bak replied in a firm voice, 'Master, I will serve as you have served.'

X

HIERARCHY OF THE NETERS

Night thinned into bright morning. Vapour rose from the ground, blotting out all shapes. The Sage and his disciple, seated on the flank of the Peak, were wrapped in mist. 'It is good sometimes,' said the Sage, 'to lose sight of Earth and be released from obsession with form.'

Her-Bak answered like an echo. 'The man who was free of it could know the Neters.'

'Wasn't it here that Chick-Pea came to look for them?'

'Chick-Pea didn't meet them.'

'If Her-Bak knew in himself the connexion of cause and effect he might find them today. The cloud is shifting . . . what do you see now?'

'A thick mist that hides the valley. The river is invisible and I no longer distinguish temples or houses.'

'Why speak of houses, river, valley? If you see nothing there is nothing . . . or perhaps everything. The mist that hides the world of powers from you is infinitely thicker than this veil thrown over what you are in the habit of seeing. If you assume the one why not the other? Still, it's one thing to know the activating powers of the world in oneself, another to study the theory that explains their functions. Schematic descriptions have no life, but men live by the powers in question: they formed, moulded, characterised and signed you. Yet whereas when you are looking into yourself you forget the multiplicity of forces that went to the making of you, it happens the other way round and when you are watching their manifestation in nature you forget the sole source of which they are names and qualities. That is why analysis has its risks. The brain is quick to appropriate things and set ideas hinder knowledge of their generative activity.'

'Is there danger of forgetting the one Neter in the many?'

'That is the chief danger. But men need images. Lacking them they invent idols. Better then to found the images on realities that lead the true seeker to the source.'

'If the Neters are qualities and functions of the unknowable One, can a man reach the source without having studied them separately?'

'The contemplative could do it by simple fusion. A man close to nature discovers certain powers, but the further thought departs from it the further it strays, and the man who ceases to worship what he sees of the eternal in it worships himself. His thinking becomes the Neter that destroys him. This danger is more terrible than any other. That's why I shall teach you now as our teachers were taught. I shall try to shew you the harmony of the Neters in a way that may itself be the key that opens a door to other meanings.'

.   .   .

'It is said that the eight Neters of the beginning, having formed the world-egg, came to sleep at the foot of this Peak, under its flank, awaiting each decade the visit of the Great Snake. Let us try to evoke them.

'All is in all, for all comes from the One that sees itself and divides. Before dividing, One is the primordial chaos that holds all possibilities in itself and these have a dual aspect, passive, active. They are there in potential, undifferentiated. This state of "fusion" is the sum of the world's activities, negatived by their own passivity, for in this state nothing has precedence over anything. I can't name them without thinking and to think is already to differentiate.

'The first name that can be named in this state of fusion is Nun, the force N which, itself negativing itself, nn, polarises itself and exhibits what was in the "water of chaos", the principle Spirit-Light, heh, and the principle Dark, kek. Then there is Nu, the celestial water that generates and nourishes the world, Amonian, invisible. Thus we have Nun and Nunet, Heh and Hehet, Kek and Keket, Niau and Niut, four dualities in one, that "are" in potential before manifestation. The duality of these Primordials exhibits the opposition that Chaos displays when it divides, an original androgyny, fused, that is incomprehensible.

'But once the Word is in action the Light-principle arises and ipso facto brings about separation and manifests the Neter-Creator that has power to separate and unite, manifest and annihilate, Atum, who makes the first evening and the first morning. Thus Light and Dark were contained in the Principle. But when there are two there is in potential a third, movement; and by cyclic movement, of itself in itself, Atum-Râ, self-begotten, puts forth the first two Qualities, Shu, principle of the dry, Tefnut, principle of the wet. And these two become Earth-and-Heaven, Geb-Nut. But the Word-Creator puts Geb in opposition to Nut; and Shu in his secret name of reh separates Heaven-Nut from Earth-Geb. Then appears the unifying Light of the Word, her. Reh, dualiser, evokes the complementary powers and Nut gives birth to Osiris, Isis, Seth and Nephtys. Then comes the Light of the ternary Word, Horus-Our takes possession of his two eyes, sun and moon. The world becomes, through incessant strife of complementary forces.'

'Why has Ptah not been mentioned?' ventured Her-Bak.

'Now I may pronounce his name, for he has manifested. I spoke of a principial creation before there was heaven or earth. Ptah is first craftsman in the material creation and gives it continuity.'

.   .   .

'Now this is the trunk of the Neters' genealogical tree. Ptah, active and causal Principle, splits the trunk in two by his fall into corporeality: hence the image of the trinity. Many branches spring from the two halves, but each keeps the character of the half it derives from, one abstract, the other, Ptah's, concrete. The first produces the Neters of cause and activity, the second the Neters of form. It may happen that the branches entwine, as in marriage. But since everything comes of One everything has One's original nature, which is incomprehensible unless it is manifest in diversity. What is real in the synthesis of functions will look, under analysis, like incoherence, an inversion of relationship. You may be sure nevertheless that the absurdity isn't in the reality but in the impotence of reason before this mystery of creation. The world is and the world was before you and your reason existed.

'These preliminary ideas regarding the hierarchy of the Neters are but a summary which will admit of considerable elaboration. I will give you an explicit example of the way we conceive of the Neters. I said that Atum-Râ, self-begotten in the *nw*, puts forth two primordial Qualities, Shu principle of the dry, Tefnut principle of the wet. But it would be wrong to see these two Neters as absolute qualities: nothing is absolute in what proceeds from the absolute Cause. Essential Fire, cause of everything created, doesn't appear before the first dualisation. Shu and Tefnut are the first results of its polarisation: the active phase of fire gives dry, the passive gives wet. But if one were to say that Shu is principle of the dry, Tefnut principle of the wet, one must add at once that the one manifests the other. Wet witnesses to dry and dry can only appear if it issues from wet: wet therefore, in the beginning, is the earlier manifestation although both principles derive from a single cause, original Fire. It is the fire of Atum that produces the fundamental Qualities, agent of their union, separation and annihilation, so that Atum signifies apparently incompatible functions, a totality of possibilities contained in a unity . . . annihilation, separation, linking. The four Qualities that are agents of becoming, Dry, Wet, Hot, Cold, are but modalities of Atum's

fire, opposite in manifestation. As all states of becoming change un-
ceasingly we can only depict a Quality in a relative condition: it is always
modified by another. Dry is the predominant quality of Shu, but Shu is
also the warmth of Wet that makes air. Wet is the predominant quality
of Tefnut and Tefnut is the cold of Wet that makes water; but it is also
the quality of contraction, cold Fire, through which Earth comes of
water. There is then a crossing of qualities between these two Neters and
because of it male Dry has a feminine aspect and female Wet a male one.
That is why you often see Shu-Tefnut symbolised by two lions, male and
female aspects of the fire-principle, which preside over the intermediate
state at the beginning of day and night as at the beginning of creation.'

'Are they connected with the dual lion *aker*?'

'The same principles are at work, from another point of view. One of
the *aker* lions looks towards the light the other towards darkness, opposites,
like the qualities of Shu and Tefnut. Opposition necessitates a reciprocal
annihilation in which a crossing of properties takes place, such that seeming destruction gives rise to a fresh unity that contains the two first
principles, a unity that will itself split into two more.'

'Why must it?'

'Because in the process of becoming none of the prime elements can
remain unchanged. Each necessarily evokes its opposite and thus brings
about mutual destruction of the two aspects that came of division. But
in this process each is seen as "founder of a line" in some determined
activity. The essential modalities of original Fire expressed in the two
first pairs, Shu and Tefnut, Geb and Nut, make of them four "founders
of a line" and each will characterise every Neter, thing and creature in
which the primordial Neter predominates. Thus Shu is in direct kinship
with Maât and certain properties of Tefnut are found in Sekhmet. Osiris
is called Heir of Geb in respect of his earth-nature, but he is Nut's son in
respect that he is the celestial Water of Renewal. Likewise Horus may be
called Son of Osiris and Heir to the Throne of Geb in his connexion with
earthly life, while he is Son of Isis in respect that he is born of marsh-water
and Son of Hathor in that he is born of the sky.'

Her-Bak had difficulty in following the metaphysical implications of
a myth of which until now he had only known the symbolism. 'Master,'
he said, 'you have explained how the primordial principles beget and
qualify what proceeds from them. But I don't see how a unity can be
split.'

'Don't be surprised at that. No one will ever understand this. It is
enough to know that Atum's separative power continues at work in all

his progeny. Just as Shu–Tefnut are born of one beginning and division in the One, so they become the principle of beginning and division in all that follows. Shu with his two arms separates Nut from Geb while Tefnut is that which is to be separated, the water of heaven and the fire of earth. Such division confronts our intelligence with a mystery that defies analysis. The crossing of qualities sets up a confusion of functions that defies our logic and can only be expressed in symbols. It is wiser to look for a synthesis in a symbology that reveals their vital effects.'

'I see the necessity for this,' said Her-Bak, 'for reason is impotent in face of the mystery. But the history of the Neters is meant to instruct us, so there must be a guiding thread if one is to get the connexions or there will be confusion for the genuine seeker, as there has been perhaps among the priests of various temples?'

'If you haven't the guiding thread it excuses such suppositions,' said the Sage. 'If you hold it you will see their puerility. Begin by accepting an affirmation of which our teaching will bring proofs. There has been no strife between successive theologies, no competition between temples and towns for the pre-eminence of their Neter, no opportunist adaptation to political ends. Human passions are always trying to interfere certainly, but the unceasing watchfulness of our Sages only allows them to affect our symbology in a measure and manner concordant with the rhythm of the time. The ground-plan, accordant with cosmic reality, was laid down in advance and no one may innovate.'

'I understand the main lines of it,' said Her-Bak, 'but I supposed that the people had multiplied the Neters of the earliest ages.'

'Theologically the people can invent nothing. In face of the heaven and nature, observing certain phenomena, they may attribute a super-natural cause to them: they will never derive a theology from it. As to the priesthood, they change nothing except when they emphasise some utilitarian aspect to increase their power. An initiatory religion never evolves by adding fresh elements to the theological bases, but by analysing them. The theological form is always given by an initiate teacher with all the essential bases. When a revelation lasts several thousand years names must change in conformity with what they stand for. To give a theology religious force an inspired initiate often accords it a historical character and this isn't contrary to truth: it is impossible for a man who isn't inspired to make a revelation that is both suitable to the time and truthful.'

'Master, will you tell me about the guiding thread?' Her-Bak entreated.

'So be it,' said the Sage. 'I will speak of it, for your happiness or unhappiness. If your heart is simple, without pride, it will lead you to secret doors. If not, you will be blinder than before.'

'Master, I've had experience of this. I listen.'

.   .   .

The sun rose. His rays dispersed the mist, his light gave the forms of things harsh outlines. 'There is,' said the Sage, 'an abstract history of the primordial creation. It pertains to the creative Power and the phases of its expression, its successive "Words", in the principial sphere. And there is a concrete history of their actualisation in a series of procreations or begettings.

'The first relates to the divine. In the original unity are *Her* and *Reh*. Each mirrors the other, as in the beginning darkness confronts the darkness from which light will spring. *Reh* looks into *Her*'s face and this is the first opposition whose clash causes the world. *Her* is the light of the Word. *Reh*, whose manifestation is Seth, is the separator, destroyer, sterile, cause of the dualisation through which the world is made. That is why Horus and Seth are called the *Two Reh*. Neither can exist without the other, for each causes the other. Their duality is repeated throughout nature: it is the principle of sex that causes birth and death.

'The first trinity, divine, original, is indivisible and incomprehensible in its one-ness. When we name the creative principle Atum, Amon or Râ we speak of a trinity. Starting with it, we come to Ptah and the celestial triads each of which is the origin of a line of becoming in continuous creation. We have Horus-Hathor-Ihi, Ptah-Sekhmet-Nefertum, Amon-Mut-Khonsu, Osiris-Isis and their son Horus. These are the principal triads and all that concerns actualisation in these lines of becoming makes part of the concrete history.

'In the first, the abstract history, you will meet again the Neters of the quaternary, the four pillars or constitutive elements of the world. They are shewn under four principial aspects, each quadruple, since a pure element is imperceptible. Their qualitative principle is given in the two first pairs, Shu and Tefnut, Geb and Nut. Their nature as innate factors is shewn by the four *bas* in the column *djed*; that of Râ or fire, Osiris or water, Shu or air, Geb or earth. Their female, substantial, immaterial aspect is symbolised by the four women Neith, Serket, Isis and Nephtys. Their organic, animal aspect is shewn by the four sons of Horus, Amset, Hapi, Du mutef and Qebhsenuf.

'I will say nothing about the abstract Number Five, which will one day be the Neter of light for you. Number Seven gives the name of

Sefekht whose signature is on everything in creation. You know already the eight primordials, associated with Thoth and the Neters of the Ennead. Number Ten is the triangle of the world of principles.'

The omission of Number Six deeply puzzled Her-Bak. He remarked on it at once . . . 'This is doubtless an oversight on my Master's part.'

The Sage smiled. 'Six is a secret Number,' he said. 'It has the character of equilibrium and at the same time of separation. It opens and shuts. But its meaning will only be clear to you later on, if you make a profound study of Number and letters.'

Her-Bak apologised for his interruption and begged the Sage to continue.

.   .   .

'The concrete history,' said the Sage, 'shews you the functions of nature in process of actualisation. The two master-functions result from opposition, which creates good and evil and teaches us natural science: they are contraction and dilatation. To understand their symbolism remember that a function in activity produces an equal and opposite reaction. Our myths and the keys to them will remain inaccessible to you if you neglect this. Thus, the scorpion *serq* is in itself the principle of contraction, concretion: by this very fact it provokes dilatation. The scorpion symbolises this dual activity in its life and in the drawing that depicts it.'

'It is strange,' Her-Bak observed, 'that it sometimes has no tail.'

'What you call its tail is an elongation of the abdomen. If this is left out of the drawing it is because the idea of poison is suppressed and emphasis laid on dilatation. The crocodile Sobek expresses a contractive quality. The idea is also shewn in the root *saq*, where the saurian curls its tail. But the perfect symbol of contraction or concretion is Sokar.

'Dilatation belongs to Anubis. Upuat stands for a particular aspect of this function. The complete achievement of dilatation is called *wadj*. Anubis as jackal is the digestion that swallows even the bones and changes putridity into life-giving substance. The digestion of seed that kills and decomposes it in order to form a new creature belongs to Mut, a female principle that cannot give life otherwise, that is to say, without giving corporal volume to the life-impulse the seed carries. The first consequence is putrefaction. If the fecundated female principle isn't itself living putrefaction becomes corruption and Mut becomes death. Sekhmet, a form of Mut in her Hathor-function, is an aspect of that which kills to give life. Apet-Ta-wart with the great belly and breasts of a nursing mother symbolises abundance, maternal fecundity and concretion. She is the body and belly that contains what is in gestation. She is also the principle of maternal and nourishing earth. Khnum is the Neter of conjunction, Heket of rebirth through renewal of leaven, and of multiplication.'

.   .   .

'If I wished to detail the aspects of the female principle I should first have to differentiate its part in the principles that govern life from its functions in terrestrial existence. But I can't do this as it is only the one that makes the other comprehensible.

'Its four chief aspects are depicted by the four goddesses Isis, Nephtys, Neith and Serket. Isis is the female principle in nature, the site and environment of all activity. She is the magnet that draws forth the male seed, the active-passivity of the feminine, mother of existence. Her fluid principle spiritualises; her tears reawaken not the earth-body of Osiris but its sublimation from which the "new Water" will flow in due season. She is the mother-substance that gestates and nourishes Horus in the marshland, Horus who will reveal the spiritual face of his father Osiris. Nephtys is the negative passivity of the feminine. Of subtle nature she corrupts to give life; she is immanent in Isis in her function as weeper who brings on putrefaction and brings the digester Anubis into action. Neith is the life-giving, spiritual feminine, the dual and luminous energy, formless, that creates form by crossing of complements. Virgin, she is the birth that precedes birth. At the extreme of dilatation she brings on contraction, which is why we place her symbol in a cobra's swelling breast. With her crossed arrows she makes substance concrete. Her shuttle weaves the prime matter of the world. And Serket is feminine sexuality, the shadowy, contractive force that provokes dilatation and breathing.'

Her-Bak made a point. 'When several functions are ascribed to the same goddess how does one distinguish them in her image?'

'Are her clothes always the same? Don't the four goddesses wear a variety of clothing, sometimes feathers, sometimes scales, sometimes womens' robes? And the fashion of their hair? If you are aware of the principles you must be blind not to see the main lines of their symbolic meaning. It will be your task to study each Neter in its cosmic role and particular functions; to assign them a place in one or other of the two histories. But you will labour in vain if you don't see their connexion in living unity. If you ignore this aspect they will seem to you as to so many others a multiplicity of particular theogonies, discontinuous, unmotivated because lacking in harmony with cosmos.'

'So it did seem to me,' Her-Bak admitted. 'I had lost all hope of understanding them.'

'If you ignore the living unity,' repeated the Sage, 'nothing I have said will explain why the gods change their names, why certain cults are modified or temporarily suppressed, why that of Amon appears late in our history, why eastern Andjeti becomes western Osiris and why certain characteristics of Mut and Hathor, Maât and Neith, are confounded.'

.   .   .

'This teaching, key to the other two, is the theogony of the heavenly cycles. It corresponds with characteristics that arise from the ceaseless revolutions of the sky-pattern and the movements of sun, moon and the decanates, giving four cycles that closely touch our life . . . the day, the month, the year and the conjunctions of sun and moon. There are other, vaster cycles, among which note the one that pertains to the shift of the polar star, the "great cycle". The Neters manifest in the four cycles: it is this that gives rise to various theogonies and the complex structure of theology.

'The daily cycle accounts for several symbols or symbolic events and explains their meaning: Râ's three names, Khepri, Râ, Tum and the character of these creative Neters; or Râ's voyage in Nut's belly and on her back . . . the Neters who accompany him are his boats of the day; or the entities in the Dwat whom he visits during his night journey; or again, the secrets of those abysses where the sleeping Neters awake at his passage and fall back into sleep until his next visit. The daily cycle is an image of what happens in the others.

'The monthly cycle explains the triad Ptah-Sekhmet-Nefertum, the lunar-solar nature of the scarab and its symbols, the meaning of Nekhbet's eye and the lunar role of Hathor-with-four-faces.

'The yearly cycle shows the passage of the decanates. The entire drama of Osiris, whose measure and key it is, is written there, as well as the metamorphoses symbolised by the ternary Ptah-Sokar-Osiris.

'Now I will tell you something you will never find written. The Twelve constellations divide in the heaven of North and South into twelve sections which correspond approximately with the twelve months. In the Great Stream they describe twelve figures, shapes or signs which are named after the animal character they give to the month they belong to. In what I have called the Great Cycle, which goes inverse to the annual

I

cycle, Earth comes under the influence of one of these signs for a little over two thousand years. This period divides into three, as the month does; but the beginning and end of an age are not strictly defined: to a lesser degree they feel the influence of the ages precedent and succedent. The quickening principle of each of the twelve ages is given the secret name that belongs to its sign. The reign of Mena took place in the age of the Bull, *ka,* whose characteristics are mass and stability, fighting-power in neck and horns, generative power so fiery that it emits seed without movement. The first symbol of the Taurian age was the power *khem* and *menw,* lightning, irresistible fire; then the generative and incorporative fire which the Bull, an incarnation of Ptah, befigures; then the Neter Min of the powerful phallus and finally Montu, who has the dual character of the Falcon, Horus-fire, and of fecund terrestrial fire, the Bull. The Bull acquired considerable importance in our symbology, for it is the animal incarnation of the principle that governed the primary organisation of the Two-Lands.'

'Statues dating from that time,' Her-Bak remarked, 'are notable for power and thickness in nape and neck. The pyramids have the same massive look.'

'Just so. The character of mass and base. However, when the new age began, with the sign of the Ram, one suddenly sees Amon in place of Montu and Osiris becomes "western". Today the Ram is at its apogee, like our own history; its images fill our temples. Western Amon's decline has begun and already the gestation of the Amonian Sun, the young fire of the Lamb, is in process. That is why our great Neter is now Amon-Râ. Thus one sign succeeds another, imposing its symbol on Earth. When Râ rises in the sign of the Fish the fish will be the new Initiator's symbol.'

'There is then neither fantasy nor utilitarian aim in these changes of cult and deity?' asked Her-Bak, to whom this conclusion brought peace.

'No. All is regulated in advance. Now study the various theogonies . . . you'll find that one of the four cycles which depend on one another, the smallest within the greatest, explains them. For those who haven't the key this creates an insoluble problem.'

. . .

'Let us seek unity in diversity. Let us find the link that unites the fundamental cults, Râ, Amon, Ptah.

'The triad of Memphis . . . Ptah, Sekhmet, Nefertum . . . summarises Ptah's incarnations in repetition of what was in the beginning, through all the kingdoms of Earth from mineral to the human egg. The creator, as

Ptah, forms Earth, Tatanen, which absorbs him and he is innate in it. He is Neter of mines, smelter of metals, craftsman of craftsmen. But he is fast bound, without liberty of action in limbs and arms. Sekhmet is the magnet that draws him, the destructive power of Earth that attracts Ptah's fire to her and delivers him. Sekhmet-Hathor's victory is the conversion of Ptah into *hotep*. His next metamorphosis that results from it is Sokar, whose chief function is contraction, concretion; after which he is reborn in his son Nefertum. It is said that Hapi the sacred Bull is Ptah's soul.

'You know the triad Amon, Mut, Khonsu. Amon in his absolute name is hidden. He appears as Râ in the Nun and fecundates that of which he was born. All the primordial earth-gods came of his body when as Ptah-Tanen he gave them form. And Râ appeared, with the face he shews to the East. Amon is the creative principle in its aspect as aerial water, the world's amniotic water, as such western. Fecundator and nourisher, he is, in nature, husband of Mut, mistress of the lunar lake Asheru, and he begets Khonsu.

'Râ is one. He has several aspects but no triad. Atum is a "moment" of Râ. In the second creation he becomes original man, adamic, androgynous, in Râ's image. Universal Râ cannot act immediately in nature, whose cosmic cause he is: it is then the Râ of nature, Atum, who works in his place and his material body is the luminous, visible globe Aten. The divine source of light we call Râ has his temple at Heliopolis. In his power of realisation, creator of Earth, he has his temple at Memphis. His life-giving power is fecundative and nourishing under the name of Amon; and in his name as Amon-Râ he sums up his dual aspect with all the Neters that are potentially contained in his name that is ineffable. His temple is at Thebes.

'These three, Amon-Râ-Ptah, are One, three in One. But man can only know One in its qualities, which vary in manifestation with the age. Heaven is the great book in which Thoth writes them; and everything born on Earth carries in Thoth's writing the astral qualities that are reflected in it. Every age is impregnated with one of them. The age that preceded our own bore the sign of the Twins and it was Thoth's domain. The Followers or Companions of Horus, who evolved with or rather within him, formed the solar-Horus seed, which corresponds in the becoming with the primordial creation: that is why the sun-temple at Heliopolis was at the beginning of our history.

'The cult of Ptah at Memphis inaugurated the constitutive age of the Bull. The reign of Thebes began in the age of the Ram and grew in glory

until the culmination of this sign. Thebes is the summit of our power and
the end of our initiative mission. Such is the sequence of heavenly dis-
pensations that influenced our development.'

The Sage gave Her-Bak time to arrange his thoughts. The disciple
said, 'When I was in the Peristyle a priest gave me a formula which I
condemned as a superstition. I'm afraid it was stupid of me.'

'Repeat it, if you please.'

'It runs, "Heaven's message is given at Heliopolis, repeated at Memphis,
written in Thoth's writing and sent to Thebes, where Amon gives the
reply that may kill or quicken. All is Amon-Râ-Ptah, one in three." '

'You should understand this now,' said the Sage. 'The theology of
Memphis repeats the actualisation of the primordial creation; for the
nomes, with their symbols in Thoth's writing are defined and organised.
The completion of our teaching is reserved to Thebes and Thebes gives
the complete revelation of abstract theology with the inscription of all
knowledge in its tombs and monuments. All that has been gained in the
course of our long mission, all that has been realised, must be summed
up there . . . which doesn't mean that other temples, thrones of the
Neters, may not inscribe details of the phase they represent. Thus your
formula is truthful: the answer is given at Thebes, where our revelation
has come to an end. That is why it is said that the primordial gods are
interred at the foot of our western mountain. The theological tree, all
of whose branches obey the four cycles, embodies the creative principles
and functions in their subtlest aspects. It reveals to the "wise of heart"
the harmony of the world of causes, inexplicable in theory. Symbols
make these living images speak and the perspicacious discover the vital
directives that flow from them.'

'Master,' said Her-Bak after long silence, 'dare I ask why you haven't
spoken about Thoth, or Maât?'

'Have I spoken about Horus? Listen then, if you are disposed not to
waste this treasure of the Sages. In the beginning, universal Horus is in
universal Râ. Thoth is his vizier, messenger who formulates his Words . . .
you find him everywhere. Maât, who links universal with terrestrial,
the divine with the human, is incomprehensible to the cerebral intelligence.
Her state is cosmic. She carries in herself the world's immaterial substance,
which is of all ages. Wedge, base, feather are her emblems. Her symbol
in the shape of a wedge, drawn horizontally, is part of a geometrical
figure that engenders the cardinal activity of Number. As such it is a
"motor". From a vital point of view it symbolises as it were a marsh
from which the earliest vegetation comes and as such it is a base, the base

of all things living. The wedge may also be drawn vertically. For Maât is the wedge that separates the heterogeneous from what has become homogeneous, as Shu separates Heaven-Nut from Earth-Geb in the beginning. And Maât's third symbol, the feather, is Shu's as well; for Maât represents in the corporal creation what Shu signifies in the principial. As the world cannot be without Shu, so it cannot maintain itself without Maât. Shu proceeded from Tum as Maât proceeded from Râ. As Shu is the principial fire of air, which gives earth the dryness of sand, and water the warmth that produces marshland, it is Maât who realises these principles. Shu, elemental, primordial Neter, is inseparable from humid Tefnut. Maât, daughter of Râ, is conjoint with Amon in nature and action, inseparable from Amon-Râ in the continuous creation where she ceaselessly regulates the two plates of a balance. She leaves the waste-products of everything to Ammit who devours the dead; and at the same time she feeds the true essence. That is why it is said that Thoth is Maât's scribe, for the fate he writes, in characters that Seshat draws, is the true signature of impulses that Thoth transmits and Maât realises.'

'I try in vain to imagine Maât's nature and role,' said the disciple. 'You speak as if she was at the beginning of things yet still plays a part in the affairs of mankind.'

'That is the truth,' said the Sage. 'But it is difficult for human intelligence to grasp the idea of unity in the creative source and the multiplicity evident in nature. The Neters are spiritual powers, qualities of divine Force, potentially all that will appear, work, develop in creatures. They are states of a consciousness which is not to be confused with the consciousness that results from existence. Their consciousness is a quality that enters into relations with things in a character that is invariable and doesn't change, as for example the quality "warmth", whereas the creature changes constantly in the growth of its consciousness, which is the road to liberation from its corporal state. Maât is the sum of the Neter-consciousness, therefore the consciousness of the creative Power. She is, in everything, the individualisation of causal activity as consciousness. She actualises it. She frames the divine Word and by her it takes its names. And by the indestructibility of such consciousness she is the triumph of life over death. But who am I that I should speak of the inexpressible. And who are you, Her-Bak, that you should listen?'

Her-Bak shook as if he had been roughly awakened. 'I don't know,' he replied, 'to whom it was said, "Maât is the food of Neters and men", but you have torn a corner of the veil. If Maât is the consciousness of creator and creature she is the world's wisdom. I can enrich her with my own consciousness and feed myself on the cosmic consciousness that she is.'

The Sage tasted with Her-Bak this moment of truth. He gazed at the Peak, lit by strong sunlight, and said, 'It seems that today Her-Bak comes close to the Neters. The vital thing is "to have known Maât". If you can hold this vision you will soon be ready to learn her true part in Man's life and you will see how real was the understanding you had today.'

·   ·   ·

'One thing still troubles me,' said Her-Bak on the way down from the Peak. 'Why are the Neters sometimes shewn with an animal head on a human body, sometimes with an animal symbol on a human head, and some of them by the animal itself?'

'Recollect that the animal is a psychically quickened body that is part of Earth. Man is a spiritually quickened animal and part of cosmic Man . . . that's why the five-pointed star is his symbol. The head is the sum of the body. Animal head on human body, even if it's the image of a Neter, indicates a functional human principle, cosmic therefore because man is the sum of the universe, but incomplete and only part of the human totality since it is limited to the functional consciousness or quality shewn by the animal's head. If the whole body is animal it is intended to depict a purely animal and therefore terrestrial function. Because the human being, microcosm, may, if he receives the supreme quickening, become a whole, whereas an animal body signifies no more than a stabilised condition in the becoming of organic consciousness. A symbol placed on a human head like a crown means accomplishment, as coronation does. It shews the quality of the man's or the Neter's nature or of the state reached.'

·   ·   ·

'What do you think you've gained by this lesson?' the Sage asked.

'The whole scheme of the world of causes,' Her-Bak replied, 'in its relation with Earth.'

'No. You have the connexion of the four most important celestial cycles with the creative principles and functions of nature. What will you make of it?'

'I shall be able to study the Neters now I know in which cycle and which branch they work.'

'Exactly. And deeply enough to get some light on the universal Harmony, which is more than those who taught you hitherto could do.

But I still haven't given you, nor shall I give you now, the secret plan shewing the connexions and interplay of these principles, no longer in symbol and approximation but with precision and in reality. This plan unveils the inevitable development of our destiny; knowledge of it is what gives us stability. It is this that has led us to foresee and adapt ourselves to each epoch, having the wisdom to abandon the values of a time that has passed and pick out the constituents of the future. An environment must be suited to the age and men to their environment. Through this we have chosen correctly, in accordance with their innate gifts, an extraordinary number of technicians and craftsmen. And we have been able to maintain a nucleus of those initiated in secret techniques and to link two thriving epochs.'

This excited Her-Bak: he tried to get light on it. 'Master, may I know whether this marvellous plan has always remained a secret? Every secret should be open to discovery . . .'

'The ancients kept this one well! Imagine, if you can, the design of a house built in many stages, whose illusive simplicity hides a trap at every step. Imagine false doors, secret entrances, a crypt from which each exit is an ambush, deceptive staircases, labyrinthine passages. If heaven doesn't put the guiding thread in your hands you'll never discover the plan of it.'

'Is silence a sufficient condition for getting it?'

'First prove your aptitude for research. Listen attentively to this, Her-Bak. Few indeed are they who have full knowledge of it; but all who proved capable of it, disciples of Thoth, astronomers, craftsmen, have been given what was necessary for their particular training. Now you know what the secret consists in: it is for you and you only to know more of it, in part or in whole, if this is your wish.'

.   .   .

'Osiris has such a high place among the gods,' said Her-Bak next day, 'that I've been surprised at your silence regarding him.'

'Osiris,' the Sage replied, 'is Neter of the natural order. His story is the story of all creatures on Earth; but his part is so complex that it can't be explained in a table shewing the hierarchy of the Neters. To know him you would have to study all his names, functions and attributes, which would amount to the whole of natural science. Without going wrong you can't isolate him from Seth, Isis and Nephtys, agents of becoming and the cycles of nature. He proceeds from Geb and Nut, the Neter-principles of Earth and the sky that holds the stars. Yet one doesn't say that Osiris is Nut's heir; rather that he is heir to the throne of Geb . . . his kingdom is that of Earth and the forms of existence that depend on it. As Nut's son he also exercises his functions among stars that are in relation with Earth-rhythms, the Moon, the planets, that are his dwellings, the Indefatigables or circumpolar stars that never leave our sky. He is Neter of Sah-Orion and all the *sâhs*. He gives Râ his terrestrial body.

'If you would understand the four principles that proceed from Geb and Nut you must study them in their mutual relationships, which will shew you some crossings in nature which they explain. I can't now give you in detail the factors and functions that are at work in such crossings . . . it would call for a treatise on natural philosophy. But I will point out the facts essential for the fathoming of their significance.

'There is a relation of nature between Osiris and Isis, as indicated by her seat, which is part of his name. There is also a relation between Seth and Nephtys as shewn by the names: Nebty, one of Seth's names, and Nebhet or Nephtys. Isis is a terrestrial aspect of Osiris when he is "the new Water"; tears and "the water of regeneration" when he appears in his terrestrial aspect. Likewise, in relation to Seth, she is light and life and all that frees from his bonds. If Osiris begets with Isis a posthumous son, Horus, he begets Anubis with Nephtys.

'In the Dwat Osiris plays a triple role: in genesis he is the black Sun; in the shadow-world he is the principle of perpetuity, witness as to what merits survival before the tribunal of life or death on which his forty-two assessors are the judges; he is the basis of the *sâhs*, whose metamorphoses and renaissances he decides. The drama of Osiris is the prototype of the drama of the human KA, in the vicissitudes of incarnation, the growth of consciousness throughout its terrestrial phases, the achievement of human royalty. Indeed it is our cardinal revelation, leading up as it does to the appearance of the Redeemer.

'The Osiris myth falls into three parts. First, the Earthly reign of the divine pair, Osiris-Isis, initiators of human consciousness as regards natural law and changes in matter. This has been called "the historic reign" of Osiris precedent to the reigns of our human kings and this aspect of Osiris is still the pattern for the role of Pharaoh. Second, his passion, in which his Earth-form is destroyed and the spiritual seed of Horus results. For there is in Osiris the seed of Horus that in our myth the kite Isis draws from his passive phallus, dead and spiritually recreated . . . note that it is after the slaying of mortal Osiris and the destruction of his component parts that Isis can recreate his indestructible body and take the Horus-essence from it. This Horus will be set apart and brought up in secret until the day when he is to "reveal his father's face", his own divine essence. Here is the terrestrial legend of Horus which follows that of Osiris. For after the destruction of his mortal body Osiris is reborn again in all earthly creatures, to die in them and descend into the lower Dwat with promise of regeneration, while Horus, son of Isis by Osiris' spiritual seed, avenges his father's bodily death by "revealing his face" and attacking the Sethian enemy in all his earthly forms. Then he comes forth crowned by Geb's order and takes up the government of the Two Banks, unites the powers of his father Osiris, master of the East then of the West. But this is still only the legend of terrestrial Horus that preludes the legend of Horus-Redeemer. Then comes the resurrection of Osiris who symbolises, in nature, the requickening of Earth and the buried seed and in spiritual fact reunion of the soul with the Osirian body, purified, indestructible.'

Her-Bak shewed astonishment that to begin with Isis and Osiris were only represented by the knot *tit* and the column *djed*.

'In the simplicity of those early days,' said the Sage, 'knowledge was give through essential symbols. Images were limited to what was strictly necessary. The first phase of our history had to shew Principles, creative Numbers, ideal Forms and cosmic Functions entering into the work of nature. This phase was necessarily theocratic. It was indispensable to assure the symbolic development of reigns and teaching in exact conformity with the character of the time and this could only be achieved with the collaboration of an instructed *élite*, inevitably a small number. The progressive development of the teaching had to follow the progressive complexity of nature, in order to bring about the realisation of the idea of a royal earthly Man, of whom our later kings will be the image. Such a programme assumed a gradual extension of the royal prerogatives, first to an *élite*, then little by little to the lowest ranks of the social scale, in proportion to the estimated advance in human consciousness. All this corresponds with the involution of Osiris and the subsequent evolution of his consciousness throughout nature by the experience of numerous incarnations with their alternate victories and disasters, light and confusion. His name was openly spoken in the age corresponding with his realisation in humanity. Having been the "first of the Westerns" he had to instruct men in the possibility of regeneration. Isis was the great redeemer in this mystery, but her part is as hard to understand as that of Osiris: don't forget that she is sister to Osiris and Seth and partakes the nature of both. She is Aset, or Set, who by her dual nature favours Seth in some cases and in others triumphs over him by giving birth to Horus. Natural magician who can take all forms, incarnate all functions, as maternal principle she causes the fall of spirit into matter and forwards resurrection with her regenerative tears. As Sopdit she is provider of life; as Hathor she is introducer of the dead and their mediatrix. She is the celestial swallow that peoples Earth's nests and with Osiris she governs the voyage between Heaven and Earth. Study all her names and you will learn the relations of Earth with Heaven. But if you would know the secret principles of Osiris and Isis go back to the primitive symbols, the *djed*, his true body and her mysterious knot.'

'Master, allow one more question. What is the difference between Amon "of whom all creatures constitute the KA" and Osiris who is the Neter of all terrestrial life?'

'Osiris is the Neter of nature, born of Earth and Heaven. Amon is celestial and is never born.'

XI

ASTROLOGY

'. . . One thing is the East bank, another the West. The same mud on both but a different light, for West is lit by the rising, East by the setting. In opposition manifestation as always . . .'

The Master's voice ceased. On the terrace of a temple on the west bank the disciples awaited Râ's coming. From within came a chant, saluting his first rays.

The disciples rose, with the Masters, to receive like all the west a baptism of golden light. The temples and palaces of the city, stretching out of sight north and south, were lit one by one. 'In eyes used to the other bank,' said the Sage, 'the land has changed, at so short a distance. But you believe in what you see on both sides . . . what man is wise enough to remain aware of relativities?'

'What point would there be,' asked Abushed, 'in living all the time in an abstract world?'

'Don't be afraid. Everyone finds himself in the world where he belongs. The essential thing is to have a fixed point from which to check its reality now and then. Here are five of you, admiring the landscape. You have visited the principal sanctuaries of the Two-Lands: will each tell me which is Egypt's true heart?'

Auab cried out without hesitation, 'Nut-Amon, Thebes, our city.'

'Its preponderance is that of its Age,' the Sage replied. 'I am not speaking of a moment in history. Every place has its nature and this decides its function: it was with this in mind that I put my question.'

'It would seem to me,' said Upuat, 'that Abydos, where men aspire to rejoin Osiris, is Egypt's heart.'

'The centre of the Two-Lands is precisely Hermopolis,' said the student of geometry. 'Isn't that the country of the Primordials?'

Abushed proposed Memphis. 'Ptah being organiser of the Two-Lands,' he said, 'I should choose the city of his temple.'

The Sage watched Her-Bak, who was silent. Answering his Master's unspoken question the disciple said what was in his mind. 'You have told me that Heliopolis is the city of the Sun and that His temple taught Râ's generation and birth. As the heart is the solar organ I suppose Heliopolis is Egypt's heart.'

'A wise answer. Your conclusion is sound,' said the Master. 'Heliopolis is the heart, the ear of the heart, that receives Heaven's message. Our geometer is right when he says that Hermopolis is the centrepoint of the Two-Lands: it is the regenerative centre. As to Memphis and Abydos, to understand their part one must study them without historical prejudice. It is always the living aspect and regard to the pre-established plan that guide us. Priests and kings have never been free to site temples and capitals. A plan, as regards time and place, is strictly imposed. The deeds and personal gestures with which they fill the framework belong to a minor human tale. We don't record details of secondary importance for posterity.'

'Tales of conquest,' Abushed persisted, 'incidents of the chase, shooting or other exploits, have no relation to real facts?'

'It can happen that some such episode or personal deed serves as base for a symbolic tale; but form, detail, dates are changed, without reference to historical fact, to shew what must be taught. The improbability of numerous incidents should have attracted your notice: does one ever see an archer transfix copper targets several inches thick as if they were bundles of papyrus? Such extravagance must throw doubt on an allegory of which the plan of the Ancients would give us the motive and detail. That only could attest the truth of what I affirm. Abydos and Elephantine saw the beginning of two great epochs, Abydos the period inaugurated by Mena, Elephantine an earlier one. But effective unification of the two kingdoms was to come about under the predominance of Memphis, which is the true point of balance between the Two-Lands.'

'Thebes ought to have precedence all the same,' Auab insisted.

'In its time, which is Amon's time,' said the Sage. 'Don't judge of such matters childishly. See our country as a whole, with the characteristics that made its destiny. Kemit is the Black Land created by the Nile which vitalises and defines the two zones, North and South, as the band of the Zodiac vitalises and defines the northern and southern skies. East and west of our valley the land extends into sterile and hostile regions, the Red Land of Seth, the desert, which isolates and protects it. The Nile divides the kingdom into two different parts: the long valley of the South doesn't resemble the North which broadens into a vast, fertile triangle, for the river that flows out of the black country, Nubia, land of gold, divides into branches that water this great garden. One branch flows west, another east; the middle one divides again and reaches the marshes that saw the birth of Horus son of Isis. The Nile opens like a flower of papyrus whose long stem is rooted among the reeds of the South in the black country, base of the land of the White Crown. Its triangular flower fertilises the land of the North with its living water, the North whose cities mark the phases of the drama of Osiris. We see this triangle as the head, the face rather, that reflects the functions performed in the land of the South . . . is it not in the face that man's nature finds its living expression? It is through the facial senses that man sees, hears, and names creatures lower than himself. And from this garden are wafted, as far as the river's sources, the fresh and vital airs of the North, while the stream bears from South to North the water that quickens seed. Thus, as in a tree and in our body, a double current sustains life. And throughout the river's course are points and regions characterised by accidents of nature, the composition of the soil, the shapes and colours of the rock, the predilection of some animal for the site: these circumstances determined the choice and name of the sanctuaries of the Neters.'

'Isn't it a childish game to deify natural fact?' asked Abushed.

'We deify nothing,' corrected the Sage. 'But we know that Neter *is* before man, idea before thing. We know that the same function, in the same circumstances, will give similar results: it is sensible to note the characters of function and circumstances that produced such and such a phenomenon. Isn't a Neter a manifest quality? One ascends from nature to Neter, through whose symbols one may get to know nature. It isn't by chance that a given temple took the falcon, ibis, vulture or jackal for symbol, but because the nature of a place attracts such and such an animal, as one sees with the falcons at Edfu, the vultures at El Kab. An animal is the living expression of the place. Men live there in the conditions that attracted these animals and there are relations of sympathy that benefit those who respect them and adapt themselves. An instinctive affinity is at work, not reason or the will. This then is the principle that governs the choice of ensigns for the nomes . . . sometimes an animal, sometimes a natural or a composite object. Whatever the image it always symbolises the nome's function in the development of our country, which is planned on the pattern of Earth's becoming. Thus, the nome of Hermopolis has for emblem the hare, which in its mode of being and living symbolises terrestrial existence. The hare is used as hieroglyph in "to exist". Hermopolis is the city of the eight Primordials, founders of primordial Earth, site of earliest life.'

'Since the subject has been brought up,' remarked Abushed, 'this may be the time to ask what the emblem of our town Thebes stands for. I find no resemblance with object or animal.'

'You might search a long time,' said the Sage. 'It is one of our most beautiful symbols, the more simply drawn the more eloquent, a tree-trunk from which springs a branch that divides in two. Reverse it and you have the head of a sceptre. Shorten the two branches of the fork and again you have the sceptre. One becomes two which again give a duality . . ."I am One that becomes Two; I am Two that becomes Four." This is the symbol of Origin. You will find traces of it in the treasuries of our kings, which include rods made of a single branch cut in this fashion, sometimes gilded to stress the symbolic meaning.'

'The head is often that of some unknown animal,' Her-Bak remarked. 'And the sceptre of Thebes is complicated with a feather and strap.'

'The head alludes to Seth's head,' said the Sage, 'which this sign must conquer with feather and strap. The ear is an ass's ear, which is the secret symbol of a primitive pillar.'

'It's all very mysterious,' sighed Her-Bak.

The Sage's voice became severe. 'You knew already all we have told you? You have grasped in a few lessons a science that is the treasure of several thousands of years' devotion? Its judgments may be better founded than those of ignorance. If it was thought well to wrap up certain truths in symbols we should be fools to unwrap them without precaution. Be thankful that we have put you on the road to their real meaning.'

Her-Bak apologised and asked if the feather in the banner of Thebes related to the feather of Amenti, the West.

'Certainly, for the feather indicates the West in the first place. All the same, one element in the temple of Karnak expresses an eastern function. Let each of you make what use pleases him of this. I have spoken truth.'

'Then the city of Amon has two aspects, eastern and western,' Her-Bak remarked.

'It has them because it is the temple of Amon-Râ. In fact it has three aspects, for the temple that complements Karnak is Apet of the South, Luxor. Both these temples have the name Apet with double meaning: Apet the belly because they speak of the mysteries of generation and Apet, Number, the laws of which they reveal and apply.'

Abushed, who tried to conceive of things as a whole, expressed a wish to study the nomes in relation to their names and symbols. 'The facts you dispose of,' replied the Sage, 'are incomplete, for their symbols and names are determined by a general plan of which you are ignorant. Yet observation of principles will be useful to you: the west or right side of your heart receives and returns blue blood from and to the lungs, the east or left side receives red blood and sends it to the body. The flow of regenerated red blood is a beginning, a renewal of life at each beat, like Râ's rising in the East. The return of vitiated, or exhausted, blue blood is an end like his setting in the West. And you can change nothing in this sequence, which belongs to the universal order. Your right hand is active, your left passive, receptive: thus it is on Earth, for those who dwell in the East differ from those who dwell in the West. Always watch and follow nature. As to North and South, I have said that the kingdom of the North reflects the nomes and sanctuaries of the South as your face reflects the functions of the body.'

Auab, having consulted Her-Bak in an undertone, risked a question. 'Is there some connexion between this symbolism and meaning of the two crowns?'

'Certainly,' replied the Sage. 'Just as in your own organism two humours, white lymph and red blood, maintain life, so our Two-Lands stand for the dual current of the life that is universal. The Land of the South is ruled by the white crown and its symbol is the reed, referring to the white fire of the pith. The Land of the North is ruled by the red crown, which refers to the red fire of the blood. The Two-Lands, like the two humours, need and live by one another. It is said that in the division of the kingdoms between the two hostile brothers the South was adjudged to Seth and the North to Horus.'

'Fair enough,' said Auab, 'since deserts are Seth's land.'

'Auab is right,' Abushed agreed. 'But why does the white crown have precedence in the desert?'

'Because,' the Master replied, 'a phenomenon always arises from the interaction of complementaries. Action sets up a resistance, which provokes a reaction: the third term is the phenomenon. Red blood needs the nourishing white humour, which is itself vitalised by the blood's red fire. Such is nature's law: if you want something look for the complement that will elicit it. Seth causes Horus. Horus redeems Seth.'

'I see now,' said Auab, 'why Seth is shewn as a Neter to whom one pays homage. For a long time I found that scandalous.'

Upuat remarked that legend placed the first victorious battles of Horus with Râ's enemies in the kingdom of the South.

'Horus,' replied the Sage, 'strives for the triumph of spirit in matter, light in darkness: thus, Horus also is in darkness. After the victory he returns to the black country from which he came . . . to start new battles. For Horus never rests, since he is the soul of the world. He has several forms, according to the work he is at, and several crowns.'

'While Seth has only one form,' put in Auab.

'What about his crocodile, his hippopotamus and the aggressive oryx?' demanded Her-Bak.

The Astronomer explained this. 'Seth is everything that tends to contract and "fix" Spirit in matter, a situation he is for ever seeking to perpetuate. Horus's struggle with him, which is a cosmic myth, is the essence of our entire history . . . his triumphs correspond with our times of illumination, while Seth's bring glories that are all too human and are always followed by long periods of darkness.'

'Since the Temple can foresee the future can't such things be avoided?' asked Abushed.

'That would violate the law of the age. The Sage's part isn't to work against nature but to safeguard the guiding thread and save men of good will from losing themselves in the darkness.'

'What liberty has Pharaoh then in this complex game? I doubt more and more whether what has been written about the doings of our kings has any relation with truth.'

'Come,' said the Sage. 'We will shew you the sources of our history.'

.   .   .

The Masters led their pupils to a terrace where the temple astronomers welcomed them. A cry of wonder sprang from every heart, for an immense gold circle dazzled the eye. It measured almost three hundred and sixty-five cubits on the outside and three hundred and sixty on the inside; its breadth was about three-quarters of a cubit. The Astronomer described the position of the decanates and constellations; then he shewed them the names of the twelve signs of the months drawn in secret writing. 'This circle,' he said, 'is a schematic image of a living and moving reality. Only the principles are fixed, not their forms or proportions. The sun travels these twelve signs in a year, with a slight retardation at each circuit, as if the equinoctial departure-point receded a little with each tour, such that after about twenty-one centuries the sun starts on his course later by one sign. As if, that is, he made the "grand cycle" on the same circuit in a direction inverse to the annual cycle. It results that while we feel the influence of a sign each month we feel also, throughout the twenty-one centuries, the influence of the sign in which the sun effects this delay and which becomes his house during the grand cycle. He is now in the sign of the Ram and receding towards the Fish. But this double movement is complicated by the passage of the wandering stars or planets and the presence of other important luminaries. The variety of movements brings about harmonious conjunctions of which Earth feels the effects. At the moment when he first draws breath a new-born child receives the signature of such influences and he will carry it all his life. It predisposes

him to certain states of health, certain characteristics and gifts, and it
endows him with affinities or antipathies for certain animals, plants and
aspects of nature. Prolonged experience has erected these observations
into a science.'

Abushed, who had seen such influences at work, acquiesced. 'It is of
the greatest help in guiding men into work for which they are fitted,'
he said. 'It should save many a wasted apprenticeship.'

'That is so. Informed selection increases the number and value of our
technicians. But its chief importance lies in the knowledge this science
gives us of the development of the four cycles and their influence on places
and people.'

'I suppose,' put in Her-Bak, 'that periodical changes in the names and
cults of the Neters correspond with these celestial variations?'

'Succeeding ages,' the Astronomer replied, 'give rise to one another
without ceasing to obey the great cosmic rhythm, in such a way that
different phases, or slices, of time have different characteristics whose
predominance alters the atmosphere of a place, emphasising or enfeebling
the character of its Neter. Take the two seasons that are so unlike . . . *prt*,
winter, and *shmw*, summer. If one nome is characterised by the Neters
of summer, another by the Neters of winter, it is obvious that during
summer the Neters of winter will be weak and the importance of their
sanctuaries will diminish. But when they regain their vigour during the
winter the summer Neters will lose their preponderance. This simplified
example of an annual fact can be carried back through the great historical
periods of a country or a world. It is a key for the man who doesn't
deny heaven.'

'It is a key certainly,' said Upuat, 'to the understanding of periodic
influences and their effects in the sphere of religion. But what is it that
determines the primordial character of a place, in such a way that it
can be related with the heavenly movements?'

'That doesn't belong strictly to the science of astrology but to another,
the science of genesis.'

'Can astrology be considered an exact and infallible science?'

'Certainly, as regards what belongs to nature, but not what belongs
to spirit. However, its accuracy depends on certain keys, secret because
sacred, without which its calculations will always amount to probabilities
only.'

Abushed shewed impatience. 'This secrecy! Why all this reticence?'

'The lessons of the past justify it. What do you complain of, Abushed?
Don't you get full enough measure?'

K

Abushed apologised. 'Master, I'm sorry. One doesn't understand what one isn't ready for. But may I ask if the names of human beings have as much importance as those of the Neters?'

'Do you not know,' the Master asked, 'that a name is a magic Word? It is for you yourself, you who know the sacred texts, to compare like with like and draw the obvious conclusions . . . a child could do it. It is the spirit of rationality that blinds you. Isn't it written that a man's name expresses his personality and the qualities of his KA? The father gives it by way of inheritance and the "signature" of his own seed; the mother feeds it and colours it with her own substance. But conception and gestation are both affected by the astral moment. It is said that "every word that proceeds from God's mouth is food which creates vital forces"; also that the bread of the gods is "spoken by Geb and sent out from the mouth of the divine Ennead". This Word ceaselessly gives out, together with the type of the seed, the name of its product; and it is most powerful at the moment of conception and birth.'

'This convinces me,' said Abushed, 'that a name has magical power.'

'It is a real power,' said the Sage. 'A name has great importance. It corresponds in reality with the being that receives it. It is a portrait that acts magically on his existence, for a name, when it is spoken, works on its possessor's KA. The higher man, the man who is spiritually fulfilled, has also several names that relate to various states of his being. That is why Pharaoh has many names, which refer to his person, his KA, his spiritual being and the "moment" he stands for.'

'Can a king's names,' Her-Bak asked, 'disclose his nature and his part in history?'

'They are in effect such a revelation. But to read them you must relate them to heavenly factors. Then you will understand why certain names were chosen during a given period, for officials as well as kings, names that afterwards fell into disuse for a time.'

Abushed remarked that this could explain why certain officials sited their tombs near some Pharaoh of an earlier date.

'Not so,' the Master replied. 'You will only see the reason for this by reference to the secret plan. But an understanding of names will give you the motive for changes in orthography and many anomalies.'

'Isn't it the same with temples destroyed and rebuilt on the same spot?'

'They were superseded rather than destroyed, to be rebuilt according to the symbolism and measurements of the age. Wisdom teaches us that it is necessary to create each new age afresh so that new seed may have new vitality. But we know that an old trunk makes an excellent base because of its deep roots: it is enough to cut off the branches and graft on a new one. This is what we do. We insert old stones in new buildings. We even choose from the resources of superseded temples such elements as may serve in a symbolic mode as vehicle for the contemporary principle. To create afresh is the rule governing the periodic displacement of key centres, not at all from caprice but in obedience to cosmic law.'

'Master,' persisted Upuat, 'may we know how such times of renewal are established?'

'It would be more sensible to ask how the phases of becoming are defined. The development of a fertilised egg is a sufficient analogy: times of fertilisation, times of decomposition, times of regermination from decomposed elements, gestation, formation, until the final accomplishment.'

'Why do you say "final accomplishment?" '

'Because each phase includes several phases each of which reaches completion. The period inaugurated by Mena is the second phase of an age.'

Abushed listened with deep interest. 'If such periods occur regularly,' he said, 'it should be simple to calculate them.'

'No, for while there is regularity as to principle there is no regularity in duration. Just as in nature the period of gestation varies with the species, so there are differences of duration in human history. But this is a complex matter for which a knowledge of our measures is necessary.'

Each meditated in silence. Her-Bak, seated in face of the entrance, was struck by the door-frame, whose carved signs, covered with gold, glittered in the sun. 'Here I see once again,' he said to the Astronomer, 'symbols one notices over many doors, the scene of the "great step". No one has given me an explanation that satisfies. Are they connected with the science of the sky?'

The Astronomer glanced at the Sage, who replied, 'The disciples here present are vowed to silence. I will tell them what they may hear.'

He approached the threshold and pointed to two designs on the framework representing the sign for the sky cut in two. 'You see here symbols of two halves of the great band of gold: they indicate what subject is treated in this scene. The two signs that accompany them stand for the solstices. The idea is simplified as usual: the curve of the sky, sometimes mounted on a long, straight stem, is most often supported by two stems of unequal length, just as the axes of the decentred curve of the sun's, or the earth's, course are unequal. Simple observation of the shadow of a vertical stem exhibits the inequality of this curve from the winter solstice to the spring equinox. The times of the two solstices mark the great turning-points of the sun's yearly cycles that are signified by the "great step". Now the curve, having two centres, is marked by two unequal lengths of extreme distance, nearest and farthest. In terrestrial life these dates are of the greatest importance for agriculture. They have also another significance, which study of the sky may disclose to you. Today I will explain two symbols that have aroused your curiosity, for they attest our astrological knowledge.'

The Sage approached the gold band and pointed his stick at the sign of the Bull. 'Our history,' he said, 'and the organisation of the kingdom under Mena and his successors, began in this sign: that's why we shall bear its character and venerate its symbol until our end. But a sign doesn't work alone, for its *vis-à-vis* acts by way of complement. You notice that the sign opposite the sign of the Bull is the Scorpion . . . we feel the Scorpion's influence at the same time as the Bull's. Note then that one of these two symbols is a scorpion mounted on a loop or knot in the circuit. The second is a composition that symbolises the bull by his *ka*, which is also the word for a bull. The four elements that give a column, *djed*, stability are shewn in the *ka*, which stands on a column, specifying the bull's characteristics, which are stance, vital strength and stability. The *ka*'s arms support a symbol which is the secret hieroglyph of the Ram of Amon, which follows the Bull and in which our history will reach its consummation.' The disciples shewed their astonishment and the Sage continued. 'We are now in the sign of the Ram. Its opposite is the sign *akh*, horizon or balance, which is connected with the balance of Maât. You know how important are the roles of the balance and of Maât in our symbolism and theology. But when the sun rises in the sign of the Fish the fish will be the new Envoy's symbol and its complement will be the sign of the Virgin.'

The light was blinding. No more was said that day.

PART II
BA and KA

XII

FIRST DAY

The cheerful brilliance of the morning lent youth to Earth's old bones, touched the peak with gold, gleamed along the river and put the gardens *en fête*. So fragrant was the hour that one forgot yesterday's cruel heat; that in a little while one would be driven to seek shelter once more, to mistrust the pitiless light. Every green thing, revived by cool night, offered dew to the sun; flowers opened their corollas confidently, brightened their hues in the sun's oblique rays.

Trees and flowers were in effervescence of sap, scent and rustling wings. Flower-beds were an extravagance of gay colour. The white of anthemis enhanced the blue cornflower carpets and the corn-poppies' resounding red. The Sage did not tire of watching the dexterity of the lapwings, the malice of the crows, the busy quarrelling of sparrows. But Her-Bak's heart inclined to other matters.

'I came to the temple at dawn, Master,' he said, 'for you promised to tell me about *akh*, BA and KA.'

'Are you sure I've forgotten? What is more living than a garden? What more real than life?' Two pairs of bee eaters took flight like green-gold arrows through the green gold of mimosa. 'Do you know what colours their feathers, Her-Bak? Do you know what gives the lapwing the instinct that detects the grub? Whence the hues of convolvulus?'

'From the seed.'

'Who formed the seed? No doubt logic can find an answer, but life can only be fathomed by life. If you colour a drawing with your brush it is artifice; but the blue of this corolla is the seed's answer to light.'

'All seeds answer light, but the colour is different . . .'

'. . . like men's hair and eyes. Do brown eyes disclose the same character as blue? The men may be brothers: whence then the difference? Have you noticed the five-pointed star in the convolvulus? If you had the patience and faith to study these characteristics and their connexions you would learn the nature of BA and KA sooner than by recording words in your memory.'

'BA, KA, *akh*, are spiritual principles. Can plant and animal tell me what animates man?'

A swarm of honey-bees buzzed round Her-Bak who tried in vain to get rid of them. The Sage reprimanded him. 'Your fear makes them aggressive. Their instinct is better advised than your reason. They could instruct you in the subject that holds your interest.'

'What connexion is there between the soul and the bee?'

'Have you forgotten their names?'

'*Bi.t* is the word for bee and for honey. This isn't the same word as *ba*.'

'You're sure? Are not *i* and *a* two aspects of the first of the *mdw-Neters*? You know too much, Her-Bak. You must learn to be a child again.'

The honey-bees, drunk with the scent of acacia, fought for the flowers, which they sucked greedily. 'What does the bee take when it plunders,' the Sage asked, 'unless it is the subtlest essence of the flower? It takes no part of the flesh. The rifled flower suffers no harm. But this golden insect makes a golden drink which is the purest of foods assimilable directly without putrefaction or loss. You'll never catch our symbols in the act of inconsistency.'

'But the symbol you speak of, honey, is a product.'

'We weren't talking of the creative Spirit but of BA. I try to make you live a synthesis but you still seek a comprehensible thought-structure. Perhaps I can satisfy you with an explanation, but after this have the sense to look for truth in the symbols. Well then, at the outset of all becoming *akh* is light proceeding from darkness. This presupposes darkness, light contained in it, and the Cause or Origin that held both in potential. When Râ rises out of Nut he is *akh*.'

'I thought the dawn of light was *kha*.'

'Listen before you argue. Through Râ's arising there is evening and morning, west and east: whence the horizon, *akht*, which we depict by two mountains with the sun between them. Always one, two, three. Can you think of east without west, or two points without horizon? Can *akh* appear unless there is light in darkness? Is there a horizon that isn't related to east and west? Remember that the third component of an original trinity is an abstract relation between two known factors.'

'The initial element may be unknown to man . . .'

'Unless you assume it as known you won't formulate the problem. Amon is unknown. Mut manifests him through Khonsu, who "reveals his face" as the plant reveals what is in the seed. But the third factor belongs as much to the first as to the second . . . that's what makes for confusion. The third is a relation of quality which makes it intermediary, like three between two and one, a thing your reason still doesn't grasp because quality is an abstraction. But it becomes comprehensible through the phenomenon it produces and the phenomenon, the third factor grown visible, becomes a fourth, or the first of a new line. Male and female may be together without relation, but the rutting season evokes a third factor and establishes their duality. This relation, which sets the sex-functions in motion, is qualitative, like the natural cause of it; and though father and mother may procreate the real cause is the power of love, universal power that acts throughout nature on seed and sex. The abstract relation between two concrete terms is always the reality. The third, real term creates the relation between the first two; but the phenomenon or product is the third factor of the trinity become visible and will be the first factor of a new one. Thus, trinities give rise to one another. Each element may change its number and function; but if you don't know how to discover the abstract factor you will understand neither sequence nor symbol.'

The disciple followed this word by word. 'Are we to regard *akh*-BA-KA as the human trinity?' he asked.

'They are the spiritual trinity that makes men. But they are not his exclusive property: we can speak of them in connexion with other forms of nature and even with the Neters in certain cases. They are three spiritual states, insusceptible of dissection like animal organs. You can't think of them as independent of one another, any more than the three sides of a triangle. Reason blunders when it tries to analyse them and imperfect knowledge of them leads to many errors.'

'Isn't it said that *akh* arises from the reunion of a dead man with his purified KA?'

'What is it in the dead man that goes to his KA? His body? He is in the tomb. His BA?'

'It is said that BA rejoins KA when KA is reunited with the *djet*,' Her-Bak replied.

'What is the *djet*?'

'The *djet* is the incorruptible body.'

'It can't interest the mummy. Is there some other element you haven't mentioned?'

'Would it be the Shade?'

'What is the Shade? Is it not a form that intercepts light? When light incarnates in substance, substance doesn't intercept light to make a shadow: it makes a body that will be light's own shadow. The Shade is a phantom. Henceforth reflect before asking questions. Popular beliefs on essential matters must be examined in order to discover the original thought. We only give the public an image they can understand . . . are you a member of the public?'

'Master, it was a thoughtless question.'

The Sage seemed content. 'Now I can reply to your first point. The appearance of the sun's rays on the horizon is called *kha* inasmuch as it affirms the sun's presence. You can use the same word for the king's appearance on the throne and the placing of the crown on his head. *Kha* is the material aspect of a power or fire potentially contained in the being who manifests it; the individualisation of such power or fire. *Kha* is not the fire but its affirmation in matter. In the word *khw* you have the same idea of a fire or force enclosed, in an amulet for instance. And *khw* with the meaning "to consecrate" gives the idea of the enclosure of fire or energy in some object such as an offering, statue or temple . . . this is vulgarly called magic power.

'Now let us resume our consideration of *akh*. It is the spiritual birth of light, spirit revealing itself; not original, causative spirit as it is in itself but spirit immanent in matter. Don't forget that *akh* is "light triumphant over darkness" at no matter what conjuncture, whether the beginning of continuous creation, the moment of a man's spiritual rebirth, or the rebirth of vegetable seed in mud. But this can't be explained openly.'

'Then *akh* has three aspects,' Her-Bak observed. 'The first is metaphysical, light generated in darkness. The second is natural, light incorporate, regenerated from decomposing elements of seed in germination, a reawakening of the fire in mud that makes what was sterile thrive. The third is human . . . but I don't know how to define it.'

'It is spiritual light triumphant over human factors that will reintegrate in unity. This still won't be the end, but a step to higher perfection; *iakh* isn't an ending, but a state in spiritual becoming that exhibits various degrees of achievement.'

.   .   .

'If you have understood the triple manifestation of *akh*,' said the Sage, 'you can understand the triple aspect of KA.

'In the beginning KA is Form that gives form to substance in the making of matter; the spiritual principle of fixity that will be the point of support in all manifestation. And it is this that throughout the process of becoming will undergo manifold changes from the lowest of forms up to the perfection of the indestructible body. KA as power, cosmic love, will be incomprehensible to you; and if I were to say it is the attractive force that causes and fixes Ptah's incarnation in matter this would be too abstract. But if I say that *ka*, the bull, is the animal incorporation of Ptah's fire you will understand by reference to the taurine properties of ardour, power in ejaculation, fixity, strength of the neck.

'KA as cosmic power is the essence of the idea of the bull. Carrier of generative potency, it transmits hereditary characters from the original creative act to earthly generation. KA then is the carrier of all powers of manifestation and activator of cosmic functions. One can say too that KA is "Father of the fathers of the Neters", for it is the realising principle in continuous creation: without it a father would have no potency and through it a son "reveals his father's face". It is thanks to KA that things are named. Râ's active properties are his KA's. The vitalising properties of food are its KA. KA is the source of all appetites. All aspects of KA are found in man, but not all are in his control. The higher qualities of KA, fed by the subtle fires of the marrow, are only incorporate in man when he has consciousness of them and mastery.'

'This clarifies some statements that seemed contradictory,' said Her-Bak. 'I have heard that man doesn't always possess his KA during Earth-life: at the same time one speaks of Pharaoh's KAS.'

'Reflect on the aspects of the KA and learn to distinguish them,' said the Sage. 'The viscera carry the animal's KAS and the appetites they embody last a certain time after death: it is for these KAS that funeral offerings of foodstuffs are made. But the individualised human KA is far higher than the animal KAS. Among our images you will often see a Neter putting his power into a man's neck: the neck-vertebrae support the head, which governs the living organism and expresses its conscious-ness. The neck is a mysterious centre. It is one of the physical sites of the higher KA, one of the centres of contact with the organic KAS. This will help you to discern three aspects of KA . . . the original KA, creator of all KAS; the KAS of nature, mineral, vegetable, animal; a man's individual KA, which comprises his inherited and his personal character and fixes his destiny.'

.   .   .

Sage and disciple walked for some time in silence. Leaving the gardens, they took the avenue of the great rams of Amon. The sunlight was grow-ing fierce, the thick shade of a sycamore seemed a good place to stop. 'After what you have said about KA,' ventured Her-Bak, 'I don't see what there can be left to say about BA.'

'In the beginning is BA,' said the Sage. 'In the end is BA. Between begin-ning and end BA is in everything; it is the breath of life. BA, Spirit, is the breath of everything that constitutes the world and its final perfection.

'KA like BA shews three aspects. First, it is the spirit of cosmos, the spirit of Fire, quickener of the Neters and various parts of the world, in which sense we are to understand the spirits of East, West, Pe, Dep, Nekhen, Heliopolis. Next, it is the natural soul in the bodily form, of Osirian character, subject to cyclic rebirth. This aspect is symbolised by the ram with horizontal horns. Lastly, BA is represented by a bird with human head. This is the symbol of the human soul, which goes to and fro between heaven and earth to range about the body until purification of the KA-*djet* allows the body to incorporate it. This is the bird that is shewn perched on Nut's sycamore, at whose feet you are sitting. You must work this out.'

The Sage rose. He took a shady path that brought them to the landing-stage, where his boat waited. Her-Bak went happily on board and sat in silence at the Master's feet, in the shade of a cabin covered with many-coloured matting. The boat went upstream, slowly, to the cadenced rhythm of oars. A breeze arose and the oarsmen stopped rowing; they hoisted the square sail, the boat heeled over and glided silently southward. 'It is easier,' the Master said, 'to go with the stream than against it towards its source. But this is possible if skilful use is made of the winds, even if they seem contrary. The succession of lives is a stream that sweeps men along without their being conscious of anything but the happy or unhappy incidents of the journey. For each the course of his life seems the whole of the way: he lets himself be carried along without noticing the current. Very few know how to overcome indolence and observe the nature of stream, wind and bank; yet this effort is the nutriment of a man's own Neter, which incarnates only with this object.'

Disquiet shewed on Her-Bak's face. 'The ideas you give me,' he answered the Master who asked what was wrong, 'are confused in my head like principles without points of application. Who is my own Neter? What is it that constitutes the individuality of that which incarnates in me?'

'The answer, Her-Bak, should be the last in a course of instruction you haven't had. But there is ground for your anxiety, for the explanations I have given you are summary and introductory statements designed to sweep a pupil's confused thoughts away. If I am to be allowed to complete the course you must give evidence of the measure of your understanding.'

'Then I'll ask you this,' Her-Bak swiftly replied. 'You have spoken about *akh*, BA, KA . . . if spirit is the absolute One, how can it be split into parts?'

The Master nodded, satisfied. 'Your question is shrewd. Now I may approach the reality of the subject.'

. . .

'All that exists proceeds from the One. One, becoming conscious of itself, divides and creates the world. In the end everything that lives will be recalled into this unity, by way of the spiritual hierarchies of beings become conscious.'

'What name has One?'

'As absolute it is unknowable, unnamable. As creator of the world we call it Atum-Râ, Amon-Râ-Ptah. In respect that it is the source of all being it is *iaaw* and every man has its image in him, like an inverted reflection.'

'Is this reflection the "person"?'

'I am speaking not of an effect but of the cause and principle of what will be personal and as it were the opposite of impersonal being, the principle of the Me, *nek*, or *inek*. The word *inek* doesn't connote a living creature or character; *nek* is the thirst for existence in and for itself, without object other than not to be destroyed. It is a transformation of the prime urge to exist into the will to continue, a tendency to the perpetuation of Me. The word *iw* expresses the impersonal principle of being. *Inek* is its personal seeming. In relation to impersonal *iw*, *inek* is "the other", *iw* being the principle of being as primal activity, *i* limited by a space *w*, its personal aspect is *sw*, for *s* expresses characteristic specificity. The earthly continuation of a "person" is given by the word *iwâ*, an heir, for *â* adds the idea of individual dimension to the idea of being. Now, Her-Bak, we have a teaching that doesn't allow any waste of words. Think well over your questions.'

Having reflected at length Her-Bak asked, 'How can the impersonal become personal? How can the One become the Other?'

'I can only speak prudently in the language of our hieroglyphs,' the Master replied. 'Our first letter, through its dual aspect *ia*, expresses Beginning with its dual potential of active and passive. At once there arises the possibility of volume, signified by *aw*, the principle of expansion, space-substance, dilatation, amplitude. The two syllables together, *ia aw*, speak of being in its original, undivided plenitude, without categories. What do the Sages say about this? "In the beginning *iaaw* lived in one sole body . . . before there could be duality, before earthly things could exist . . . when there was as yet no birth, when there were no gods . . . when the desire of *ikw* had not yet been spoken."'

'What is *ikw*?'

'It is the reflection of primal activity in a tendency to personification. *Ikw* is the power that precipitates abstract substance into matter, being into becoming with all its phases and turns of fortune . . . whence the name of the scarab, *kheprer*, which symbolises these changes. *Ikw* causes the fall into matter, duality, procreation and the rest. Becoming is universal genesis, the summit and term of which on Earth is man. Then follows a supernatural process, a taking possession by man of his spiritual elements, BA and KA, which means a new quickening, the birth of a conscious man who has "learnt to know", acquired "higher reason, *rekh*". This word is exact, for *kher* is the relation between thing and cause while *rekh* is the consciousness of it. This new birth is accomplished in spiritual renaissance after death.'

Her-Bak made a point. 'Master, you say BA and KA must be reunited in a man. Being spiritual, they are part of the One from which comes the Other. How can the Other exist without the One? How can the One be separate from the Other that was formed of it?'

The Sage rose. 'This is too abstract to be resolved at once. There are more concrete matters to be clarified: if you can formulate them I will answer tomorrow. But remember, when you are trying to state the problem, that its basic elements can never be clarified by the brain but only by the intelligence of the heart of Osiris in man.'

XIII

SECOND DAY

By favour Her-Bak passed the night in a room in the temple devoted to study. The atmosphere was propitious for meditation, as if the ideas under attention impregnated the walls.

When the Master came looking for him next morning Her-Bak put a question. 'You say genesis begins with division. Division is dualisation of a prime unity. Can there be division if there is no difference of nature between the parties of origin?'

'Your language is inexact where rigorous exactitude is called for. Genesis, in the created world, begins with division just as creation itself comes about through an incomprehensible scission of unity. The mistake is to carry over into unity the idea of duality. Still, you can't think otherwise: you have here the mystery of creation, a reality the Sages alone can demonstrate. But you should know that the prime mover is the spirit-word whose power is fire; the principle of impulsion itself, not common fire, which is only its image. We can only perceive its qualities when they have called forth their complements, which constitute the water-principle ... one could also call it the resistance to fire-activity that creates the first "space" in which the world is situate. You cannot without going astray imagine the abstract qualities of these two principial factors; but if you study the hieroglyphs you will learn their mutual relationships and their effects, according to the part the hieroglyphs play in the formation of the relevant words. Four letters symbolise the part of these elemental qualities in creation, N, H, S, M. The first two, N and H, refer to the activity of the quickening spirit; the other two, S and M are their product in nature. But you must bear in mind that N symbolises cosmic energy in wave-form: it is its characteristic of alternation that produces manifestation. By extension, N stands for the wave-principle, whatever kind of wave it may be. N as pure quality, pure energy, divine life, is inconceivable. It is the principle of fire in action, the very essence of form, cause of all forms. Whereas H is the principle of substance, having the nature of the water-principle, in which essential fire, source of form, works. But this substance H, proceeding from the divine source, not created, is abstract, spiritual, like the cosmic fire that quickens it.

'The two *mdw-Neters* N and H, considered in the abstract, are attributes of the cosmic Virgin, mystery that can never be put into human language. Perpetual Virgin, united with the divine Word-Fire that fertilises her and which she bears eternally, she is the mother of that uncreated light we call divine Râ.

'N is more easily comprehensible in continuous creation as an alternation of energy in Neith, the feminine principle, whose two arrows signify the alternation that gives "aspect" to everything in time . . . light and dark, warmth and cold, up and down, expansion and contraction. Their manifestation in nature is symbolised by the double letter S; the affirmative, generative aspect by S vertical; the negative, destructive, Sethian, by S horizontal, the bolt formed by two papyri as it were in opposition. The crossing of Neith's arrows and of her shuttle signify the neutralisation of opposite activities, while crossings of H signify the activation of primordial functions through which prime substance is engendered and which will be the metaphysical causes of becoming in matter. This substance is the earliest state we can conceive as substance quickening and quickened. It is the second meaning of H, the best synthetic symbol that can be contrived, a cord that seems double because it twines about itself.

'H-crossings determine moments of neutrality in causal activity and set going the reactivity that causes phenomena. Neutrality is the principle of M. As S arises from N in the world of becoming, so M arises from H. We must also distinguish between alternation and crossing: alternation gives time, crossing gives states. M in the abstract is neutrality, impassibility, the dead point of balance; it is the principle of the passive contained, formless, that gives birth to form created by an activity that fills it. M is the Idea of the contained, the receptive environment, in itself inert, that an activity may quicken. In the concrete it is the passive character of water, which will take the shape of anything that holds it. As environment M will receive and contain every kind of seed and let it fructify.

'H and M together express a living passivity, apt through its neutrality to receive impulsion but capable, when the reaction is stronger than the passivity, of letting the activity it localises take shape.

'Remember that NH signifies the perpetuity of universal life while SM makes up the name of what can take form, *sm*, and what is born of it, *ms*. Finally, the four letters together give the word *hsmn*, natron, the world's basic salt.'

'I can imagine the principles *HM* and *M*,' said Her-Bak. 'Remembering what you said about Thoth and Horus I can see the true meaning of *H*. But I find it difficult to conceive, without confusing them, the nature of the fires of *N*, Neith and *S*.'

'Are we not concerned with the very foundations of the world?' asked the Sage. 'Never pretend to understand them until through the intensity of your desire you have forced their meaning out of them. Today I'm giving you the simple ideas that are necessary to the understanding of man's make-up. Receive them as such, without confusing symbol and reality.

'*N* is always qualitative, but at various levels of manifestation. Reason can distinguish three states of *N* in this sense. First, original *N*, pure quality, pure energy, incomprehensible. Second, essential but indeterminate energy which, by polarisation, produces the complementary aspects that are symbolised by the two columns *àn*. It is *Nt*, Neith, with two arrows. It is the quickening energy that maintains everything in the universe. It gives blood its red. The red crown is its symbol. The third state of *N* is manifestation in the terrestrial world in wave-form, whatever the wave's nature and properties: wave that carries one of energy's manifestations, wave that environs, wave that refracts and reveals appearances. But *Nt*'s two arrows become concrete in nature through the dual fire of *S*, active principle that produces form; and this expression of duality, potential in *N*, decides the choice of the letters *S* and *N* to signify "double," the number two, *sn*. *S* is the active principle, essential and immortal fire, innate in matter but differentiated by the seed in and through which it works, which seed acts as character-giving leaven.'

Her-Bak savoured every word; but he felt out of depth in abstractions and sought an image. 'Master, what you say about *N*, Neith and *S* is confused in my mind with the idea of Ptah and I can't disentangle it.'

The Sage, who seemed satisfied with the point, advised Her-Bak to make a profound study of the matter. 'When you were observing the sky, *pet*, you learnt that it is the region where the power-functions we symbolise by the Neters are active. Imagine them, no longer as principles but at work in every germ, every fertilised egg . . . you will see Ptah as the smith who forges everything in the universe. Ptah is the active and causal principle who is captive through his fall into matter. The heat of his activity is the source of all life . . . we symbolise it by fire. Just as the fertilised egg carries the specific form that will be the embryo and contains the nutritive substance that will progressively increase the matter in the embryo's body, so is the world's prime matter perpetually manufactured by Ptah: we call it *pat*, or *paw* if the idea of volume is present. This is the corporal or continuous creation.

'The fertilised egg carries the principle S, essential fire as differentiated by the species, of which the egg is the product. The egg also contains the spermatic fire, S, of the father: this makes the chicken a chicken. And throughout gestation the egg will be quickened by the non-specific fire N, as is our blood throughout life. Such is the difference between the modes of action of the fires N and S, S that determines the particular, N the perpetual and universal quickener. The complementary action is symbolised by *meh*, the cow *meh-wrt*, passive and universal water-mother who conceives and carries what the fires engender. Now you are in a position to know the four bases of the world, N, H, S, M.'

.   .   .

Her-Bak tried to relate this to what he knew and his face shewed such perplexity that the Master was astonished. The disciple explained. 'Your definition of S, which gives all creatures their form and character, seems the same as what you say about KA . . ."form that gives form to substance in the making of matter . . . the hereditary specification".'

'You confuse time and phase,' the Master replied. 'This isn't surprising . . . it is difficult to grasp the idea of simultaneity in successive events. In origin S and KA *are* simultaneously; but in the process of becoming S precedes KA and KAS. Yet it would be wrong to expound with logical argument a reality the Sages have been content to state in principial terms. If you have matured your thoughts on the hierarchy of the Neters you have some insight of the principial functions. Yesterday I gave you a few succinct ideas on the spiritual factor in creatures and the causes of becoming. Now that you have a glimpse of the leading features of the problem I shall try and sketch a synthesis of principles, so that you may set in order, after the beginning of the beginning, first the origin of man created by God, then of man born of woman, then his return into cosmic Man, which is the history of consciousness.

'The first stage is a decline of the sole Cause, primordial and indefinable, into the corporal. We cannot see it otherwise as we are part of the corporal. It is impossible to invent any combination, any system, that would describe or account for it. What I shall give you will be no more than a few words, a few letters, but a faithful, precious extract from the Scheme of the ancients. What I am conveying to you is truthful but as it were detached from the treasure itself like a stone from a necklace, to give you a sufficient account and one into which no opinion or arbitrary interpretation can make its way.'

.   .   .

'In the Origin are three principles, three in one. They are unnameable and we can only designate them as *A, N, H*. No one precedes other, for though each has its properties they are perfect unity. One is inconceivable without other and proceeds from it; yet *A* is the action-principle, essential, original, source of all activity. *N* and *H* proceed from *A* and by *A* have their being, yet one can only speak of *A* through *N* and *H*. It is in *N* and *H* therefore that we must look for what constitutes the scale of powers and their manifestation.

'*A, N, H* is a triangle, three in one. *A* is in *N* and *H*, which proceed from it. *N* or *AN*, two in one, is divine fire, principle of quality and source of form. *H* or *AH*, two in one, is spiritual substance in whose passivity *AN* can work. In all three the powers that derive from them are latent.

'From *N* comes *NT*, which contains the causes of heaven and earth, the principle *S* in its primal unity, the ternary principle of the original KA. From *H* comes *M*, neutral passivity, principle of the container, and principle of the Word *Her*, the Face that is in the image of the Whole. But all these principles, not yet having interacted, are united in themselves and there are no opposites.

'Next, reflected in their own image, they are seen in their effects. From *N* proceed *NT* and Nut that contains *NT*, the energy *NR*, living light, energy come into action through meeting the resistance that equals it, with its qualities and properties; the principial element fire, which holds the different fires of the world in potential; the principles of the characteristics; the divine KA and the dual fire of *S* undivided. And through these the name-principle, the father-principle, the principle of time and all possibilities of forms and names.

'From *H* and *M* proceed the quickening word *Her*, principial water-element, womb of spirit, the mass-principle, womb of fire from which matter comes; through these the mother-principle and womb of humanity.'

.   .   .

'There is not yet the division of forces that causes nature. But the creative power of forms-in-potential is known to each of them, being fused with them, inherent. The ultimate form, the human, image of the divine Totality, knows and names all others. That is Maât-consciousness, Maât being daughter, spouse and mother of omniscient Light and source of all divine KAS that will take flesh in human wombs, to become conscious there of inferior forces and awaken the human Horus who will accomplish the return into cosmic Man. And this new consciousness, discriminative, is the second Maât, the Maât of judgment. And this "necessity" becomes the possibility of separation, through the Self's evoking the Me, the Selfsame's evoking the Other, with the desire to exist. The initiative in this is symbolised by the serpent, prime agent of choice.

'If the Me identifies itself with the Self through consciousness all will rest in eternal life; but if the Me puts itself in opposition to Self then comes the fall into matter, at which point Maât's great struggle begins: Maât must suffer in corporeity through life and death until the original condition is regained. Now N becomes the Wave, which refracts and reveals particular qualities, and Neith's arrows polarise them. S divides into the fires of Horus and Seth, HM becomes the womb, SM becomes the form or seed, and M becomes Mut, femininity pregnant, and the death that comes of it. All this, the work of Ptah, is continuous creation. Ptah is the smith who forges everything, father of the kas of nature, carrier-intermediary of human KAS.'

.   .   .

The Sage fell silent and Her-Bak waited. 'When you meditate this,' said the Master, breaking silence at last, 'you will compare it with what I said about the hierarchy of the Neters and you will be surprised over the differences in names, words and mode of instruction. Here is the reason. From the Neter-theme you learn about the genesis or successive appearance of powers and qualities that proceeds from the eternal Cause and their projection, living, into nature. The synthesis of Principles is related to the laws of Number-Entities which, contained in the original One, spring from the primal division and constitute the abstract structure of concrete nature. The two teachings refer to the same reality, but the synthesis comprises knowledge of the spiritual elements in mankind and shews the possibility of a way of return into the Source. Now we will consider the principles in their third phase, functioning in nature, so as to understand their part in the human being's make-up.

'Everything that exists is what it is through the reciprocal action of the two primordial factors S and H. Each gives the "thing" the character of the appropriate elements. You see an example in the co-existence of the yellow yoke and white water in an egg, swht. The two principles are associated in every living being, neighbours, like yellow and white in the egg. But if there is to be a chicken the yellow and white must combine, go rotten together in a chaos in which the germ will develop: the germ takes shape through the active essence *sw* and is fed by the passive substance *ht*, which is the egg's living base.'

'What you say,' suggested Her-Bak, 'seems to exhibit a second aspect of duality: *SN* meaning "*two*" and *SH* the double principle.'

'There are yet other aspects,' the Master replied. 'But those two are fundamental. Their difference lies in their part in the creature's history, of spirit, body, consciousness.

'The spiritual history of the creature is only conceivable through meditation, fusion; but you may try to grasp it schematically by means of the abstract ideas you have just been given and our symbolism. Its corporal history can be understood through study of the process of gestation throughout nature. The history of consciousness is intelligible through our own experience, regarded in the light of various states of the universal consciousness . . . ignorance of these matters increases blindness. In fact the history of consciousness is the history of BA and KA. The passage of the spiritual into the corporal, like that of substance into matter, is a mystery, the mystery of incarnation.

'Now this happens continually in nature, *N*, *H* and *S* play a quickening part in it. Never lose sight of this. The difficulty is to avoid confusing two roles expressed by the same letters: here the *mdw-Neters* will be a help to you through the subtleties that diversify their meanings.

'As to the two expressions of duality, *SN* and *SH*, I will say that *SH* plays a part in the corporal history analogous with *SN*'s in the spiritual, but with a seeming reversal of order among the factors, which results from the law of crossing. And as the spiritual and corporal aspects mingle in the mystery of incarnation, then in the mystery of quickening, so do the corporal and consciousness aspects mingle, because it is through the body that consciousness arises.

'The role of *SH* is incomprehensible unless you take account of simultaneity, for *S* and *H* are at the same time two immaterial principles and the same principles incarnate. They constitute the "egg" of everything living. Although every kind of matter is formed by the action of *S* and *H*, which is a first effort at union, every material factor that results shews the characteristic of the principle that predominates in it: thus it is with the egg's yellow and white. All natural history arises from this togetherness of two complementaries, whose attempts at union, whose successive separations and reconstructions, cause the perpetual form-makings, incarnations and rebirth of existence. Osiris, Master of Orion, is the Neter of this cycle. He suffers the vicissitudes that arise through attempts at union between *S* and *H*.

'The egg, *swht*, is an image of the human egg whose body, the only visible part, makes us forget other causal factors, energetic or spiritual, as well as their pre-existence as substance and their existence *post mortem*. The whole becoming of man and the phases of his metamorphosis have for determinant the confusion of active and passive principles, S and H, in his being and their efforts at union. It comes about little by little through an alternation of buildings-up and breakings-down, in the course of which the antagonism between dissimilar elements diminishes. In this way you can explain the progressive transformations of gross nutritive matter into the subtlest particles of the marrow, provided they find at each stage the leaven that works the change. KA plays the part of leaven throughout the metamorphosis. This happens every moment of the day and the sequence of lives; throughout the various states of the creature, its consciousness, until the state of total consciousness is reached.'

'Then my earthly life is a moment in the life of my egg?' Her-Bak asked.

'A phase in its development. The egg *was* before your body and the fruit of the egg is a first liaison of S with H through *â*, the individuality's, becoming conscious. Now the individuality is *sâh*, no longer subject to decomposition and final destruction at death but ready for spiritual evolution, as we shall see.'

'Then why,' asked Her-Bak, 'possessing so fundamental a science, don't we have it written down intelligibly instead of giving it out in riddles, incomprehensible to one who isn't directly guided?'

'You don't know yet that what is written down intelligibly is addressed to the thought of the "Other", who is always opposed to the impersonal being whose voice is the intelligence of the heart? Whereas a symbolic enigma awakens consciousness of analogies and vital functions, perception of abstract through concrete. Tomorrow we'll talk about the natural history of earthly man in subjection to the Neters; but never forget, as regards the metamorphoses of the human being during life, at death and after, that nothing one can say by way of argument and speculation has real importance. Anything one may say about it on the basis of visions and imaginative ideas is fantasy. The reality of spiritual states and their changes in man is effective and knowable. What we say about it in myth and symbol is the fruit not of arbitrary composition but of positive knowledge of the states. Part of what is affirmed is verifiable in personal experience from the beginning. The rest becomes progressively accessible to the man who, being "open-faced, open-hearted", has grown mature in the rejection of prejudice and a relentless search for the real.'

XIV

THIRD DAY

The Master said, 'Man depends on the Neters, the power-functions of nature, in all that concerns the natural evolution of his earthly life.

'You know that every part of your body is an incarnation of one or more of these functions: thus, every part is endowed, in its kind, with characteristic affinities and the reactions that belong to it. The mineral, vegetable and animal principles are found in man, with the consciousness inherent in each and their disposition: these are the elemental bases of instinct. But to organic consciousness are added the personal characteristics that attach to a man from the moment of birth through hereditary and celestial influences. All this constitutes the instinctive, emotional and organic disposition of the new-born, who bears the marks of it in his skin, chiefly the face, the palms of his hands and soles of his feet. It is the KA that shews itself in this way, a fact expressed by the word for the animal skin, *meska* product of the KA. The KA in question is that of the earthly animal-man, the instinctive-emotional being who suffers the influence of the animal KAS of the viscera. It is to him that funeral offerings are made, to appease appetites that survive the animal body a longer or shorter time depending on the man's spiritual condition. Although this KA works throughout the body its chief seat is the belly, which contains the organs of nutrition and reproduction. This is why the word for belly, *khat*, designates likewise the body regarded as an aggregate of elements in continuous gestation.'

'A corpse has this name as well,' Her-Bak remarked.

'True. Doesn't a corpse give birth to fresh animal lives? *Khat* means a vessel, container and generator of material life. The human body comprises other vessels that are called higher because they carry subtler elements and energies, the heart, the vertebral column, the blood, glands and nervous centres. They are in contact with the living air and vital fire of the universe, the breath of Amon-Râ. They correspond with higher functions and tendencies, in accordance with the divine harmony of the world of which man is the living image and sum.

'Blood, *senef*, washes your whole body and returns to the heart charged with exhausted or impure matters; the heart sends it to the lungs for revitalisation. There it is in contact with *nef*, Amon-Râ's fire and air, which consumes what is tainted and renews the life. *Ib*, the heart, and *sma*, the lungs, are the vessels in which this change takes place and are called *hati*, in which several centres of activity of your higher disposition are found. The solar plexus, near the heart, is a centre of concentration for nervous energies which react to your emotional impulses; it is also the mysterious site in which the understanding or intelligence of the heart is expressed, *sia*. It is there that a relation is established between the call of the ego and the call of the spirit and battle is joined between man's two wills.'

'But isn't it my brain that discusses and decides?' Her-Bak asked.

'Your brain is an instrument for spinning thoughts and arguments, in which partiality and error are always to be suspected. The real motive forces are your passional disposition or lower KA on the one hand and your spiritual tendency or the urge to be free on the other. Besides, rational judgments don't write themselves into you as unforgettable experiences . . . only vital reactions are agents of the immortal consciousness. Unless you take account of this you will never attain unity, *wâ*.'

.   .   .

'What do you mean by that, Master?'

'Man is more complex than you imagine. However, there is but one source: all comes from One, Amon-Râ-Ptah, three in one. The man who reunites these three factors in consciousness is himself unified, *wâ*.

'You must know how unity becomes diversity. Ptah is first craftsman of the material creation, an active and causal principle bound through his fall into corporeality. But while imprisoned in the lowest depths of the matter in which he works his active heat is the hidden force in generation. Ptah then is the hidden drive in your life; but Khnum is the potter who shapes your form, the power that mixes human seeds which Amon-Râ has blessed with his breath, that the male and female complements may be fitted perfectly together. Khnum moulds them "with his two hands" in order to reactivate the enswaddled Ptah and give effect to the gifts of the seven Hathors. For several powers or functional entities are present with Khnum at the moment of birth, the two principal being Renenutet and Meskhent. They bring to the child the characteristics of his inner nature, his KA . . . that is why in the birth chamber of our temple of Luxor, Khnum is shewn shaping the child and his KA as well. The KA then is the specific character, his particular specificity, with which the incarnating spirit must conform, the permanent factor which assures the identity of the human being throughout the process of his becoming.

'But as soon as the KA has taken flesh it arouses a personal urge, a will to live, that becomes the Me, *inek*. *Nek*, primitive blind force of human animality, quite without higher sensibility, is the principle of egoism; and this, growing with the child, crystallises the KA's tendencies to its own advantage, to affirm its existence and assure its continuity. This *inek*, this Me, that seems to be the true individual, is in fact nothing but a reflection of KA and the individual's KAS. It is this that deludes a man as to the importance of his thoughts, which likewise are nothing but a play of ephemeral forces and relative values. Thought is "the other" in relation to the intelligence of the heart, as *nek* is "the other" in relation to *iw*, the true being. Every real value appertains to the KA. It is KA that individualises and so to say binds the spirit. KA is the only factor through which immortality can be gained, the only guarantee of perpetuity to the human entity, the characteristic that only has affinity with the forces that created it. And only forces of the same kind can come back to quicken it.

'But the Me, on the look-out for what is agreeable to its egoism, doesn't concern itself with such affinity. It adopts without scruple any heterogeneous impulse that will serve its egocentricity. This creates for the individual a mass of impure and destructible factors that hinder possession of his KA on Earth and reunion with it in the Dwat.'

'The understanding of this,' said Her-Bak, 'has involved long preparation on the correspondence between parts of my body and those of the universe.'

'You may go further. You may speak of assimilation. It is the fusion of all parts of your being with those of the universe that will turn your consciousness from egoism to selflessness. All the monopolist tendencies of the Me lose their reason for existence when you become universal, aware of the cosmic harmony, aware that neither your qualities nor your knowledge are personal to yourself but imperfect reflections of the attributes of your creator.

'One may preach this, but it remains a fictitious belief as long as the individual hasn't awakened in all his members, all his being, a consciousness of functional identity with the Neters. As our ancient texts say, the doors of the blessed regions of the Dwat are closed to the dead man who doesn't know their names or the names of their guardians; but the man who absorbs the Neters, performs their cosmic functions with them, identifies his KAS with theirs and feeds himself with their qualities can say without blasphemy, I am Shu, I am Nut . . .'

'Isn't it only to a dead king that these words are attributed?'

'What does a king matter unless as a fulfilment, the perfect man? There's no question here of his Me, but of Osiris remade through the virtues and functions of Nut.'

.   .   .

'It surprises me,' said Her-Bak, 'that you should have been able to speak of all this without mention of BA. What is its connexion with KA?'

'Since all proceeds from One,' said the Master, 'we must start again from the beginning if we are to understand the matter you raise.

'Original *ia* is the causal principle of breath in its dual movement, inspiration, expiration. It is the first aspect of the one and only Spirit *iaaw*, whose second aspect is BA, divine intermediary between Heaven and Earth as original KA is the third aspect, Spirit creative and concretive. BA is the passive agent of this life-giving trinity, but it becomes an active, life-giving power in nature. It is the life-giving breath whose departure causes the death of the creature. It is also the sensitive spirit that is carried by the blood and when it has gone the blood coagulates and the heart stops beating. It is the carrier of *nef*, N-energy of Neith and F-breath of Amon. When BA gives life to *senef* and through breath and blood to the marrow it changes into energy *ner*, and in its vital quality *nefer*, which is the essence of all qualities in a living creature. This energy, active fire of the world, specialised in our marrow, is *sa*, a man's fire or vitality; a man who succeeds in becoming conscious of it can augment and use it at will. We call this controlled power *wser* and the higher man, *ser*, is one who has mastered it. Note that it is one of the KA's powers . . . KA, as you see, remains ever in relation with BA.'

.   .   .

'Now I will speak of the individual soul that is proper to man. But I can't speak clearly without discussing consciousness, which is the subject of a subsequent lesson. Today I can only talk about BA in relation to the KA through which it becomes an entity.

'BA, pure, formless spirit needs an objective means if it is to manifest. The means is the selective affinity of the thing that is to receive it, arising from the KA and its characteristics. It is the particularity of the KA that picks among the elements of foodstuffs or of an atmosphere, because there is only affinity between things of like nature: the KA acts in the same way after death of the body as regards the vital constituents of offerings and environment. The KA, stable factor in a man, differs from another man's in the particularity of its selective action. Universal BA is in continuous relation with the man to whom it gives life, and with his KA; but the KA assimilates BA and generates a new being which is his individualised soul, divine, incorruptible, immortal, yet conditioned by the acquired affinity with the KA's particularity.'

'Then the individual BA is man's spiritual factor?' asked Her-Bak.

'Surely. In its divine nature it is his kinship with the Creator. For that reason it is always incomprehensible to the cerebral intelligence, whose habit of relativity can never bring it into relation with spirit. That is why it is impossible to locate and define the individual BA, or to confine it in a body: it is immeasurable, indivisible, infractionable, free, mobile and relatively impassible to human vicissitudes. Its relation with the man is a relation of consciousness.'

'It is depicted sometimes,' said Her-Bak, 'as a bird with human head, in free flight, come to visit the dead man without letting itself be caught. Now I understand this.' He paused. 'But they say it's a question of making sure that the soul can shew itself freely and openly, which suggests that it might find itself in prison.'

'The spirit-soul can by no manner of means be imprisoned,' the Sage replied. 'The symbol refers to a struggle on the part of the dead man's higher consciousness to be free of the lower elements that haunt it "like a Shade". It is in fact through his Shade that he is involved in struggles which delay reunion of the higher KA with BA. For the divine soul, BA, can only be held by the man's particular KA in an incorruptible body when all that is foreign to it, corruptible, has been eliminated. But remember that before you interpret a symbol, such as the bird with human head, you must fathom every aspect of what it stands for and study the circumstances and the accompanying text.'

Her-Bak took good note of all he was told, but he felt impatient that he couldn't co-ordinate so much at once. 'I try to understand and obey,' he said. 'I won't try to grasp what I find incomprehensible. But could my Master not give me some information that would seem indispensable? Isn't my KA my real personality that doesn't die with the body, with which therefore I ought to concern myself above all else? I very much fear that I have often taken the Me, sad figurehead, for the KA; and I shall certainly succumb to this illusion unless I learn to discriminate what you call man's higher KA from the lower.'

'Is this not the final aim of the teaching? Wait until you have grasped all the elements of the problem.'

XV

FOURTH DAY

The Sage sat for a long time in silence. When Her-Bak shewed uneasiness he said, 'If yesterday's lesson suggests no question we have no starting-point for today's.'

Her-Bak leapt at the opening. 'Master, I didn't dare press for a definition of the KAS . . . I was waiting for the moment you might think suitable. But another problem plagues me. What is this Me that survives a man's death? The texts say it must return to its KA, keep its heart, not lose its BA nor its earthly name. Who is it whose body lies in the tomb, who isn't the man's BA, his KA nor his heart since his aim is to get possession of them? His sole attribute is his name, which he can lose, since BA, KA, *akh* and body are separate from that which is named.'

'The name,' answered the Sage, 'is the particular designation of that one to whom the constituents of the person who bore it belong. Ter-restrial birth brings them together in an individual, death dissociates them. Existence between birth and death is a loop or knot in the cord of destiny and what determines the loop or knot determines the name. But death doesn't cut the cord. Destiny continues in the Dwat, a fresh existence is prepared there, until the necessity ceases.

'The Me is the desire for personal existence; and this, though it arises through the incarnation of a spiritual being, will absorb the inclinations and appetites that belong to the KA's affinities. The Me is neither the body nor any of the spiritual factors. Its will to exist draws to it the vital attributes that clothe it. And this is the holding power of the cord that lasts as long as the will to exist prevents the soul's final liberation. There may be twists, knots, loops in it, changes of direction or name; but it remains the link between one life and another as long as the name borne in the life that precedes isn't erased before the new life begins, which would break the terrestrial destiny.'

'What happens,' asked Her-Bak, 'when a man changes his name during life?'

'The new name, if taken deliberately, maintains the continuity but alters the rhythm and the man's relations with the world. *Nek*, the Me's will to exist, is a blind force of cohesion and continuity: in every organic creature it arouses the copulative tendency *nk*. It is one of the consequences

of the seven Fatal Powers . . . you can call them "fatal" because they are
constructive and indispensable. You can also call them the seven points
of the star of Sefekht that is sealed on every creature.'

.   .   .

'We touched on the division of One into Two. Consider now the
formation of the four directions that One contains in potential. The first
syllable of *iaaw*, *ia*, denotes polarisation in the Source: north and south,
high and low, everything in nature that exhibits it, as a stick, standard,
dorsal column, a grave. The second syllable, *aw*, gives the idea of
extension, amplitude, through the possibility of volume . . . think of a
sphere rotating on its axis. Nothing can explain the why or how of the
separation of *ia* from *aw*, which produces volume through the four
directions; but we know that *ikw* denotes the tendency of One to seek
and see itself in another, a principle expressed by *ki*. *Ikw* then is the first
of these mysterious powers that are inherent in the original movement
of division. The outcome is manifestation in corporal existence. The
product of *Ikw* is *nek* and *inek*.

'The second of these powers is *Mer*, universal principle of attraction,
affinity, love. The extremities of an axis differ; north differs from south,
male from female, and one attracts the other. *Mer* is the force that urges
two complements separated by *Ikw* to rejoin. It is the motive force in
nature that has "become" through division and it works by the conjunction of complements. Selective affinity is *Mer*'s mode of action,
through the attractiveness of a given thing for some vital element conformable with its nature. This is what we mean by the phrases Merit of
the North and Merit of the South in reference to the selective affinities of
the Two-Lands that receive from Nut and Hapi the gifts appropriate to
their nature. The opposite of *Mer* is *khesef*, repulsion.

'The third power is *Sekhem*, third agent of becoming. *Sekhem* is the
power that creates darkness by annulment of two abstract principles
from which the concrete proceeds. *Khem* is the secret place of generation,
the dark and hidden centre that hides the Neter or incarnate Word until
the time for manifestation.'

'It would seem,' suggested Her-Bak, 'that the place for this should be
the womb, *hem.t*.'

'No. *Hem.t* is the container of *khem*. *Hem.t* meaning womb is the passive
container of the living chaos, *khem*, that arises with the incarnation of an
active fire, destructive or generative, such as the fire of lightning or seed.
Khem is the dark chaos that gives birth to light without knowing it, as a

mother doesn't know her child until the moment of delivery. That is why, in the vulgar tongue, *khem* means ignorance. *Sekhem* is its effective power, the destructive power from which conception arises: the male and female factors would make nothing without this pitiless force that wills the destruction of one form for the conception of another and the appearance of a new life. *Sekhem* is the liberator of the constituents of the KA. It is *sekhem* that effects the difficult disengagement so as to prepare a basis or form for the BA and the conception of a new spiritual being in the Dwat. The personification of *sekhem* is Sekhmet, who is the disintegrative aspect of Hathor in the gestation of the new being after death and of Mut in the gestation of earthly creatures.

'The fourth power is *Kheper*, the power of transformation that creates the germ. The fifth and sixth are effects of *Ikw* and *Mer*, the powers *Ab* and *Tekh* of which we shall speak in the fifth lesson. The seventh is *Seshat-Sefekht*, power of crystallisation of characters in nature, or concretion of ideas in matter. It is the expression of the characteristics of KA in the form of an individual.

'It is impossible to understand the development, first corporal then incorporal, of a human life without learning to know these seven powers. The first three are causal drives in becoming; the other four are agents of actualisation, activities that derive from the three causal drives and bring out their effects. All are incomprehensible as to principle, for they spring from substance in its abstract state, the laws of which human thought is incapable of conceiving. But the results are perceptible and it is important to make a profound study of their character and functions if you wish to penetrate the mysteries of the Dwat and to understand the spiritual metamorphoses of the human being. They are the movers that regulate all life in our universe, but they are not to be confounded with the properties of KA and the *kas*, which are active qualities of celestial bodies modified by their influence on one another. Reflected in every earthly body according to its seed, they become its *kas* or particular vital qualities. But in a world of opposites every quality has its reverse and these, as regards the *kas*, are passive attributes, *hemswt*, which manifest as resistances.'

'Râ has fourteen *kas*,' said Her-Bak. 'Has he passive attributes?'

'He has them in respect of his material body and all that is part of him on Earth. But the glorious beings that have achieved unity have no resistances.'

.   .   .

'Does the resistance of passive attributes make them evil forces?'

'There is no such thing as absolute evil. Their inertia is baneful and can be deadly if it neutralises the activity of the *kas*; but life results when resistance provokes reaction and the reactive force *nekh* prevails. Note that the root *hm* signifies living passivity, while *hms* signifies inertia, *hm* having subdued the activity *s*.'

'Why was the word *hm* chosen for royal majesty and the seer?'

'You don't see, thoughtless disciple, that it is precisely this inner passivity that gives the king his majesty and the seer his vision? It is in a state of not-willing that they receive an impulse of wisdom, capture a ray of light, recognise the true law and the true path. Woman and womb are the passive factors in animal humanity that receive and carry. And it is the passive resistance of the helm that steers the boat.'

'Master, I see how the *mdw-Neters* give the "right view", the "right idea". I see that one must seek out the meanings of passivity. Shall I be given instruction on the principle of activity?'

'The male activity of the bull, *ka*, symbolises the active qualities of the *kas*, inherent in every body and organ, since Ptah created them. And though the organs may be cosmic functions incarnate they share in each individual the characteristics of his particular KA, which I haven't yet discussed. When you are trying to fathom this subject by your sole effort note the nuances of what I have said. When I speak of the *kas* of celestial bodies I don't only refer to the stars but to all glorified bodies like the sun from which light streams. Their spiritual KA is different . . . it is no longer a question of natural vital qualities.

'As to Râ, the powers of his *kas* vary as they proceed from his material or his divine body. Here is a precise example of symbolic analogy. Râ's eye, the sun, is the visible body of being that creates Earth and gives it life; centre and master of our world. It is the perfect body that sums up the qualities and functions of the stars that depend on it, in a state of intensity, subtlety and equilibrium that indeed makes him ruler of these imperfect subjects. That is why Râ's "incorruptible" body is the type of what Pharaoh should be for our land, a being who gives life, equilibrium and strength, the leaven of his people, whose physical body radiates his active qualities or *kas* as Râ's body radiates his, which are fourteen. Râ is the living heart of the organs or worlds that depend on him: thus also Pharaoh, KA and chief of all *kas* in his realm.

'Let us sleep on this. Tomorrow we will try to learn more about these states.'

XVI

Her-Bak tried to envisage the connexion between the human personality and its spiritual elements, BA and KA. 'How can they live separately yet find each other again? How can the Me, having neither its BA nor its KA, seek and recover them?'

'Your question lacks depth,' answered the Sage. 'You look at effects without having examined the causes. The key to all problems is the problem of consciousness.

'The first business of consciousness is perception, the second registration. With the plant perception is an organic necessity. Lacking water a tree withers; it registers the withering; the effect in consciousness will be a pushing of the roots deeper. Perception and registration in this sense constitute a progression of consciousness in every kingdom and every live creature from the most primitive up to man. And all these degrees of consciousness are found in man, who is for the most part unaware of it. But note that the whole possibility of consciousness calls for a process of perception, with an instrument for the purpose and a centre of registration, of which the human being has several. The brain, that registers ideas, is the least durable seat of memory because, dependent as it is on brain-matter, memory ceases at death with the organ that was its instrument. When in order to recall an item of knowledge we appeal to memory and other cerebral faculties it shews that such knowledge is not yet written into the deeper consciousness that survives bodily death. If what we know is to last the getting of it must have affected us in such a way that we can no longer exist without taking account of it: it must have penetrated the entire being and reached into the non-mortal constituents. Organic consciousness is the consciousness that is innate in all kingdoms: it appears as instinct. In the individual it is the function-consciousness that finds expression in appetites and passional tendencies. The relation between instinctive-passional and cerebral consciousness brings about emotional and vital consciousness. What the brain records of an emotion-memory disappears on the death of the organ. But what, in the emotional sphere, is caused by life-consciousness and the organic, instinctive and passional appetites makes its impression in another mode and lasts a longer or shorter time after death.

'The sphere or mode of registration that pertains to acquired consciousness changes with the evolution of the creature, passing from a physical event to states that are less and less corporal: this, true as regards organic functions, is true also as regards higher states created in man by the spiritual quickening that is proper to him. Consciousness evolves throughout nature. In man it reaches the possibility of liberation, freedom in handling personal experience, which is the mastery or consciousness of all degrees of consciousness.'

'This is the privilege of higher man?' asked Her-Bak.

'Obviously. It is individualised consciousness. Throughout this progress, from the most primitive organism to man, it leaves traces of a lower instinctive consciousness behind it; but after a man's death it quits the body and lower *kas* and awaits the discarnate entity in the higher world to which it belongs.

'A man may accept or refuse relations with this higher consciousness and its quickening action. It is the frequency and intensity of such relations that constitute the richness or poverty of his sense of responsibility as to the choice of motives he will obey. This sense is the agent of the highest consciousness; little by little it teaches a man the connexion between cause and effect. The man who feels himself responsible, without excuse for failure if he yields to instinct, writes the meaning of experience into his consciousness in indelible characters. This is the third mode of registration. Now let us look at the effects of the various procedures.

'As to the cerebral memory that doesn't survive death, you are simply to note that if we call it *sekhaw* we also use this word for the second memory, the writing of innate tendencies into the KA that is held in incarnation and the inscription of instinctive consciousness acquired during the life. This takes place in the Shade, the dead man's instinctive and emotional body, and because of this process his image and likeness.

'The organic consciousness of the viscera, which embody the four great functions of animal existence, may be distinguished. The viscera are usually taken from the mummy, embalmed and enclosed in separate jars because they don't follow the same process of evolution. If a man has been aware of these functional entities during life they become subtilised constituents of his future being: this is what is meant when they are shewn lifted up on a lotus before the throne of Osiris. If not, they return into the consciousness of nature. The organic consciousnesses constitute the animal KAs and are part, along with the Shade, of the dead man's lower KA.

'I have described the third memory and sphere of registration as the

M

taking into consciousness of the real meaning of experience. *Tekh* is the site of this heart-consciousness, which is related with the highest part of the man's spiritual being and is his higher KA. But it is in touch with the lower KA, the aspect of Ptah imprisoned, which the consciousness of the spiritual KA alone can liberate, with the help of BA, thanks to the affinity of the one with the characteristics of the other. This is what we depict by the image of the bird-soul that returns to range about the tomb, hoping the Shade will emerge free.'

.   .   .

'It is time now to speak of the symbolism that brings together all the phases of the drama in which the dead man's fate is decided. We shew him present at the weighing of his heart in the presence of Maât, Thoth and sometimes Anubis. Generally present also are two whom we shall know shortly, Renenutet and Meskhent; *shaï* the dead man's destiny, in his own form or as a block with human head; and BA, the bird-soul, perched apart on a door or sanctuary. A monster of animal nature opens his jaws to swallow, reabsorb, everything in the man that hasn't been integrated. It is called *âmmit* or *âm-mwt* the devourer: *âmm* is the greed of nature ever ready to reintegrate with its own element all that becomes dissociated in the process of decomposition. Its anomalous structure, crocodile's head, lion's chest, hippopotamus's hind-quarters, signify elemental states each of which absorbs what belongs to it.

'Now look at what is being weighed, a heart on one plate of the balance, a feather or an image of Maât on the other. But don't overlook the third object, the plummet or weight attached to a line: this often takes the shape of a heart and is called *tekh*, which also means drunkenness, saturation by imbibition. It is the heart, *àb*, sometimes called *hati*, occult centre of the emotional life, that is being weighed.

'The counterweight that "judges" the heart is Maât, symbolised by the feather. But Maât herself is present, though not the same Maât: one is the divine, universal principle, while the other, who counterbalances the heart, is the individual Maât whom the dead man should have realised in himself. Listen to what our Sages have taught on this subject, for it is the highest in our theology: "Maât is cosmic consciousness, universal ideation, essential wisdom, proceeding ceaselessly from divine Râ, whose nourishment she is. From Maât come all incarnate rays of wisdom, all human KAS. That is why the dead man is sometimes made to say, "I came from Râ's mouth".

'Maât then is in truth the highest consciousness man can make his own, that which comes to him at his quickening. She is the agent and the vehicle of Râ's essence and a man only lives in spirit when his lower KA unites with the higher, a ray of Maât becomes his own Maât in his own consciousness.

'Think this well over. Nothing can be assimilated to Maât that is not of Maât's nature, true and indestructible consciousness. All that comes of the lower personality, all that is mortal, fictitious, cerebral, alien to the individual's essential KA, is rejected. Whence "the judgment of Maât". For Maât, judge of the heart, is his own Word in the man in whom Man has become conscious and realised. If the heart, centre of emotional and intuitive life, is not identified with this Word there is grave risk that it will be lost in the adventure of the Dwat. Thus, it is essential that you should recognise the functions of the two hearts that play a leading part in your life.'

'But Master, I haven't got two hearts,' Her-Bak protested.

'Not I but the hieroglyphs say it,' the Sage replied. 'I am not speaking now of your spiritual and fleshly hearts, for the one is nothing but the symbol and physical organ of the other. By the "second" heart I mean that which governs the oscillations of the balance, the plummet, to which the Neter who supervises the weighing gives all his attention. The symbolism of the plummet, *tekh*, touches one of our most sacred mysteries . . . still, I must speak of it or you will find everything I have yet to say incomprehensible. I will try to clarify matters by the parallel between its symbolism and that of the word *àb*. In both there is a double play of word and idea which puts the physical and psychic functions or states in relation with one another and with an object or organ that explains the double meaning, concrete or abstract.

'In the words *àb*, thirst, and *ab*, desire, although their determinants may differ, it is *àb*, heart, that gives exactly the relation between them. *Àb*, written with the concrete à, means thirst; *ab*, with the abstract *a*, means desire. This dual aspect of a function, physical need on the one hand and emotional desire on the other, is found again in the meaning given to the word *àb*, heart, according as one has in mind the organic heart that drinks blood or the centre of psychic activity. The symbolism of *tekh* likewise contains a double play between the word for an object, *tekh*, and the state of drunkenness or saturation denoted by its homonym, between the role of the plummet, *tekh*, and the absorptive capacity implied by *tekh* as a state of saturation. There is then a direct relation between these two ideas: drunkenness conveys the idea of imbibition to saturation-point. Again, when something dry is soaked in liquid to saturation-point it can't absorb any more . . .'

'Like a sponge in water,' put in Her-Bak.

'The image won't do. There is no question here of container and contained: if one said that a jar filled with water was *tekh* it would be wrong. The idea of drunkenness suggests extinction of a fire. A thing's absorption-capacity depends on the measure of its dryness, caused by its inner fire. The fire that brings on dryness is Seth's. Whether in the sands of the desert or in a consuming fever or in the bitterness of egotistical passion it is always Seth's fire that tends to make use of natural forces on behalf of natural passions that are its fuel.

'As against this destructive activity our symbolism presents the compensative action of "the waters of heaven and earth", the "water of rejuvenation" that revives the dead, the tears of Isis and the "new water" of Hapi that restores vegetation to arid earth.

'Next, imbibition supposes an absorption-capacity in that which drinks the reviving water, the greater as the fire is the more intense. It is true then to say that the absorption-capacity is a measure of the fire, that evoked compensation. It is the part of the plummet, to shew this.

'The laws of generation shew that every living thing is formed by the alternate action of fire and water. Seth's fire never seeks, of itself, to absorb the compensating water, but rather to consume everything and increase its combustibility. But in a living creature its very aggressiveness awakens a reactive and defensive power which calls out the compensating factor. It is this reaction that makes the creature "absorbent" to the point of satiety or exhaustion of the fire's greed. The reaction can work in the reverse sense if the inimical factor becomes predominant.

'*Tekh* then, in the process of generation as in the weighing, is the witness or intermediary that guarantees the free play of contrary forces in the measure that is possible. The part of witness between the emotive heart *àb* on one plate of the balance and the individual Maât on the other gives *tekh* an important part also in the determination of the destiny *shaï*, sometimes shewn in the judgment scene as a block with human head. *Shaï* measures the individual destiny, the foreordination of which, prenatal and natal, Seshat writes in the embryo and the man's will and actions sign it daily.'

.   .   .

'I see that,' said Her-Bak, 'but I still find the spiritual aspect of the heart a riddle. Even more enigmatic are the words, "O my heart of my mother . . . you are the KA of my metamorphoses." '

'Consider deeply what has just been explained,' answered the Sage.

'You will understand if you study the parallel between the role of the heart *àb* and the role of *tekh* once more. The heart *àb* is the equilibrating agent of the blood-stream; *tekh* that of the elements fire and water in every generative process, witness and intermediary as regards their fluctuations. Now just as *àb* means an organ as well as a function so there necessarily exists in the human organism a centre that performs the *tekh*-function, and an equivalence of function as between a man and his KA. The higher KA plays an analogous part with that of the "water of rejuvenation". The lower KA, which comprises the psychic characteristics of the personality, and suffers the animal urges of the organism, suffers also the aggressiveness of Seth's fire and the compensating reaction.

'*Tekh*, point of contact between these impulsions of the two KAs, is their witness. It plays the part of a heart-consciousness that keeps the record of this perpetual vital experience and in consequence survives death. Likewise it is the "KA of the changes" that incarnates in the embryo, ever-present witness of the successive metamorphoses of the creature.'

'This throws light,' said Her-Bak, 'on the text that troubles me, "O heart of my mother, O KA of my transformations!" But as to the heart, the complexity of the subject still leaves me in some confusion.'

'It isn't surprising. Your difficulty is an imagination that dissects and labels the constituents of a spiritual being. All is in everything. Each part contains the principle of the others, with accent on properties that are its own. Cut off a man's leg and the physical member disappears: not so the principle, which lives on so that the man feels sensation as if the leg had never been amputated. Don't assume discontinuity between various states of the organism, from the most material to the most spiritual. Every part of the being, physical or spiritual, shares its entirety: with all the more reason do we say that the heart, a man's sun in a physical sense as well as in reality, cannot be independent of the rest of him . . .'

'. . . any more than the sun is independent of Earth?'

'Precisely. There are continual exchanges between them on which the harmony of the system depends. In the formation of the universe all necessarily "becomes" in accordance with one sole harmony: if the planets have a share in the sun's heart they themselves have a sun in their own. Man's constitutive elements are in relation with their cosmic analogues. Your divine KA, ray of universal Maât, and your BA are in the same relations with spirit as those which link Maât with the divine Râ whose daughter and nourishment she is. Your physical heart, in respect that it is a sun in your body, contains the double, active-passive principle we depict as a solar egg surmounted by a crescent moon. The heart in its passive or lunar state is feminine, maternal, so that in this aspect I can say "the mother is in the heart"; but if I wish to separate the idea of "mother" and study her in herself then the heart is in the mother.'

This exasperated Her-Bak. 'What use are these riddles except to complicate what is already complicated enough!'

'You ask to have the mysteries explained: is it your wish that I should use the superficial formulas of the Peristyle?' Crestfallen, the disciple bowed. 'Solar activity in the heart,' the Master continued, 'gives the creature form and makes him tributary to Râ. Lunar passivity gives understanding, if it reflects light. Solar activity brings light if passivity elicits it. Crossing is the law of laws: this is the key to all enigmas. Enigmas are for those who have the key. Logic is for the blind who only touch ground with their stick.' The Master fell silent.

.   .   .

Eyes closed, Her-Bak wrote these principles in his consciousness, hoping for confirmation in that experience. At last, calm, respectful, he spoke.

'I have but glimpsed what is hidden in the imagery of the heart, but I see already what accusation heart-consciousness would bring against my human heart if it rejected this lesson. Every detail in the judgment-scene must be thought out . . . thank you indeed for what you shew me. May I hear again what part *inek* plays?'

'The Me,' answered the Sage, 'is the bearer of the name, *ren*, who stands helpless at the weighing. The name is the word of the human personality manifest; correctly given it should express his KA and his nature. It is the magic formula that preserves his image in man's memory. It is the clothing of *inek*: that is why when this egotistical Me effaces itself and a man becomes conscious of his real aim, which lies in selflessness, we modify his name so as to put it in harmony with his true being and function.'

'Why does the bird-soul stand aside during the weighing?'

'The divine soul is neutral, impassible, indifferent to personal matters. If a man has failed to cultivate the affinity of his KA for the soul, if he hasn't established by constant appeal to his spiritual being a relation of reciprocal consciousness, the soul returns to its own country and its unified being can't be realised.'

'You haven't explained the role of the two personages Meskhent and Renenutet who attend the weighing.'

'Her-Bak, you ask too much for one day. Moreover, you wouldn't recognise those two without having understood what we mean by "forms, envelopes and skins." If you wish to speak of a thing as eyes and fingers perceive it, how do you name it?'

'We have several words . . .'

'Those that matter are *irw*, *qd*, *sem*. There is a great difference between these words, whose sense the profane often distort. In *sem*, *m* is what retains form: *sem* in its absolute meaning is "to make a thing take form," form specified by *s* . . .'

'*Sm* also means "to bless",' put in Her-Bak.

'In reference to the spiritual meaning. If you wish to learn wisdom through language you should look for the basic meaning of syllables and not be led astray by vulgar usages that enable us to convey secret teachings and veil them at the same time. The basic principle of form is expressed by *qd*, the essential character of the thing, the innate form round which the apparent form is constructed. The absolute meaning of *irw* is the present state, what has been made, shaped; state and quality being changeable because not innate but acquired. Our texts play constantly on these words: see that you don't neglect them.'

'Doesn't the word *kheprw* refer to form?'

'*Kheper* is the becoming of form, the manifestation of change. There is a subtlety in our thinking that comes not from a child's game of analysis but from knowledge of the profound motive that appearance hides; and we try by choice of words and images to awaken discernment in the reader. Our Masters always considered what is contained and what contains: what is contained is what is hidden, what contains is what hides. Thus, as regards the human embryo, *ànm* is the skin while *àmn* is what it hides, everything Amon formed, membrane, air, water, with the stable element *mn*, contained in Amon. *Khen* is our leading symbol for that which encloses and for the natural force that makes its own envelope. This force is the reactive energy *nekh*, the effect of which is expressed by the word *nekht*. The symbol of *khen* is a quadruped's skin, all but the head: it took and has kept that form because the skin is an emanation of the animal nature. This shews the meaning of envelope and skin. Skin takes an impression of personal characteristics, which is why it serves as symbol in the funeral scene of the *tikenw*, and in the mysteries of Abydos, which demonstrate the necessity of "returning into the skin" to be reborn to a new life. This isn't a purely notional image. The skin is the living and perceptible image of the imperceptible envelopes that preserve a man's form. *Khen* is the perfect material expression of this because it shews the identity of within and without, this being the creature of that. In speaking of "within" I don't only mean the organic body but the vital powers and the action of the two hearts *tekh* and *àb*, the factors that express individual characters and qualities. Just as the skin, *khen*, preserves the animal form so the invisible envelopes that emanate from a man, while part of his inner being, preserve impressions after death . . . they are centres of registration.'

'How is it we can't perceive these envelopes?' asked Her-Bak.

'Can you see the air you breathe? Yet you are aware of it as you are aware of a man's sympathetic or repellent atmosphere. You must come back to the *mdw-Neters* if you are not to mistake what we mean by envelopes.

'The causal principle of an envelope is *wt* . . . try to see the profound meaning of this. We depict *wt* by an empty skin, which is shewn sometimes wrapped round a stem rising from a pot. Another image for it is the principle of the gland. *Wt* means limitation, definition of a space by limitation in matter; whence the use of this word for embalming, which holds the mummy in a condition of incorruptibility and preserves its form in bandages. For the same reason *wt* signifies the Sethian skin of Anubis that holds the spirit in prison. *Wt* is heaven enclosed, a thing limited by volume and that which takes volume. It is the germinal idea of an organ, gland and incarnate function. That is why we say the Shade is purified if there is no *wt* left in it; that is to say, no germ of an organ or animal function in a state of becoming.

'Now consider all words constructed on the *wt* idea. *Nwt*, or *Nut*, is the energic, aerial container of all the *wt* in the world. *Mwt*, *mut*, is the material container of *wt* that preserves form and fixes it in a containing space. *Twt* is the manifest form of an image in which *wt* is displayed. *Swt* is *wt*'s concrete specification. Finally, if you recall the dual principle *SH* you will see that the egg, *swt*, is the perfect type of *wt* concretised and quickened by those two vital and essential principles. This will corroborate for you the exact meaning of *sâh*, in which *wt* is replaced by *â*, the letter of individuality: you won't find the *t* of concretion. *Sâh* is the state of the man who, after death, has kept the two vital principles together, though not conjoined, as you've heard.

'It is interesting that we define *swt* by the form of an egg and *sâh* by the seal that fastens an envelope. Our ancient texts often speak of the dead man who must "break his egg". It happens in such texts that *swh* is given by the sign for a city, *nwt*: it isn't a question of a city but of the dead man's own *nwt*, his egg, his surviving envelope.

'A man's *nwt* is like the celestial Nut whose physical organs are the constellations of the zodiac. Their functions differ, in man's body as in hers; but their influences interpenetrate, though they can only communicate with essentially identical states and through an intermediary.

The heart is in sympathy with the intermediary and plays the same part in man's body as the sun does in our universe.'

.   .   .

'Then whether it is a man, a city or a sky, *nwt* is the energic container of all the *wt* in it.'

'You are right to insist on this,' the Sage replied. 'For a thorough study of *wt* will save you many mistakes over the envelopes. It is a subject that lends itself to too many fantastic interpretations. To obviate this danger we have varied Nut's symbol, in case the student fixes his thought on one only. Take Nut as the night sky. Earth is surrounded by a sky in which groups of stars make a belt of light and life: Earth receives their influences turn by turn through the annual cycle. The sky, Earth's Nut, gives birth every day to the sun, which returns every evening into her womb. Night follows day and Earth sleeps until morning. But during her sleep terrestrial creatures live another life of which they have no memory on waking: in the same way the lives of men, who are born, die, or rather sleep to awake to a different kind of life in the Dwat, succeed one another. The nightly sleep may end sooner or later in an eternal sleep if KA and BA are not reunited in the lower man who has failed to cultivate an affinity with them. As for the discarnate man who "passes to his KA," all he has taken into his consciousness, vital, spiritual or instinctive experience, is written in his personal Nut; and what is written affects, in its kind, the centres, forms or spiritual states of his being, which thus become his creations. We shew this personal Nut as a tree whose fruits are the sum or harvest of lives lived by a human KA. Thot-Seshat writes the name of the man whose KA this is on the last of them and its celestial Nut feeds it with these same fruits, harvest of its lives. The root of the tree is in Earth as long as the man works out his terrestrial destiny in a series of rebirths. Its trunk is Nut's body, or the man's if he has become fully conscious. Its branches and interlaced leaves are in the sky; they are his own emanations, envelopes, energic or spiritual states in which he was at one with cosmic states of the same kind; they are centres or planes of registration which preserve and sum up the experience of the "person" and decide his fate.

'I should detail these centres or planes; shew you the relationship between the human egg and each fruit of the sycamore. But to do this would go beyond the scope of this lesson. Sleep, Her-Bak, if you are to hear instruction tomorrow. It will be the same subject under other names and from another view-point.'

XVII

SIXTH DAY

Her-Bak waked more than he slept, possessed with anxiety lest he forget what he had learnt. He welcomed the Master, saying, 'If I have really understood what you have taught, the human body is a perceptible appearance of other forms, more or less spiritual, whose togetherness constitutes individuality. The survival-time of each differs according to the degree of its harmony with the man's Maât.'

'This is correct,' said the Sage, 'if your understanding of "form" is correct likewise.'

The weariness of sustained effort marked Her-Bak's face. 'Master,' he begged, 'how without error can I imagine states so complex? Our symbols shew the bird BA, the KA, the Shade, Destiny, in separation, yet you speak of their simultaneous presence in the human being, you talk about their differences and their kinship. If death parts them, what becomes of them in the Dwat? What happens to the Me that was their image on Earth? We name places where they sojourn, the island *neserser*, the field of reeds, the field of offerings: are they symbols or realities? It troubles me. Can you give my heart peace?'

The Sage understood the true measure of his disciple's effort, but he was unwilling to compromise an intuitive awakening by soothing his disquiet. 'Symbols,' he said, 'are always a mystery for the man who isn't "open-faced", whose inner senses aren't awake, so that he can only perceive the earthly, tangible aspect of things. Call the Mistress of Heaven Hathor, to your aid, Hathor, who holds Earth, Heaven and the Dwat in contemplation, Hathor, mother of your God, house of divine Horus, of "your Neter that is in your egg". Make her eyes yours that you may see the celestial Luminaries. Make your ears so quiet that they may hear the word of the celestial Bull. Let your nostrils, obedient to the rhythm of its breath, inhale Life and know it. Let your mouth, scorning idle words, learn to utter the words of Maât. Then you will see the meaning of symbols that were drawn by the open-faced and open-hearted, those who can see Hathor's other aspect.

'It was wise, when you framed your question, to associate the idea of various regions with that of states of being in the Dwat: you can't separate them. Just as a *nwt* or city is an assemblage of "atmospheres" emanating from heaven and from men, which give the city its character, so also a man's *nwt* is a complex of influences and impressions that sum up the states of his successive personalities. In the same way a region of the Dwat is an environment, clearly distinct from another, to which those whose disposition and state are in affinity with it are drawn. If you see this you will understand the idea of coming, or passing, from one atmosphere to another, by which we indicate the action of an ineluctable power, the law of selective affinity that imposes itself between things, states and beings of the same kind. It was in this sense that the texts say of the dead man "He has come to the land of life . . . you have come living . . . he has come in his name of . . . in the capacity of such and such a Neter or function." As if you said "He has passed into the state of . . . he has taken the nature of . . ." '

.   .   .

Her-Bak gave his mind to this. 'It means that I have to develop another way of thinking. May I ask whether there is space or distance between these places?'

'Space and time are relative to conditions. A gnat's life seems as long to its time-consciousness as its many years to an elephant. For the immortal spirit there is neither time nor space. Through its human situation it is in relations with both, but remains unaffected since in its divine nature it is simultaneously aware of all dimensions and all durations. But this, Her-Bak, can't yet penetrate your intelligence. That is why you must teach yourself by symbols, for they are the quickest way from the world of appearance to the world of reality. Remember that to speak of the regions of the Dwat is to speak of the states of a being and his metamorphoses. If you visit known or unknown countries in sleep it is your astral body that travels while your physical body lies on the bed. The two bodies are linked by a subtle cord the breaking of which causes death. The "form" that goes out of you is part of what will be your Shade. It has properties your physical body lacks because its subtler substance is not subject to the same laws. It can wander space without physical means. It can go through walls . . . physical obstacles don't exist for the non-physical. But spiritual states, worlds, bodies, are inaccessible to it in the same way as a wall is impenetrable to your body. Time and space have a very different relation with it from what your intellect conceives. Besides, you have certainly had extraordinary adventures, lasting a long time, in dream, brought on by some incident a moment before you woke up: in this case your mental and intuitive consciousness evokes images of scenes lived through by your astral body, shewing the difference between your physical concept of time and space and what the astral body knows of them. You can have consciousness, then, of the lowest of such invisible bodies or states.

'If, moreover, you awaken your inner ear and succeed, through the intelligence of the heart, in perceiving the qualitative analogy between certain vegetables and certain living beings you put your KA in contact with theirs, and this mode is the more subtle as you seek the experience after elimination of the mental factor and without making it depend on your personal impressions and tastes. Such consciousness of the KA is of a higher grade than the astral or emotional consciousness; and although the Shade may be as it were the clothing of your lower KA it necessarily shares the higher experience, which makes it subtler and less tyrannical in its earthly affinities.

'Climb a step higher. Try to relive some experience in which your lower inclinations fought with the heart's wisdom . . . remorse over some fault, or the quenching of an egoistic desire . . . which wrote a memory of real importance into your consciousness. Consciousness of this order directly touches your divine KA and enriches your fate-body. In yet higher states the lower personality is liberated. The wise man can attain them on Earth, and they are perfected in the Dwat by those who gain possession of their KA. Our texts refer to this when they "hail Nut in the name of a ladder." It is his own ladder the man must climb, the progressive consciousness of his own Nut, whose richness grows with each metamorphosis.'

'I see this,' said Her-Bak. 'I catch sight of what we must understand by the regions of the Dwat . . . certainly not fields, rivers or islands.'

'We have to present men with familiar images, since for the most part they are incapable of the abstract. However, another example will shew you the reason for the symbols we choose. You have seen desert-mirages: if they seem to depict real landscapes they are deceptive and upside-down. Thus it is with illusory pictures of the Field of Reeds. Everything that is registered in the emotional life is reflected in the "robe of Nut" or akashic screen and lasts for a time that is determined by the life of the lower consciousness involved. Those who live in the Field of Reeds are such as still feel drawn by their Shade to the attractions of Earthly existence; they relive the mirage that was their life still in the grip of hostile forces that prevent their passing to a higher state. It is in the other world as in this: slaves of the Me, whom the tyrannical inclinations of the lower KA hold back from the higher, strive to increase the number of their companions in slavery. The Field of Reeds and the Field of Offerings are to be regarded as inferior heavens. They are shewn with lakes and streams because men float there in a state of uncertainty, awaiting successive changes; with islands to signify that one is stuck in certain conditions; with fields because it is a question of "making one's own plant grow in the marshes", a new subtle body that is conformable with the new state of affairs, fit to shew the "true face".

'Now comes a term in the island *neserser*, which can't be located in time or space but is intermediary between Earth-life and the Field of Offerings. To sojourn there is a first beatitude. *Neserser* means a state created by the ceaseless play or circulation of the two fires or energic forces *n* and *s* which take shape in earthly creatures. These are the fires that colour and specify a man's nature or disposition . . . that is why it is said regarding *neserser* that "the heir rejoins his father to make sure of his inheritance and the continuation of the paternal name on Earth". There is reference here to the occult link and instinctive affinities of character between the discarnate father and the son who bears his name. One might think of *neserser* as a subtler Earth that reflects tendencies, dispositions, in their universal aspect. It is in this "place" that the discarnate man must exhaust and consume his instinctive desires until the time comes when having quenched his thirst he is free and recovers his "true face".'

.   .   .

'Has this,' asked Her-Bak, 'the same meaning as something else you said: "Wholly to recover his own Word, which is to realise his own Maât?" '

The Master shewed satisfaction, 'You have taken the point. That is why the weighing of the heart is said to take place in that region; for when purification is accomplished it is no longer the Me that is in command but the *sâh*, that one who having mastered the "fires" possesses his heart, his KA, and may pursue the development of his consciousness through the metamorphoses that take place in these lower regions in peace.'

'Why must there still be such changes?'

'Before he gains the supreme bliss of the higher heavens the man must have renewed his consciousness of all intermediary stages, states of becoming that are reflected on Earth in various states of life. If during earth-life he has succeeded in identifying his whole being and all his functions with the functional Neters and cosmic powers, further metamorphoses are unnecessary and he is ready "to become like one of them", free from the world of appearance. But if his experience is still incomplete he will await in the beatitude of the Field of Offerings the time for his return to Earth, gathering the fruits of experience without being separated from his BA or his KA. In this way there is reborn a being who will incarnate on Earth as a higher consciousness than before.'

'Is it true that a man may return to Earth several times?' asked Her-Bak in surprise.

'Many times if he hasn't "acknowledged" his KA. But the "person" doesn't benefit consciously from this. It doesn't know it, for individual consciousness only lives through the KA. In such a case it can hardly be said that there is reincarnation, but continuity of instinctive life in confusion with other instinctive lives. It is useless to teach this to those whose life is only instinctive.

'As for a man who has acquired the consciousness of the KA, he must learn to increase his sense of responsibility and of the fact that everything he does will have its consequences. He must be personally instructed in those matters we generally leave to be understood by words and allegories that conceal in the broad idea of the renewal of life that of a repetition of births. It is for such a man we symbolise the regions and states, the judgments, that determine waiting-periods in the Dwat, with the tests or beatitudes appropriate to the measure of his liberation. It is for him that we insist on the necessity of preserving the memory of the Earthly name, for it is a factor in reincarnation. Statues, tombs decorated with scenes of daily life, have the advantage that they attract the KA and assure its reincarnation in the same region or line of descent.'

.   .   .

'This isn't the moment to give proofs and the reasons that justify this. But I will explain two relevant symbols. I spoke of Meskhent and Renenutet who are present at the weighing of the heart. They are present at birth as well.

'You remember that the name, *ren*, if judiciously chosen, is a formula indicative of individual identity and defines the personal cycle in which "possibilities" are realised. Also, well or ill-bestowed, the name, being pronounced, becomes the image that the man who bears it will evoke in men's memories. *Ren-nutet* is the perpetual movement in the functions of nature. It is the necessity of the cycle, every function giving rise to the next so inevitably that the end sets up an analogous rebeginning at the point where the cycle started. It is Renenutet who turns the humours of a mother's blood into milk. It is she who makes the sap rise when the time of Osirian lethargy is over. It is she who feeds the radicles of the buried seed and the grain in the ear of corn, the root of the tree and its fruit. It is through Renenutet that the *djed*, the pillar of Osiris, is raised in nature or man; and it is she who when he has reawakened the fire of life in his *djed* leads it to the summit, the frontal uraeus that is the third eye of Horus. Then "the Neters fear him", for this eye of fire masters them and rules their blind powers. Thus Renenutet is an agent of all renewal, as for instance of the annual cycle in the sky. She wraps the newly born in the orbit of his personal cycle, cradles him in his own rhythm and supports him within the limit of his possibilities. She preserves the name of every species and individual, since she is the compass of the particular cycle that governs their periodic return.

'Meskhent is the expansive force that makes outer arise from inner, brings things to light, causes what was within to be born, the child, the skin, the subtle envelope every man spins from himself and thanks to which he can respire, breathe in radiant light.

'During terrestrial life these two powers form an integral part of the individual and his Nut. Death separates them from the body but they remain attached to the surviving entity by affinity of the name with this "Meskhent" or skin that conserves his imprint. If there is rebirth they reappear and make the link with the previous life, Renenutet as guardian of the terrestrial cycle, Meskhent as the womb in which the being who is to reincarnate is reborn in the Dwat. This is what is meant by texts that speak of the "Meskhent-house" inhabited by the discarnate in the lower heaven: "house" or "jar", they call it; "this house, in this night of birth, is a jar", they say. Such a place of sojourn, house, or subtle envelope is the Meskhent in which the Me should efface itself without trace and give way to the *sâh*, the essential principles of the living entity. This will be realised when all thirst is quenched, all dust swept away: you understand that thirst is the power of passional tendencies, dust the heterogeneous residue of the Me. At this stage the *sâh* can ascend in the Field of Offerings, where it will find the spiritual abundance of a higher state and will eat the fruits of consciousness acquired during life on Earth in beatitude. The characteristic of the Field of Offerings is the possibility of becoming spirit among spirits. When the trials of the Field of Reeds are over the spirit can emerge from the darkness of the swamps.'

Her-Bak interrupted. 'Is it written that it will find its Meskhent there?'

'Yes, but purified and glorious. Don't let these images trouble you, Her-Bak. The awakening of a higher consciousness wipes out illusory forms, replaces them with vision of the causes that bring about these effects. The new being's vision develops and is purified in successive stages as different from one another as the stages of transformation from grub to chrysalis, nymph, butterfly. Shall we call these stages worlds, regions, or bodies? Each has its particular life, with creatures of the same disposition; this constitutes its world. And each change is only a purification, a divestment of transitory forms acquired on Earth that shut out the vision of a luminous reality.

'But listen again to what you must know about the lower heavens. Access to the Field of Reeds is by purification in water and in the marshes: then, our texts say, the purified one is thought of in heaven as Sah, Orion, with whom he now identifies himself, and Sothis will be the third element of the triad that leads the happy *sâh* to the sources of life, *nefer* of the heavens. Note that Sah, Orion, is with Sothis the constellation that rules the Osirian periods of Earth and men; thus, the human *sâh* is Osirian and should be reborn on Earth as Osiris is reborn in vegetation at the time of renewal.

'The characteristic of the island *neserser* is the fixation of consciousness of that which has the nature of earth and fire: that is why we locate there the struggle between the fires N and S, which accounts for the judgment there of the dual heart *âb-tekh* as well as the presence of the terrestrial ancestors and animals. It is there that a man becomes son of Geb, the Neter of Earth.

'But there is one other possibility in the Dwat. We are advised to "avoid the water-ways of the West and choose the ways of the East". That has to do not with the way of Osiris but the way of Horus and it will be the seventh day's lesson.'

XVIII

SEVENTH DAY

Her-Bak asked his Master to summarise the factors that constitute man
on Earth and in the Dwat.

'If I could put everything in a rigid scheme,' the Sage replied, 'what would
it amount to? Words. Notions evoking images that don't conform with
reality. You can't isolate the bodies and states we have talked about: the
human being is an egg in perpetual gestation. The names we give them
merely denote transitory conditions which pass into one another often
enough and can be named otherwise. Earth receives the light of the sun
and moon but they are the same light. Throughout these talks I have
discussed each state at the suitable time: you will be able to connect what
is relevant, but resist the temptation to define and separate or you will
go wrong.

'It is the dispersal of our theme that troubles you, because you try to
grasp it outside yourself. If you would build something solid, don't
work with wind: always look for a fixed point, something you know that
is stable . . . yourself. Your bodily form is an illusory solid, perishable:
what caused it is a real solid, the *djed*, word of Amon-Râ-Ptah, established
in you and become your own. This *djed*, word or pillar of Osiris, is the
base of relative stability, principle of whatever is durable in the Osirian
world, the world of becoming and return. It is for you to make it eternal,
your own *djet* secure against agents of destruction.'

'Master, what is the *djet*? You've said nothing about this.'

'Can I speak of the end before the beginning? The *djet* is the inborn
Word, shut up in the lowest depths of mortality, awakened, freed and
become your essential, incorruptible body. This awakening is the mystery
of mysteries, the secret of resurrection, and I shall only speak of it because
it is a link without which the chain would be incomplete. But if the rites
of Osiris teach men how to form the immortal body we teach also that
the *djet* remains prisoner of Earth and Osiris unless Râ comes to deliver it,
"unties the ropes" and "undoes the knots".

'The two principles Râ-Osiris have been from the beginning the life-
givers of the human *djed*. We symbolise them as the souls of Râ and
Osiris shut up in the physical *djed* or pillar. They are two currents of
universal life whose source is one though they are two in the creature.

They differentiate the two fires, *nefer*, of the dual Osirian *djed* as they differentiate the two eyes and the two luminaries. This duality is the cause of terrestrial continuity, recurrent existence and the endless metamorphoses of the Osirian way. To escape from such slavery the solar soul must absorb the Osirian; the universal must vanquish the particular.'

.   .   .

'You have two eyes, Her-Bak. Their function is sight, *maa*. It is by insight that this word is sometimes written with two eyes and the falx or sickle-shaped membrane between them, for looking would give a double image were it not joined up in the brain. The two eyes are stimulated by the dual fire that runs up the dorsal column; the light of Râ quickens your right eye, while your left belongs to your Osirian KA. When a man is united with his higher KA the left eye becomes the eye of Maât from whom this KA derives: then may take place the union of Râ with Maât which lights the third, the Horus-eye, the eye of intuitive vision. There is no longer double sight and union in the personal Maât follows. You understand now the symbol of Pharaoh's frontal uraeus?'

'It is the third eye, the eye of Horus. Does this image symbolise an extraordinary power that is Pharaoh's?'

Say rather that it belongs to the perfect man of whom the ideal Pharaoh is the symbol. It is power itself through the victory of real over illusory sight, when the personal KA is taught and ruled by the higher KA and the two consciousnesses are fused. The texts tell us that this total KA, one with its indestructible *djet*, will with the soul's help become the leaven that can work in the other and lower KAs, feed on them and transmute them to its own spiritual nature.'

'Does this refer to man's life on Earth or in the Dwat?'

'It can only be done in the Dwat if it has been more or less accomplished within what is possible on Earth. Note that I have drawn special attention to what is the aim and perfection of human life. In the mass of earthly men only a few, who are of "those in the know", can aspire to it. The rest, ignorant or still governed by instinct, must still suffer the troubling alternations of Earth and the Dwat. For them, ignorance of the end that makes man the centre of his world renders beginning and end, birth and death, incomprehensible . . . they know nothing of the factors that come together in the human being or of the dissociation that terminates his existence. If you would know yourself, Her-Bak, take yourself as starting-point and go back to its source: your beginning will disclose your end. In reality you are the sum of the life of Amon, because you embody the

KAS of all nature in your humanity. Now Ptah, KA of the trinity Amon-Râ-Ptah, creates nature's bodies and KAS and it is the KAS of nature that make the body of Amon.'

'Why do you say Amon, not Amon-Râ-Ptah?'

'Because, while the three are one, Amon is the western aspect of which one phase is fulfilled for Earth. At one time the worship of Ptah and the image of Min symbolised an earlier phase of incarnation. Now there rises on the horizon a hope of a solar dawn of which Râ will be the symbol. This cosmic sequence is repeated in the successive phases of an individual destiny. Look on your ostensible self, Her-Bak, as a statue of flesh that encloses and hides the multiple aspects of the living you. At your beginning, from the moment of conception, Khnum shaped your egg as he shaped the world-egg; but before it could take bodily form he shaped it in essence with the ideas of your limbs and organs, helped by the forces at work when you were conceived. Then he wrapped it in skins and each fold took the impress of the cosmic force that was relevant.'

'What am I to understand by the "skins"?'

'Here it isn't a question of membranes but of exudations more or less subtle, aerial or fluid, that derive from the embryo or its mother, from Earth or Heaven that is. Each is a state, atmosphere, envelope or skin that sometimes surrounds, sometimes imbues, an embryo, a star or a grain, according to its function and subtlety. Whether it is the amonian water of *Nw* or the aerial envelope of Amon, they correspond respectively with the liquid that bathes the embryo and the membrane that contains it. Another envelope, formed later, derived from the embryo, by means of which the mother transmits nourishing humours, is equivalent to the lunar atmosphere that surrounds Earth. Finally, an outermost envelope produces all the child's skins, external and internal. The new-born keeps only the latest of the material skins, but all the cosmic "states" that made the embryo's envelopes in their image remain part of the child and become subtle states of the living being. When you know how to read our riddles you will discover innumerable details regarding the connexion of these states with the organs and nervous centres and their becoming in the Dwat. Just now I must limit myself to strictly necessary examples.

'Renenutet and Meskhent play their part in the formation of the egg-embryo. Your essential name was transmitted by Renenutet, who, "in the name of your own cycle and personal rhythm", formed and nursed the KA of your human personality, whose character resides in the liver. Meskhent is the "skin of rebirth" that relates, through the mother, to the form that will be the Shade of the spiritual KA, as the moon is Shade to the sun. This has its cradle in the spleen, where the white blood of Osiris is made, whereas the red blood is made in the liver but gets its life from heart and lungs through *nefer*, the life of Amon-Râ. The sensitive soul, your animal BA, is thus carried by the blood. Your heart *ib-hati*, emotive and intermediary centre between your divine and your lower KA, is its seat.'

.   .   .

'How difficult it is,' Her-Bak exclaimed, 'to distinguish the aspects of the KA!'

'Aspects is the right word, their diversity isn't in the cause but in the effects. If you reflect the sun in mirrors of different metals it will take different colours and qualities. Each KA that proceeds from Maât takes its character in the man who embodies it from the vital forces, or natural, organic and instinctive *kas* it finds there; and from the innate conscious-ness of the *tekh*. When there is reincarnation Meskhent and Renenutet contribute earlier registrations and the destiny that flows from them. The man who is ignorant of his spiritual world has few or no connexions with his divine KA; his personal KA is reduced to the sum of his lower *kas* and after death it will be his Shade. But the quest for spirit and the develop-ment of consciousness gradually changes the quality of the personal KA until the time comes when through the awakening of the spirit the man gains contact with his divine KA and the tyranny of the lower diminishes. This is the simplest explanation I can give of the KA's reality, after many repetitive statements regarding relevant forces without which the terms of my explanation could have been misconstrued.'

'I understand!' cried Her-Bak. 'It isn't possible during life on Earth to define the aspects of the KA precisely because they have a part in all the activities of the being.'

'It is the agent of the *tekh*'s consciousness, ever-present witness to the metamorphoses of the creature,' said the Sage. 'It is the personality written in the liver and signed in the skin by Seshat. It shares the emotional reactions of the heart and the animal KAS. It is fed by the *kas* of foodstuffs and enriched by the dual fire of the vertebral column. It gives the energy or vitality called *sa*, while its divine consciousness or knowledge is called *sia*.'

'I see now,' said Her-Bak, 'how much a man can gain during a lifetime. But what becomes of the envelopes or centres of registration at death?'

'It depends on the state they are in when the man leaves them. The disengaged Shade is seen as the impure form of the individual KA . . . the word impure is used in the sense of double-natured, not homogeneous, destructible, because while it contains an admixture of spirit it is affected by the body through unexhausted instinctive affinities. It has memories of the desirous Sethian thirst and the exultant thirst of the heart. It holds something of the hereditary germ that the mother embodies in the spleen and something of the personal form inherited from the father by incarnation in the liver. The first will be felt in the emotional reactions of the heart and written into the heart-consciousness, *tekh* . . . that is why it is said, in allusion to the mystery of the *tekh*, "O my heart of my mother, you are the KA of my metamorphoses." The heart-consciousness is the permanent witness to vital experience in a man's lives and transformations. The second inheritance, paternal, personal, permeates every cell of the being and disengages at death, keeping the dead man's form. This duality constitutes the Shade. In the case of an ordinary man it lasts as long as the carnal body; but the man who is master of his KA frees himself from the Shade more quickly, having exhausted the instinctive affinities that made him its slave. Our texts are full of details regarding the becoming of the higher emotion-body.

'One can also speak of the liberation of the *djet*, the body of functions or functional Neters, become conscious in such a mode that a man can say truly, "My thighs are like Nut, my feet like Ptah. I am Nut in her name of . . ." '

Her-Bak held his breath. 'Is this then the mysterious *djet*?'

'It is the aspect I can shew you today. Its name should seize your attention: *djed* means a word, then the Word . . . isn't every function a Word, a functional Neter or attribute of the creative Cause? *Djet*, conscious of all these *djeds*, is Master of the Neters.'

.   .   .

'When a man has liberated his Neter,' said the Sage, 'he becomes an "emitter", like Ptah, and does the work of "those who are in their caves". That is, he shares the work of cosmic powers with the acquired consciousness of cosmic Man.'

'If I have really understood,' said Her-Bak, 'this is realisation of the human Horus.'

'Remembering that it isn't accomplished in a moment, but by patient weaving of the Horus-soul in the Osiris-body.'

This occasioned Her-Bak some surprise. 'Weaving . . . is this what those famous fabrics the steles often refer to mean?'

'It is one of their meanings. You will understand as well the meaning of the symbol *shems* as applied to the Followers of Horus. The curved point represents a falcon's head. The body is a tissue of thread, which is universal Horus, Word of divine Râ, taking consciousness and possession of the man in whom he is weaving the human Horus. It is thus that he incarnates in man, bringing the supreme awakening to those who are ready for it.'

'Horus is given many names . . .'

'As many as the transient states between his quality as universal quickener and his realisation in the man made perfect through what he has gained in the course of existence. He is called Hor the remote as the Horus-principle in course of becoming. He is called Hor *remet.t* as "proceeding from man's members", and in this name he struggles with the enemy, the Sethian personality. It is he who gains consciousness of his members and functions, first on Earth, then, with greater difficulty, in the island *neserser*.

'The enemy is that which resists the urge to freedom, clings to ego-centricity. It is the principle of cohesion in the elements of the Me that work against fusion with the universal consciousness of the divine KA. When resistance is overcome the personality is subdued to the higher KA's divine reason: this is the conscious union of the two KAS that awakens the higher reason in man and promotes a coming together of intuitive knowledge and ideas.

'What I have just said concerns mastery by the spiritual being, that other part of the being which is as it were the fixed centre that becomes the *djet*. This, purified as I said, will be the agent of resurrection, the leaven that precipitates and "fixes" the spiritual being. Now the divine *wât*, the Unity remade, will appear like the Sole Star, Venus, that unites the dual fire in herself and accompanies Râ at his rising and setting. This perfect being, ever increasing his light, can at last be independent and self-radiant like an indestructible sun.'

'Then there is nothing absurd about the texts that shew a dead man as a star in the sky,' Her-Bak remarked.

'What is absurd is to mock at texts because one doesn't know how to read them.'

'But may I ask where Horus is seated in myself?'

'Haven't I shewn you clearly that when this process reaches completion he is your soul, BA, become conscious little by little in your incarnate KA? Our texts tell you that "he rises from your vertebrae"; from the dual fire in them, that is. That "he quickens your spiritual heart, opens your mouth and eyes to the Real"; that "being realised in you and having at last stripped you of your transient names, freed you from the humanity that is in your members", he will "reveal your true face", your face of Maât, and "make you one of the KAS of universal Horus".

'But just as Horus, son of Isis and Osiris, undergoes many tests and regains his power stage by stage, so it is with him in humanity. The Followers who weave him in themselves incarnate him little by little in their lower being as weft and warp make a fabric by means of the shuttle.'

.   .   .

Having reflected the disciple said, 'This is more than an explanation, it is a programme for getting at the real aim of existence. But what happens to the dead man who hasn't got very far?'

'He undergoes long tests in the Dwat. When his Me is purged enough to become *sâh* he awaits, in the relative bliss of lower heavens, the moment of rebirth, spiritual or physical. His dwelling is his *meskhent*, for it is she who preserves the memories of his acquired consciousness and the images of his aspirations, emotional or spiritual. This is what pictures shewing a dead man's life in the other world as a reflection of his earthly life mean. If there is reincarnation it is Meskhent who recalls the KA that Sekhmet had freed. But I repeat what I said at the beginning of this lesson: it is the difficulty of describing states of spirit and consciousness in concrete terms that necessitates the use of so many images and symbols. Images are nearer reality than cold definitions. The symbol of the "skins of rebirth" that preserve the consciousness of the being in the Dwat and pass it on to his future lives is expressed in the image of the word birth, *mes*, which depicts three jackal skins tied by the sign for the placenta: three skins, envelopes, on which I can't usefully now expand. In the ancient text that says, speaking of Meskhent's role, "This house, in this night of birth, is a jar", the word jar is as apt as the word skin. It confirms the meaning and gives it precision.'

.   .   .

'I am only giving you now,' said the Sage after a silence, 'what is essential if you are to understand the writings of our Masters; the mode in which they expressed the harmony and identity of function between the visible and invisible worlds. You may be sure that analogies between words and the play of letters can reveal the profound meaning of the mysteries of the Dwat.

'They named the constellations in the neighbourhood of the fixed point in the sky, the pole, which are always visible at night, "Imperishable". Among them are Meskhetiw or Great Bear, and the Hippopotamus that leans on a mooring-post, *menit*, stability. They liken Meskhent to the lower heavens, where metamorphoses take place and rebirths are prepared. The word *Sah*, Orion, name of the constellation next to *Soped*, Sothis, is very close to *sâh*, the condition of the blessed, Followers of Osiris. Each of the three constellations Meskhetiw, Menit, Sah, has seven principal stars, the number of every terrestrial and Osirian manifestation. But while Meskhetiw and Menit are always visible, turning on the fixed point of the northern sky, Sah-Orion, appears and disappears: it accompanies Soped-Sothis in the south bank of the Great Stream, the band of the zodiac. It rises at the beginning of our winter and is seen in the night sky at the time of the feasts of Osiris in December, in opposition to the Sun.

'Wisely did our Masters liken Sah-Orion to Osiris, for its annual cycle corresponds with the cycles of Osiris that rule Earth's vegetable life according to its distance from the Sun. Their history is the history of the world since the creation of the primordial Types, as it is written, "O ferryman in the primordial world, take us speedily to the land where the Neters were created at the beginning of the cycles." The dead *sâh* is submitted to cyclical alternations as Sah-Orion to the seasons of Osiris . . . that is why it is said, "he was conceived with Sah-Orion in the west and brought forth with him in the east". The alternations of the Osirian state are successive transitions from darkness into light, sojourns in the dark west, rebirth into day. But rebirth needs a point of recall which our Masters liken to the action of the Imperishables Meskhetiw and Menit, constellations that are identified with three principles. First, the principle of perpetuity which links effects with fresh causes and leads memory-consciousnesses to a rebirth determined by affinities with the *sâh*'s KA. Second, the principle of stability, shewn in another symbol, the thigh of Osiris, the resurrection of which and re-erection of the pillar the water of revitalisation will ensure. Third, the principle of stability signified by the mooring-post, which draws KAS back to the affinity of their earthly *djed* or their spiritual *djet*. Menet is the port into which the boat returns to be moored. It is the swallow, the migrant that leaves its nest to return next year. Study once more the symbol of the *djed*, the pillar of Osiris, which alludes sometimes to the ending of these alternations by the inscription of two eyes surmounted by one single *nefer* instead of the third eye.'

⋅   ⋅   ⋅

'If I have understood,' said Her-Bak after prolonged reflection, 'the Way of Horus is a development and the term of the way of Osiris, to whom he brings deliverance.'

'It is the ascendancy of the spiritual Sun,' replied the Master, 'that brings triumph. The sacred word says, "Take the roads of the East; follow Râ not Osiris . . ." for "the man who is tied to his house of Earth dies . . . the man who leaves it and follows Horus-Râ is unbound. Râ returns him not to Osiris and he dies no more." '

The disciple was deeply moved. 'Although you have filled me to the brim during these seven days,' he said, 'my heart urges a last question. Is man condemned to follow this long road of disengagement and purification for ever?'

The Master hesitated. 'This is in truth the last question,' he said at last. 'There is indeed a purpose of perfection in the first creation: the mystery of Horus-Redeemer lies in it. The time for revelation is not yet. But there is nothing to stop your seeking the way yourself. There is no higher science on Earth.'

PART III

PART III

XIX

THE LEGACY OF EGYPT

This morning at the hour of instruction the Sage looked Her-Bak through and through as if he were transparent. 'My son,' he said at last, 'You have completed the first stage of the great journey. Not a heroic phase of it certainly . . . it is easy to receive, harder to make something of it in a spirit of gratitude. We have put a few simple keys in your hands. They open the door to exact knowledge, hidden in symbols. Now it is for you to advance by your own effort.'

Her-Bak was seized with fright. 'Master, your teaching is indispensable. What can I achieve alone?'

'We will guide your researches. First find the doors, prove your discernment, your respect for the eternal wisdom. Then we shall open our treasuries.'

Seeing the importance of it Her-Bak quickly got his feelings under control. 'Master,' he said, 'your conditions are just. To get without labour is to usurp and I know these treasures aren't for all men. I would win wisdom, not get it by subterfuge. I'll work for it, without forgetting who taught me the beginning of it.'

'Seek peacefully, you will find. Light goes out in face of an ingrate.'

'Am I to have a last piece of advice on the method of search?'

'You have understood the first condition of success. The second is this: make it your constant endeavour to awaken your higher consciousness, your divine Maât, in whom is all knowledge. Without her you have but your cerebral faculties and if rational thinking is your only guide it will bring you to a philosophy of negation. We have always refrained from giving the people an intellectual training out of key with their nature, but if some child of the people shews evidence of intuitive gifts no door is closed. We always act prudently and never lose sight of him. If the "heart's vision" doesn't awaken he will work according to his possibilities under surveillance, as you have seen in various places of outer instruction, for every mode of thinking is admissible in a theocratic state, which is governed finally, through a process of selection, by an *élite* of the people. But if under the influence of texts and symbols the intelligence of the heart lights up, the way is wide open to him and he has full liberty.'

'Haven't there been times,' asked Her-Bak, 'when selection became impossible, the people being independent?'

'There have, there will be again, crises of egalitarian wilfulness. They always lead to vulgarisation. The feeling for perfection deteriorates, Sages are reduced to silence, the *élite* is used up little by little and disappears. Then comes a really black phase when there is no longer an *élite* and the people build without foundations. They try to reorganise their lives, but without foundations they can only proceed by trial and error. Unfruitful experiment aggravates their misery and trains their consciousness. And it is they who by degrees will raise up a new *élite*; they themselves will call for leaders of quality. And the new age will never resemble the old, because the new *élite* springs of new necessities.'

'This seems to say that Evil is necessary to Good,' Her-Bak remarked.

'The people, like an individual, develop consciousness through experience. But organisation and stability are impossible unless those who know the laws of harmony lay the foundations.'

'Do the priests, who pretend to know them, abuse their power?'

'It isn't the priests who withhold the fundamental answers. They perform the rites, assure the maintenance of tradition, assume all religious and funerary duties. The wisest among them study certain high sciences, but the master-keys are never in their hands . . . those who hold them must be independent of authority, for Wisdom, or the science of universal harmony, must guide all other powers to prevent abuse and maintain harmony among men.'

'Isn't this Pharaoh's role?'

'You don't yet know Pharaoh's role, we shall return to it. Today is the day to sum up the purpose and method of our teaching.'

.   .   .

'Our Masters came to perform a work of reconstruction, in an isolated centre among deserts that nothing might contaminate this new small world. They said to the desert, "You are our frontier, Red Seth, hostile to life." They said to the barren mountains, "You are Evil; no man may pass your gates, quitting this land." They said to the great river, "You are the benefactor; your source is in Heaven and the chasms of Earth; we shall live by you." They said to the mud, "You are black earth, the magnet that will attract Heaven and all the Neters." They said to the sky, "You are the bull that begets and the cow that nourishes; you are our country; your regions are places of pilgrimage for our souls. When the day comes for us to be rejoined with Earth our souls will ascend with many great ones, not find themselves in exile. For our kingdom will be made in Heaven's image; our roads will be your roads, your cycles will rule our lives, what is below will be as what is on high." They said to men, "Live with the heavens and with nature and nature will give you knowledge of Heaven. Your, *nwt*, your city, is like the Nut on high; never depart from it for it is yourself. Do for it what it does for you; feed it with your labour as it feeds you with grain and you will never know distress. Do not dread the day when you go to your KA, if you have lived to possess your KA on Earth. Evil comes to the fool who lives for his belly and sex, but the man who seeks his Neter returns to it. Each country has its Neter; the Neters of your city are your own, but above them is the Neter that is in Man by knowledge of whom he becomes master of all things." They said to the workers, "Make the perfect gesture in all you do and in each task sing the song that belongs to it: your labour will be joyous." They said to the craftsmen, "Thoth has set up a balance that gives equilibrium on Earth; the man who knows it will be master of matter. Everything made in measure and proportion proves the mastership of the one who made it. Every work of art should express number, measure and quality. Monument, statue, no matter what object, every perfect work, is an initiation and its own reward. But the glory belongs to the Masters who bequeathed knowledge and it would be wrong to write the maker's name on it." They said to the leaders, "Each of you represents a mode of authority the principle of which images a power, functional quality or Neter. Your sceptres, rods and insignia are symbols of it; know them and use your authority within the limits of such function. The crook-bearer will be the leaven of the people he governs; such as he is such they will be: may he know himself. He who wields the sceptre must conform human justice with the divine justice of Maât: may he know both. He who wields the rod will direct the work he has in commission: let him order and punish as may be necessary so that there shall be no misconstruction: the rod will be his honour and his own punishment." They said to themselves, "We will set the pattern for all other countries and the generations to come. Conform with divine Harmony and we have nothing to fear from foreigners or invaders. They must adapt themselves to us, for cosmic Law is more powerful than the arbitrary decisions of men." '

The Sage fell silent. 'This plan is awe-inspiring,' said Her-Bak. 'But men are feeble, the people ignorant. How could such a programme be realised and maintained in spite of whatever crisis?'

'What turns man from justice,' the Sage replied, 'is the violence of his passion: greed, bodily pleasure, ambition, vanity in personal performance. It is useless to try to suppress such passions, wise to direct them into the quality of living. It is good to diminish greed by removing its object: we have reduced the causes of desire by reducing daily needs and personal luxury, even for the leaders and Pharaoh himself, to the strict necessities of existence, the due exercise of functions and the prestige of authority. As regards ornament, wealth has been concentrated in images and temples, in symbolic representation of the Neters and Pharaohs, objects used in initiation and funeral rites. As to bodily pleasures, it is true that evil comes to the intemperate man through his belly and sex; but it is true also that imposed sobriety provokes passionate reaction. Liberation of instinct is authorised at the time of certain liturgical feasts. As to ambition, it is a stimulant that we render innocuous: appointment to posts responsible for harmony, tradition and perfect craftsmanship is not susceptible to favouritism. Vanity in personal performance is transformed into the legitimate pride of the craftsman in his knowledge of rules and canons and in the master-touch. The grandeur of a work is proportional to its conformity with cosmic example: it is perfect if it is a perfect symbol. In this light private fantasy looks like a child's meaningless game, human genius like vision of the Real. Thus, individual vanity brings no gain . . . we offer vanity no nourishment. We know that all comes from Heaven; it is Heaven we glorify when we say, "I have succeeded for I have done all according to Maât." But we don't charge our sins to Heaven, and to repair the harm they do we count only on ourselves. The stars shew us men's dispositions and we obey. There are several aspects of the KA in each individual; each answers what interests him: animal man works for his belly and profit, but higher man seeks his food in the world of Soul and Cause: his sustenance is Maât. You don't ask a dog to know Heaven, but he will serve you for his food. If you, a man, put care about your subsistence first you will lose your knowledge of Heaven. Man is a microcosm. Self-knowledge shews him that he is made in the image of Macrocosm and being conscious of this he develops a sense of the universal. Thus, we point his gaze to the Neter and the Neter comes down to the man who attracts him. It is no use whatever preaching Wisdom to men: you must inject it into their blood. For blood carries the sensitive soul; eyes and ears are its windows and you must watch what they tell it. It isn't what reason appreciates, judges, accepts or refuses that impresses the human being but the daily sight of objects, the hearing of words and familiar names. The connexion between its name and the nature of a thing, between its form and its function, this is what writes itself in the heart. If the name and form of an object correspond with its reality, his sense-perceptions shape a man according to Maât; if not eye and ear deceive him. Thus forms, words and names are established and changed to suit every age. In this way we have achieved Maât.'

.   .   .

'Happy is the man who can say, "I have spent my life watching Heaven, the laws of Maât." All truth is in him. A man's history is of no interest to posterity; his destiny means nothing to anyone but himself. But while man passes Heaven remains. If his name, his rhythm, his mode of action are in accord with his time, or a given phase of it, then his name may serve as a theme of instruction: it will be the history of a name and a moment in becoming.

'Our genealogies shew relations of principle. They give the evolution of an epoch, not individuals. But we take care to see that relations appropriate to the necessity of the age are assured at important conjunctures, for kings should be prototypes of man made perfect.

'Pharaoh is a leaven. It is our duty to guard its integrity, a duty beyond the criticism of the profane. We know the laws that govern the transmission of blood and the incarnation of souls; we order everything accordingly. We have obeyed, in every particular, rules established long since and we shall obey them until our mission on Earth comes to an end.'

XX

PHARAOH AND SAGE

The companions climbed the path that turns the foot of the Peak. Slackening his pace the Sage put a hand on his disciple's shoulder. 'Do you remember the double event whose anniversary this pilgrimage commemorates, Chick-Pea's first ascent to the summit and the presentation of Her-Bak to his king?'

'Could I forget the moments that decided my path? Yet when I recall them I feel shame, congratulating myself on praiseworthy decisions . . . who was really responsible for them? Wasn't it your light that lighted the road? Could I have refused? I often feel as if my will entraps me and my decisions are an acceptance of which I am a helpless witness.'

The Master stopped short. 'This gives you the right to speak of consciousness. Do you appreciate, Her-Bak, the full meaning of this insight? The commonest error among men is to think they are free, whereas they receive impulses of which they are blind slaves because there is in them no observer to note what goes on.'

'But this denies the validity of voluntary effort.'

'The point is too important for juggling with words. Habit misleads you over the meaning of "effort" and "will". Your will isn't constant because it is far from being single, but multiple, like the animal forces in you and the powers of your lower KA. Each is capable of effort to achieve its desires. Each obeys a thousand circumstances that derives from within you as well as from external conditions. The animal too makes an effort to achieve its desires: your "intelligent" purposes, the "rational" intentions of your Me, are not less relative than the motions of your animal will. To which of your wills do you attribute validity when you speak of voluntary effort?'

Her-Bak hesitated, refusing evasion. 'I see only one that deserves to be called valid,' he said at last. 'It is the will of my higher KA, or of that in me that serves as a magnet to draw it to myself.'

He stood without flinching under the gaze that his Master, deeply moved, bent on him. 'This shews that the magnet is at work,' the Sage responded. 'This is the observer. If it is he that chooses, gives orders, you can say "I act, I decide, I wish"; otherwise you are driven, you do what you are told, without discerning the source of your impulses, from within or without.'

'The magnet you call witness is my desire?'

'The word is too vague and desire too subject to illusion. The witness is consciousness arising from relentless control of your various Mes. Strictly, it is the awakening of that Light in you which deprives impulse, speech, action, of their disguise and unmasks their real intention.'

'The awakening is transitory,' said Her-Bak. 'When the light fades one forgets it, at least for a time.'

'The light can't go out, but man can sleep and not see it. That's why its awakening is the disciple's constant aim. When through shock a man is roused out of his torpidity he may, before he falls back, see the difference between slavery to an anarchic complex of wills and the being able to co-ordinate them in full consciousness. And this gleam of consciousness, if you can hold it in view, becomes a magnet to your divine KA, your immortal witness, who will arouse in you the necessity, what you call desire, for his constant presence. Fortunate is the man who succeeds in making it his true will.'

Her-Bak flushed. 'Master,' he exclaimed, 'at such a moment as this one can see the distance travelled. Between the unthinking enthusiasm of that first ascent to the Peak and the serene certainty of a decision that today is my own. And my impertinence before Pharaoh . . . I don't care to recall it.'

'Was the sight of your king such a shock?'

'And I had the presumption to judge him . . .'

'You did. What came of it?'

'It was that I was defeated . . . to the point of losing consciousness and collapsing lifeless. Yes and when I found the courage to look up all my pride was in revolt at having given way. It melted when you spoke and I had a strange vision. In Pharaoh I saw the fulfilment of a Power, the summit of the kingdom, its limit, its end. In the Sage I saw no end, no limit to his power. I looked at the king. I looked at my Master . . . I no longer knew which was ruler.'

'Make no mistake,' said the Sage. 'Pharaoh and Sage are aspects of one Power. Pharaoh is its right arm, the action of human will. The Sage is the left arm whose hand grasps the key of life. This is never openly declared, but your own destiny obliges me to tell you that a Sage guides every Pharaoh. If it is said sometimes that "the King gives the plan and the canon of a temple" he takes counsel of those who know what is really designed. The Sages pass on this legacy to one another . . . the plans are flexible and there must be true knowledge if proportions and symbols are to be modified according to the real requirements of the epoch. The Sage translates the laws, the King executes them. To the King belong outward pomp, human glory and earthly rule; to the Sage spiritual reality, inspiration, detachment from the world. The Sage's life is a unity, whatever his apparent functions, in harmony with his role as teacher, for he is the slave of Heaven. Pharaoh's life is a double one. In his royal life he is slave to the function or phase he stands for. Symbol of a cosmic moment, he reveals it by his name, by the symbolic facts to which he must adapt the outer facts of his reign. In his personal life he is human and independent, in as far as transmission of the royal blood and power isn't affected. Thus his private destiny may touch the particular destiny of his people.'

'If the King goes wrong may the Sage intervene?' Her-Bak asked.

'If what he did harmed our work. Otherwise the Sage has no right to interfere with a personal destiny from which the kingdom is due to suffer. But he may subsequently redress what was done wrong or modify a historical account if there was danger of its falsifying the symbolism.'

'Is there no danger that this might create misunderstandings?'

'Doesn't misunderstanding arise if one man tries to usurp another man's function? Does your right hand dream of rebelling against your left? In a country organised in Heaven's image the two powers rest on universal Harmony. Necessity unites them. It is the stable basis of authority.'

'By what right does a man claim authority?'

'An essential point. Knowledge is consciousness of reality. Reality is the sum of the laws that govern nature and of the causes from which they flow. Nothing in it is arbitrary. Maât is its perfect concordance: she is equity and truth. Authority is the power to impose thought and will on others. Personal thought, arbitrary will, are an abuse of it, but authority in accord with Maât governs by reality. The King is its representative; he is action and the man who acts is subject to personal impulse. Royal authority is the power of Himself, a corporal person who is the conscious embodiment of his KA and the KA of his kingdom. This will colour his actions. The Sage is a channel of universal wisdom. Neutral because impersonal, he establishes the relation between the particular destiny of king and kingdom and the destiny of the world. His consciousness is the King's light. His judgment isn't affected by the will to action; if he acts it is in obedience to the King. His vision remains impersonal, without doctrine or prejudice. It is his knowledge that legitimises the King's authority.'

'It is a harmonious and impressive collaboration,' said Her-Bak. 'But is anything on Earth indestructible?'

'Everything changes because everything is in perpetual gestation. Wisdom would be at fault if it didn't foresee this. Troubles may come. A foreigner may usurp the throne. Anarchy may for a time upset the established order. What may happen seems incredible to a man who is unable to verify what I am going to tell you, that even this is foreseen in the inspired picture in which the Ancients wrote the development of various levels of the world. One day you will see this for yourself, as well as events to come. During such black times the Sage remains hidden, as it were in an oasis, guarding the thread that disorder itself may conform with the order of its Age. This explains why every invader carries on our traditions in spite of himself. And so it will be until the inevitable end of our mode of teaching.'

'Didn't you say that the time had come?'

'Not yet. We are at the end of our work of revelation; we hasten to record the last proofs. Those who follow us will only be able to copy what has been said and repeat it until Egypt's last days.'

'You are my Master for ever, and Master of Masters,' Her-Bak cried.

'I am a link in the chain. Above us are the Masters of Principle, incarnations of Wisdom, Imhotep and Amenhotep son of Hapu.'

Her-Bak shewed astonishment, 'Amenhotep, called Hui . . . was he so great a being?'

'He was our second Grand Instructor. The first, the great Master Imhotep, King Zozer's genius, came to bring an earlier age of Wisdom to its conclusion. He gave the ground-plan for the times and phases of the age then beginning and those that would follow to the end of our history. This comprised its application to architectural proportions, to changes in the language and in names, as appropriate to each phase of the era. His knowledge of the human body and the methods of Wisdom warranted his reputation as a divine doctor.

'Amenhotep, son of Hapu, renewed and in his own time used what Imhotep passed on, inscribing in monuments the proportions and functions particular to the current phase and his King's symbolic role. This referred to phases past and to come, for it reached its accomplishment with the generation of the royal Principle which ended the age of Amon and preluded the coming revelation. But this great being's mission outlasted the merely temporal, for Imhotep and Amenhotep son of Hapu are for ever the two pillars of our Wisdom.'

'Then wisdom,' murmured Her-Bak, 'is an edifice that defies time and man's inconstancy.'

'I spoke not for men but for a disciple of the Masters.'

Her-Bak replied in a low voice. 'The disciple is troubled by this perspective . . . the duration of this teaching . . . the Presence to which it testifies . . .'

'Are you afraid of it, Her-Bak? This Presence of which you become conscious today guarantees that Reality leads you.'

'Master, it measures the weakness of my animal self. How shall I master my violent impulses quickly enough never to stray from this road?'

'It isn't the animal in you that will be your difficulty,' the Sage answered, 'but the human who is proud of his own thinking, the arrogant critic, who would judge us, dissect us, our morality, our history, our religion. For us reality is otherwise.' He was silent, taking river and valley into his gaze, temple and village, all flooded with light that obliterated detail. 'Listen, Her-Bak. Man's life is an apprenticeship of his consciousness as an organism made in the cosmic image, of consciousness in his harmonious connexions with the cosmic organism and with the social organism of which he is a cell. That is our morality, our history, our religion.

'Social good is what brings peace to family and society. For the individual good is what leads him to possession of his KA during life. The supreme good is the realisation of his BA, giving birth to his own Neter. Evil is all that hinders him in these purposes. Our programme is to avert evil and promote good by all natural means, from the argument of the rod to education through symbols. Enhancement of consciousness is the aim and result, but getting it demands proof in experience. Obligation provokes revolt. Law gives sin power. Theory brings out the counter-argument. Confront a man with the consequences of what he does and he will work out his own morality.

'Death is the door into a life conditioned by earthly existence, which a man could hardly forget. Funeral rites remind him of the survival of the KAS of his own dead. People, nobles and kings know that they live by the Neter. The mortal feeds on the grain of Renenutet, the living on divine symbols. Every man dies in Osiris and looks to him for the promise of resurrection. His sarcophagus is the Nut that holds him in her two arms. Man communicates with his dead by means of funerary gifts, with his Masters by libations in their name, and with Heaven by feasts that celebrate its dominion. Heaven and Earth, gods and men, Pharaoh and kingdom, are bound inseparably together by threads of Neith's weaving and our real history is written by Seshat's reed. Thus, morality and religion are inherent in daily life; and history, the legend that attaches to a king, is but the necessary translation of symbols.'

'This will save me from the temptation to analyse and dissect,' said Her-Bak.

The Sage gave a sigh. 'That won't be your only temptation. Men will say to you, "What use is this science wrapped in so many mysteries? What point is there in writing the secrets of Number and the entire cosmic mechanism on the ground if it's only shewn to a few initiates? Of what avail is it to hide the key to relations and measures on the inside of walls and tombs supposed to be sealed for ever?" '

Her-Bak's face clouded. 'Have you an answer?' he asked.

'Yes, Her-Bak. We have written it all down to the least symbol, even where the human eye may never see it, that our work may be done for its own sake in conformity with the creative Law. It is the first title to nobility and highest witness of truth, to work for the Useless, without open reward, even moral, that the work may carry in itself the signature of the Real as completely as the plant conforms with the idea in its seed. And for nothing. For simple joy it shall be, even if no eye sees it, no ear hears it; that a perfect thing may be accomplished and stand for ever. What an affirmation of the divine sense in man! What a victory over imbecile vanity! What a triumph of the impersonal, art without usefulness, love for love's sake without object! What adoration of what is, in contempt of what seems to be!'

Joy blazed in Her-Bak's eyes and the Master knew his disciple. But he knew as well that the gem must be stripped of its gangue; his voice grew severe. 'Among those who glimpse Light very few have the courage to love it in this absolute sense. Several, learned men, had died still putting the question, To what end? This proves that knowledge isn't necessarily wisdom. You who will have to travel this road, bear in mind that it will be long before you come to the end of it, which is to have the power of what you know. Its length is measured by tests: you will be submitted to various temptations. After doubt will come that other danger, the danger of believing in the reality of monuments covered with silver and gold instead of seeing in them nothing but the sure evidence of wisdom, the reality of the Word which is Earth's soul and energy. We have learnt to know this power through ancestors whom God inspired and we use it to put nature in man's service without doing violence. There have also been men who put it to evil use. More of such black savants will seek to exploit it by negative and destructive means.'

'How is this possible?' asked Her-Bak.

'Fire can burn or give life. Truth is one. It can be approached by search into cause and creative power, which is the only way that opens the eyes of consciousness to the divine thought and the secrets of becoming. It can also be sought through matter and by violence, the way that leads to destruction. A curse on those who yield to this temptation! It is the most dangerous of all, for progress on this road flatters a man's pride so that he attributes the glory of his discoveries and his accursed science to his rational mind. While that other path means simplicity of heart and thought, acceptance of the fact that one is but a link in the becoming of the divine consciousness in humanity.'

'It means the death of all personal vanity,' murmured Her-Bak.

'Clearly. That is the indispensable condition of the revelation of Spirit in nature.'

'Today,' said Her-Bak, deeply moved, 'I know what acceptance means'.

.   .   .

They stood on a spur that dominates the valley of royal tombs like a ship's prow at the mouth of a river. At its extreme end a strong breeze from the north completed the illusion that they were making a voyage. Her-Bak filled his lungs with it, joyous, exalted. 'There is no sadness in this place,' he said. 'It seems to me we are travelling towards a new sunrise.'

Gravely the Sage replied, 'It is indeed in this spirit that you should envisage the future. At our feet the last of our kings with a mission are buried. Their successors will only reflect them, until the waves of an acquired rhythm die down. As for you, accustom yourself to the scale of successive ages, ages past and the age that will follow your own: you must get beyond consciousness of the present if you would escape from the habit of separating whole into parts. Look beyond valley and mountain for the reality in which three become One; look beyond your time. A guide must see further than those he leads and understand the connexion of things if he would know where humanity is going. Learn first the five ages of incarnation of the great Neter. The unknowable One descended into Heaven: that is the first. There he became the Neters of Heaven: that is the second. The Neters of Heaven came down on Earth: that is the third, in which they created and became the kingdoms of nature. There will come an age when God, incarnate in divine Man, will be the revelation of the Creator: this will be the fourth. And finally it will come about that men in whom the great Neter is conscious will leave Earth with its temples and gods to worship Spirit in fusion with it and in truth. This will be the fifth.'

'Could this be hastened without derogation from the Law?'

'That is the object of initiation, but it is only possible for the few.'

'If cerebral intelligence is the obstacle couldn't men be convinced of it?'

The Sage watched Her-Bak, smiling: then, with pitiless severity in looks and voice, he replied. 'Are you strong enough, Her-Bak, to hear what I'm going to say? You will never bring truth to men with argument, for cerebral consciousness, being Sethian, demands opposition and choice. How should it understand Maât-consciousness, which is fusion without opposites? If you attain absolute being by fusion of your own with it, duality ceases, intellectual comprehension ceases: what is the point, men ask, of seeking fusion in which you're no longer you but That and therefore don't know That in yourself? It is this disillusioning thought that prevents men of this world from engaging in the search.'

A new storm of doubt smote the neophyte. Head in hands he struggled with it, now yielding, now refusing a rebellious impulse. At last light came. He linked up the sequence of teachings once more, then looked his Master in the face and said, 'You have shewn me the sole Source of the world. You have proved that one who knows this Source can overcome matter. You have opened to me the secret of the ages, which makes everything flourish in its time. You have taught me to think with the heart and to translate what I learn with my head. You have discussed the mystical mathematic of Number which solves insoluble problems in arithmetic and geometry. You have sketched the philosophy of our language-structure, a guide for our whole life. You have put me on a road which with the Neter's help will lead me to Wisdom. Now you test me by shewing the inanity of all effort, the vanity of purpose. It only remains for me to affirm my faith. I can't contradict you . . . you seem to be right. But against all reason I believe. I believe in all you have taught me, in what is despite what seems to be, in Spirit that takes form in matter, in the divine seed that awaits resurrection in man's heart, in the celestial kingdom towards which humanity tends, in the continuous passing on of Wisdom throughout the ages. And my faith is a certainty that passes my understanding.'

.   .   .

The Master gathered the first-fruits of his labour. His voice, vibrant with controlled feeling, was less an answer than an echo. 'And you will never understand it. Such faith is the intelligence of the heart. This is another world than the world of thought and the two cannot be transposed. This is truth in relation to error: error can isolate truth and make it appear, but it can never itself become truth. Truth and error aren't interchangeable; one can only negate negation and affirm what affirms itself. Faith willed or imposed isn't faith, but discipline of thought. Faith is the consciousness of the soul, acquired by identification with the object. And each acquisition is a victory over the Me, which is wrong when it detaches itself from the object to understand it. When faith ceases to be mere belief, when it is no longer a matter of understanding, when it floods and envelopes us, it is the "gift of Light" that possesses us. When the flood rises and swamps the banks, that is belief; when it overflows them it is conviction; when it drowns everything in itself it is faith with divine peace, and becomes absolute certainty. By knowing one reaches belief. By doing one gains conviction. Through fusion comes faith. When you know, dare. Then will no longer to know or to will. Surrender your Me to know Self: this communion will be light and faith.'

Her-Bak's face shone. 'I have regained my Master and my joy!'

'You never lost them,' the Sage replied. 'But pain awakens consciousness, which is faith. Rebirth is prepared in this way. When a man has outlived himself, when, being simple, a child, poor in science he has surpassed, rich in experience he has proved, he draws to himself the Neter, then the life in him is reborn and true science is his.'

Silence followed. The Master tested Her-Bak with his inner eye and at last spoke the decisive words. 'Her-Bak, where are you going now?'

'At your side, Master, from summit to summit.'

'No. First make your own way. My word is in you; you are furnished with all you need. Go alone and make use of what you have learnt. We have said all that a Master may say to his disciple before he has proved his insight. Mut and Amon have shaped the components of the egg: go back up north, to Heliopolis, Râ's chief sanctuary, and learn to be alone. Then you will come back here and ask Amon for life.'

Her-Bak knew that argument was useless. Eyes closed, he took the shock, listened, saw what the words meant and in faith accepted. He regarded his Master steadfastly, measured the distance between the one who knows and the one who begins. The inevitable now lighting his path, he asked his last question, seeking a viaticum. 'Master, shall I be alone in reality?'

'The man who seeks the very truth of truths is alone with himself. You will be alone among men, like the kernel in fruit, but you will be one with those who belong to it. Become a living germ in it and you will draw to yourself those who may become part of it likewise.'

'And the others?'

'If life rises in you they will receive of you what all creatures may receive from the sun, according to their hunger and capacity.'

'Shall I be independent?'

'You are dependent on what you can't do without. Your tyrants are the desires and necessities that impose their will on you, habits, sicknesses, needs and desires whether material, affective, passional or spiritual. Learn to face them, adopt or refuse them.'

'Have I always liberty of choice?'

'Natural man is subject to the Neters, forces of nature, destiny, the stars, Earth itself. Conscious of their influence you will gain liberty.'

'What is the measure of my responsibility?'

'The measure of your consciousness.'

'Is ignorance of the Law and the means of knowledge an excuse for unconsciousness?'

'Before what judge is it valid? An act and its intention are judge and judgment. Every intense desire has repercussions in the world where it is formed. Every action has its source in the latent disposition of its author: its effects appear on the screen of fate, it may be long after.'

'Are not the deeper motives of personal disposition written in each of us at birth?'

'Shewing the qualities of the KA. Every quality has a good and a bad aspect. Evil consists in its egoistical and untimely use; good is a use of it that conforms with Harmony.'

'One ought to be warned of this! The two causes of evil would seem to be ignorance and egoism?'

'They are. Altruism is the mark of a superior being.'

'Isn't such a one responsible for the ignorance of his inferiors?'

'Her-Bak, a bright light has dawned! Knowledge is vain that hasn't taken the measure of human suffering and communed with man in his misery. It was consciousness of this that forged the Masters' hearts and sustained their courage. Ignorance will not suffer attack without resisting. The intellectual is happy with the science of appearances. The passionate are afraid of losing their pleasure. The crowd distrusts all that lies outside its capacity. Your chief test then will be solitude. You will have to pursue your researches alone. I have given you the instruments. What you have learnt gives a language for what you will find. Nature will be your school, Heaven your Master. Create silence around you. Don't listen to men, their praises, sarcasms or reproaches. All is in yourself. Know your most inward self and look for what corresponds with it in nature. Then there will be communion; you will have knowledge and obscurity will cease. Work, to confirm the truth of what you have heard and to prove that our philosophy is unassailable. Success will be the sign of the Neter's blessing. Then faith will radiate from you. It will feed the hungry. And in this happiness, this victory, you will meet your last test.'

Her-Bak knelt at the Sage's feet. 'Master,' he asked, 'will this be the temptation to ingratitude?'

'No. Ingratitude would affect not the Master but the ingrate, who would forthwith be turned from the road. The last test is the test of detachment even from the work, if you are to reach your own peak of perfection.'

'How can a man work without getting attached?'

'Nothing true is achieved unless Light drives and Light is its own reward. One must learn to surrender all that brought it.'

The Sage collected his thoughts. Power flowed from him, serene, virile, penetrating. He put his hands on the disciple's head, saying, 'O Her-Bak. O Egypt. You are the temple which the Neter of Neters inhabits. Awaken Him . . . then let the temple fall crashing.'